"Release me from the contract and I will make certain Papa pays you every penny from the estate."

"No. Jilt me and you will be ruined, your father and sister with you."

"But why?" Lottie was puzzled.

"Because I need an heir. One woman is as good as another in the dark. Your father owes me and you chose to deceive me. You will keep your part of the bargain whether you wish it or not."

Tears were stinging behind her eyes, but Lottie refused to let them fall.

"Have it your own way, sir. You hold all the cards it seems but you may come to regret this…" She walked past him and this time he let her go.

* * *

Bartered Bride
Harlequin® Historical #303—March 2011

ANNE HERRIES

Award-winning author **Anne Herries** lives in Cambridge-shire, England. She is fond of watching wildlife, and spoils the birds and squirrels that are frequent visitors to her garden. Anne loves to write about the beauty of nature, and sometimes puts a little into her books—although they are mostly about love and romance. She writes for her own enjoyment, and to give pleasure to her readers. She invites readers to contact her on her website: www.lindasole.co.uk.

Bartered Bride

ANNE HERRIES

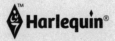

TORONTO NEW YORK LONDON
AMSTERDAM PARIS SYDNEY HAMBURG
STOCKHOLM ATHENS TOKYO MILAN MADRID
PRAGUE WARSAW BUDAPEST AUCKLAND

Recycling programs
for this product may
not exist in your area.

ISBN-13: 978-0-373-30612-1

BARTERED BRIDE

www.eHarlequin.com

Printed in U.S.A.

Available from Harlequin® Historical and
ANNE HERRIES

*Banewulf Dynasty
**The Elizabethan Season
†The Hellfire Mysteries
††Melford Dynasty
‡The Horne Sisters

Prologue

Nicolas, Marquis of Rothsay, nine and twenty, tall, strong, handsome, and known to most of society as a cold heartless rake, looked helplessly at the diminutive lady before him. Henrietta, Countess Selby, might reach no higher than his shoulder in her heels but she was the only person he would heed, the only person he truly cared for in the world—and, he sometimes thought, the only person who cared two hoots for him.

'Marry to get an heir, dearest Henri?' he murmured, looking at his godmother with a sceptical expression. 'Who do you suppose would have me? The match-making mamas take one look and stay well clear of me for fear I may corrupt their little darlings.'

'More fool them,' Henrietta replied, a sparkle in her eye. 'Besides, it is no such thing. You know very well that there are many young ladies who would be happy to become your wife.'

'Why, for the sake of my fortune?'

His dark eyes smouldered, a mutinous, brooding expression on lips that could at certain moments be sensual and passionate, but were, these days, more often set in lines of disdain or disappointment. His memory strayed to a woman he had known some years previously, when he was first a green youth on the town.

'The lady will give you an heir—or more than one to be safe. In return, you will keep her in comfort for the rest of her life. Surely an heir is worth a little effort? You owe it to the family, Nicolas. Also, you should remember your father's last request. He did not exactly make it a condition of his will, but it was his dying wish that you should provide the estate with an heir. You are in your thirtieth year, dearest, and while I would not suggest you are past your prime, I should hate you to leave things too late.'

'Should you, dearest Henri?' Only his beloved godmother would dare to say such a thing to him, and only she could make him smile at the idea that he might soon be past his prime. 'I suppose Cousin Raymond might be called my heir?'

'That nincompoop? He has no more brain than a peagoose and thinks only of his appearance and what is the latest scandalous tale upon the town.' Henrietta fixed him with a compelling stare. 'If you will not do it for yourself, then do it for me. Had I to refer to Raymond as the head of the family, I should soon find myself in my grave.'

'Poor Henri.' Nicolas smiled affectionately, becoming in that moment a very different man than was known in the clubs and certain drawing rooms in London. 'Has my cousin been lecturing you on my morals again? He tried to remind me of my duty to the family name recently. I fear I sent him about his business with his tail between his legs.'

'Perfectly understandable. I should have done the same in your place. He has no right to tell *you* how to behave, Rothsay. Yet, do you not see, that makes it all the more important for you to set up your nursery? If Raymond begins to imagine himself your rightful heir, it will make him more conceited than ever—and perhaps resentful if at the last minute you produce an heir. Besides, the children of old men are often weaklings.'

'Henrietta, I adore you.' Nicolas swept his godmother from her feet, planting a kiss on her cheek. She gave him a mocking wrathful look and he set her down carefully. 'Forgive me, but you tempt me so.'

'Remember I am more than twice your age and to be treated with respect,' Henrietta said, but there was a smile in her eyes. 'Will you at least consider marriage, Nicolas?'

Nicolas caught the hint of tears in her eyes and realised that the matter of his heir was important to her. She had no children of her own and, although not precisely lonely, for she had many friends, she must wish for a child to dote on. He suspected that his godmother had not been truly well for a while now. She might be thinking of making her own will, and, while he knew himself her favourite, he believed she would leave her fortune to his son if he had one. She was forever telling him he had more money than was good for him.

In his heart Nicolas knew that her pleas made perfect sense. It was time he produced an heir for the family. His father had begged him to do so on his death bed and Nicolas had pushed the memory to the back of his mind, a little resentful that his father should make such a demand after the neglect of years.

The trouble was that he had become used to his life as it was and had no wish for a change. Love caused more trouble than it was worth and he would avoid it at all cost—but perhaps a marriage of convenience might suit him? It was, as Henrietta said, his duty. He was not yet in his dotage, but if his lack of a wife was causing his godmother distress, he must certainly give it some consideration.

'For your sake I shall give the matter of an heir some thought—when I return from Paris.'

'You intend to visit Paris?'

'Yes, for a few weeks. The company grows stale in London. I need a change of air.'

'What you need is a passionate adventure,' Henrietta replied. 'I do not mean your opera dancers and actresses, who oblige you for the sake of the money you lavish on them. No, Nicolas, you need to fall desperately in love and to be brought back to life. I fear you have no real interest in anything.'

'Love is a myth,' he replied, withdrawing from her, a look of disdain upon his mouth. 'If I marry, it will be to a woman who understands that I must be free to live my own way. As you said, there need be no more than a token marriage on either side. She will give me an heir. I shall give her a home and jewels and there it ends—if I find anyone foolish enough to take me, that is.'

Even for Henri's sake, he had no intention of surrendering his heart and soul to love. He had witnessed the way love destroyed a man, making him a shadow of his former self, and causing him to withdraw into a lonely place inside his head. Nicolas's father had worshipped his mother; when she died, he had shut himself off from everyone, including his only child—leaving Nicolas to cope with the loss of both parents alone.

As a young man he had briefly believed himself in love but learned a sharp lesson when the young lady laughed at his offer of devotion. After Elizabeth, he had decided that he would never let another woman under his skin.

'Believe me, I can do without a romantic attachment, Henri. Love is for fools.'

'Well, I have said my piece. You must go your own way, Nicolas—and now I shall bid you good morning.'

'Leaving already?' The smile had come back to his dark eyes. 'Stay and have nuncheon with me? It is rare enough that you honour me with a visit, Henri.'

'If you visited Rothsay Manor occasionally, I dare say I should see more of you. London is too much of a racket for me these days.'

'You are not truly unwell?' For a moment real anxiety flashed into his eyes.

Henrietta smiled. The boy she had loved was still there beneath the cold aloof manner he had assumed these past years.

'No, dearest, I am not unwell—and, yes, I shall stay and eat with you since you ask…'

Chapter One

'What have you there?' Lady Hoskins asked as Charlotte Stanton entered the parlour carrying a letter. 'Is it from your father?'

'From Clarice,' Lottie answered with a smile. 'She apologises for not having written before, but they have been too busy.'

'Too busy!' Aunt Beth gave a snort as she looked at her favourite niece. 'Too busy to write to her own twin? Well, is that not typical of them both? They leave you here and go gallivanting off to Paris while you have the bother of an invalid.'

'I did not wish to go to Paris with them,' Lottie replied a little untruthfully. She might have wished to go had her aunt been in better health, or if Clarice had agreed to remain at home with her this time. 'Besides, you were quite unwell, dearest Beth. I could not have been happy knowing you were here alone.'

'Nonsense, I have Muffet and the maids,' Lady

Hoskins replied, but the tone of her voice told Beth that she would not have wished to be left alone to cope.

'I would much rather be here in the country with you than racketing around all those hotels and gaming halls with Papa. Besides, someone had to give an eye to the estate, though Mr Jackson is a very good agent and does his best for us.'

'Well, I certainly hope that your sister is not racketing around gambling clubs,' her aunt said looking alarmed. 'It would be quite improper for a young woman of her age. Your father is a confirmed gambler and will never change. It was the death of my poor sister, never knowing where the next penny would come from. That, my dearest Lottie, is what you get for marrying a rake and a gambler.'

'Papa did break Mama's heart,' Lottie admitted, sadness in her eyes. 'She had to follow him all over Europe, never knowing whether they would have enough money to pay for a roof over their heads or the next meal. It was fortunate that Papa was left this house. At least Mama was able to rest here in peace for a few years, though Papa did not stay long with her. He does have a small mortgage on the house, of course, but the bank will not lend him any more. That is just as well, otherwise, I fear we should not have a roof over our heads.'

Lottie looked round the charming room. Although the soft furnishings and curtains were faded and showing signs of wear, it was a comfortable place to sit in the afternoons. At this precise moment the sun was pouring in through the French windows, which they had opened to allow for some air. The furniture was for the most part old, some of it belonging to an age long gone, heavy carved Jacobean pieces that gave Lottie a feeling of permanence, of belonging. However, the previous owner had been an admirer of Mr Chippendale and there was a very handsome bookcase in the best parlour, as well as a set of good chairs in the dining room. Aunt Beth sat in a comfortable wing chair, her sewing table to hand and a book of poetry on the wine table at her side. Lottie, too, had been reading earlier, and her book lay on the small elegant sofa.

'What else does your sister say?' Aunt Beth enquired as Lottie sat down to read her letter.

'She says that Papa lost a large sum of money to an English marquis playing piquet…' Lottie turned the page, scanning some lines of rather indignant writing from her twin. 'Oh dear…that is too bad of Papa. No, no, he really has gone too far this time. No wonder Clarice is angry.'

'Why? Do not keep me in suspense a moment longer!'

Lottie handed the letter to her aunt, who frowned over it for some minutes before returning it to her.

'That is both ridiculous and disgusting,' Aunt Beth said. 'How dare he?'

'What, you mean how dare Papa accept—or how dare the marquis make such an outrageous request?'

'Both,' Aunt Beth said, looking affronted. 'I have never heard of such a thing—to suggest that your father should give him Clarice in payment for a gambling debt—it is the outside of enough!'

'The marquis has said he will marry her,' Lottie said thoughtfully. 'I suppose in a way it might be a good thing for Clarice. Besides, it could be worse—he might have demanded she become his mistress…'

'How can you think so?' Aunt Beth shook her head. 'The marquis must be a rake. He is probably old enough to be her father—a lecherous old devil who will lead Clarice a hell of a life.'

'If he is, she must not marry him.' Lottie got to her feet. 'We shall know soon enough—they are coming home in a few days. Clarice said the marquis provided the money for their return. Otherwise they might have been stuck in France until we could send more money.'

'And where would we get that, pray? I have nothing left but my pearls—which are for you, Lottie, when you marry—and fifty pounds a year. Clarice had the garnets when she was engaged, and she did not return them when she broke off her engagement. What little I have is for you, my dear.'

'Do not speak of such things,' Lottie begged her. 'I pray you will live for many years yet. Besides, I am not sure I shall marry.'

'Why ever not? You are the equal of your sister in looks, and your character is superior. She has had chances enough—why should you not?'

Lottie sighed. 'I should wish to marry for love, but then poor dear Mama married the man of her dreams—and they very soon turned to ashes.'

'My sister was a silly little thing, though I loved her dearly,' Aunt Beth said. 'However, I married a man who had both background and money—and look where that got me.'

Lottie nodded. Her uncle had not gambled away

his money at the tables, but on a series of bad invest-
ments—including being caught in a scandal that had
been almost as calamitous as the South Seas Bubble,
which had ruined so many people in 1720—and had left
his widow with very little fortune. Aunt Beth had been
forced to sell her home and come to live with her sister
and nieces after her husband died in a riding accident.
Then Aunt Beth had taken care of her and Clarice after
their mother died, and Lottie at least had become very
fond of her.

'I suppose if one of us were to marry a rich man we
might all be comfortable.' Lottie frowned. 'But Clarice
sounds very angry. I do not think she will agree and if
she does not...'

'Do you think we might lose the house?' A look of
anxiety crossed Aunt Beth's face. 'Where should we go
then, Lottie?'

Lottie had no idea. She had lain awake more than one
night recently, worrying about what would happen if her
father lost what little money he had at the tables. She
had begged him not to go on this latest visit to Paris, but
he could never rest in the country for more than a few
weeks at a time, and Clarice had demanded to go with
him. Now her father owed more than he could pay and
both he and Clarice were on their way home.

Nicolas threw his gloves and hat on to the sideboard
in the spacious hall of his London house. His boots clat-
tered on the marble floor, the resulting sound echoing
to the high ceilings. He was not in the best of tempers
and it showed in the set of his mouth and the brooding
expression in his eyes.

'Did you have a good journey, my lord?' his butler dared to ask.

'No, damn it, I did not,' Nicolas snapped. 'Have Harris lay up some things for me. I shall be going into the country for a few days.'

'Yes, my lord—certainly. Is there anything more, sir?'

'No... Yes, you can wish me happy, Barret. I am to be married, and quite soon I think.'

'My lord...'

Nicholas left his butler in shock as he took the stairs two at a time. He smiled grimly. The one consolation in the whole sorry business was that it would set the cat amongst the pigeons once the story got out. A reluctant smile touched his lips. At least he could still laugh at society and himself—but why the hell had he done it?

It was true that he had promised Henrietta he would consider the idea of marriage, but to ask for the hand of a woman—he would not call her a lady, for she was an adventuress—he had only just met was ridiculous.

Nicolas had at first refused when Sir Charles Stanton had offered him his daughter as payment for the gambling debt. However, after a night of reflection, he had decided that one woman was as good as another. His memory of being ridiculed by Elizabeth when he declared his love had made him determined never to offer his heart again. Therefore Sir Charles's offer was a convenient way of solving his problem. Clarice had been brought up as a lady, of that he had no doubt—but he had not known when he'd agreed to the deal that her morals were those of an alley cat.

It was on the night after he had signed the contract Sir

Charles had hastily had drawn up with their joint lawyers that Nicolas discovered his mistake. One of Nicolas's friends had been visiting Paris and they had gone out to a gaming club together, both of them drinking more than usual. Ralph Thurlstone had been three sheets to the wind and Nicolas rather more drunk than was sensible when he discovered his friend in a back room of the club. Ralph was lying senseless on the bed while a very pretty young woman with long spun-gold curls emptied his pockets of what money he had left. From the look of her hair and crumpled gown, he suspected that she had been on the bed with Ralph prior to robbing him.

'What the hell do you imagine you are doing?' Nicolas enquired dangerously.

'Taking what belongs to me,' the woman replied, her green eyes flashing with temper. 'He owes me and this is scarcely recompense for what he took.'

'Are you telling me you were a virgin before this evening?'

'Would you believe me?'

'No.'

'Then I shall tell you nothing,' the woman said and passed him, going out of the room.

Nicolas had let her go. In truth, he was still stunned by what he had seen. Returning to the main rooms a little later, he discovered Sir Charles at the tables, and standing at his back was the young woman he had seen going through Ralph's pockets moments earlier. Nicolas had thought he must have been mistaken, but there was no mistake. Clarice Stanton, his bartered bride-to-be, had robbed his friend while he lay in a drunken stupor.

'Ah, Rothsay,' Sir Charles said, looking up. 'Sit down and join us, won't you? Clarice is bringing me luck tonight. I was down to my last guinea but she brought me ten more and I have won the pot of two hundred.'

Which he would no doubt lose before he rose from the tables, Nicolas thought.

Nicolas looked the young woman in the eyes and saw her flush. Until this evening, he had not met Stanton's daughter, not bothering to propose to her but leaving it to the father to tell her of their arrangement. He supposed that he had intended to speak to her in his own good time. When he recklessly signed the marriage contract, he had been acting on impulse. He had heard on the rumour mill that Stanton's daughter was pretty, but as he was engaged to her already, sight unseen, her looks were not his primary concern. He had thought only that she was available and would give him the heir everyone said he needed.

To his horror, he had contracted himself to marry a thief and a wanton. What a damned fool he had been!

Henrietta had begged him to marry for the sake of the family. He hardly dared to contemplate what she would say if she knew the truth.

He must find a way to withdraw—but how could it be done? Anger smouldered inside him as he saw the young woman continue to encourage her profligate father at the tables. When Stanton rose a winner of some two thousand pounds or more, she flashed him a look of triumph, as if daring him to expose her to the world.

Needless to say, Nicolas had kept his mouth closed. It would have exposed him to ridicule, as well as Ralph, whom he knew to be newly engaged to a respectable English girl. His friend had been feeling a little hedge-bound, because his mother-in-law to be was demanding he dance attention on her daughter the whole time. Ralph had escaped to Paris for a last fling, and would never know that he had not spent all his guineas at the tables. The loss was one he could afford, but Nicolas was affronted by the idea that he had agreed to marry a woman of such low morals.

Nicolas had left Paris the next day, sending his would-be father-in-law a sharp note dictating that he take his daughter back to England to await his further instructions.

As soon as he had set foot in town, Nicolas visited his family lawyer to discover if the contract was watertight, and apparently it was. Nicolas could of course withdraw and compensate the girl for breach of promise. He would no doubt have to pay through the nose to be free of her. His mouth drew into a thin line as he contemplated the scandal.

No, better that he find a way of forcing the woman to withdraw. He would be ridiculed in the clubs whichever way it went, but if Miss Stanton withdrew it could all be settled by a payment for her bruised pride—if she had any—and there would be less scandal.

It was his own fault for giving in to a wild impulse. He could not blame Henrietta, who would certainly not have advised such a reckless affair. Nicolas smiled wryly. The irony of it was that such a marriage would have suited him had the woman not been a thief and a cheat. She was certainly pretty enough, and, if compliant, might have had her own house and done much as she pleased once she had given him a couple of heirs.

So for now, it seemed that he must go through with the formal arrangements. Henrietta must be told of his impending marriage and in due course an announcement must be made in *The Times.* Yet he would hold back on the announcement for a while; there was still a chance he might be able to persuade the young woman to withdraw. He must post down to his country house and put some work in hand. Nicolas seldom bothered to pay more than a flying visit to his family home; it would certainly need some changes if his wife were to live there.

His wife… Nicolas felt as if a knife had struck at his heart. There had once been someone he hoped to make his wife, but Elizabeth had laughed in his face and married an older, richer man. For years he had allowed his hurt pride to eat away at him, but it was time to put it aside. When this fiasco was over, he must look for a suitable wife in earnest.

'I shall not marry him. I told Papa in Paris that I would not. He refused to tell the marquis that the contract must be broken. I know there is a debt, but he won a little before we left Paris, after I wrote to you. I dare say if we sold this house he could pay the debt.'

Lottie looked at her sister's flushed face and wondered how Clarice could be so selfish. Did her twin never give a thought to anyone else's comfort but her own?

'What about Aunt Beth and me?' she asked. 'Where should we go if the house were sold? Aunt Beth has little enough income as it is—and I have nothing at all.'

'I will find a rich husband and rescue you both.' Clarice flashed a beguiling smile at her sister.

'Surely the marquis is rich enough? Papa said he was rolling in the blunt.'

'Well, I dare say he is, but I do not like him. He is arrogant and cold—and I shall not marry him.'

Clarice took up Lottie's hairbrush and began to brush her twin's hair.

'I hate him, Lottie. Papa is mean to say I must marry him. I would rather die—besides, there is someone I really like. I met him in Paris and I think he is in love with me.'

'Oh, Clarice…' Lottie sighed. 'If the marquis is that horrible, I should not want you to marry him. Is he very old, dearest?'

'Oh, middle-aged, I should say…thirty or more.'

'That is not old.' Lottie frowned at her. 'Is he ugly?'

'No, not ugly…stern, I suppose.' Clarice put down the brush. 'You must agree with me or Papa will make me marry him.'

'If he is presentable and rich…' Lottie looked thoughtful. 'It would be the answer to Papa's troubles, Clarice. Could you not marry him for his sake and ours?'

Clarice made a face at her in the mirror. 'If you think he sounds presentable, you marry him. He would never know the difference…' Clarice stared at her in the mirror and her expression became one of excitement. 'Why not? Why do you not wed him in my place? You could be certain that Aunt Beth had a decent home and Papa could come to you whenever he was in trouble.'

'Don't be ridiculous, Clarice.' While it was true that

they were almost identical in looks, apart from a mole on Lottie's right breast that Clarice did not have, they were very different in character. 'Surely he would know the difference? I know that many people cannot tell us apart but he must know you better than most.'

'We have only met once—and he does not know me at all, though he may think he does.'

'What does that mean?'

Clarice shrugged. 'He is so arrogant. I suppose I cannot expect you to marry him, Lottie. Yet I shall not. I would rather run away.'

'You will not change your mind?'

'No, not for the world,' Clarice declared. 'I am sorry if the house must be sold, but I dare say Aunt Beth can find a little cottage to rent.'

'Is that all you care—after she looked after us for so many years?'

'Well, I should not like her to be homeless, but I refuse to marry him. If you are so concerned, Lottie, you may marry him yourself. I do think you could for it would be better than being stuck here in the country the whole time.'

'Do not be so ridiculous. It is you he wants—how could I marry him?'

'You could pretend to be me.'

'No, no, that would be cheating him. It is a foolish idea, Clarice. I cannot consider it.'

'Then Papa will have to tell him the wedding is off,' Clarice said and looked mutinous. 'I shall not marry him and that is an end to it.'

'Have you seen your sister this morning?' Aunt Beth asked when Lottie came back from her walk the next morning. 'Your father wanted to speak to her, because the marquis has written to him, but she was not in her room. I knocked, but she did not answer'

'I expect she is sulking,' Lottie said. 'I'll go up and speak to her at once.'

Taking off her pelisse and bonnet, Lottie went to her own room first. She was thoughtful as she walked along the hall to her sister's room. She had been thinking about Clarice's suggestion that she marry Rothsay in her place ever since their argument the previous day. It was a mad idea that they should change places, yet if Clarice truly dug her heels in, what was the alternative?

Lottie knew her sister well enough to be sure that Clarice would never marry to oblige her family. She must dislike the marquis very much, which meant that he was probably a most unpleasant man. Yet if Clarice refused, their father would lose everything.

Knocking at her sister's door, Lottie waited for a moment, then opened it and went in. The room was empty; by the look of things, Clarice had left it in a hurry. She had clothes strewn everywhere, an odd shoe dropped on the floor—and all her silver combs, brushes and perfume bottles were missing from the dressing chest.

Feeling cold all over, Lottie went to investigate. Looking in the drawers of the tallboy, she saw that some of them were empty of all but Clarice's oldest things.

As she glanced at the bed, she saw a letter lying on a pillow. It was addressed to her. Tearing it open, her worst fears were soon confirmed.

Clarice had run away.

Tell Papa not to try to find me. I shall never come back and he may as well sell the house because I do not wish to marry that awful man.

'Oh, Clarice,' Lottie sighed. 'What have you done now?'

As a child Clarice had always been selfish and thoughtless, and, because most people could not tell them apart, she had formed a habit of making people think it was Lottie who had broken their vase or knocked over her milk or put a stone through a window.

Glancing at the letter again, Lottie saw the post-script.

Why not do as we discussed and marry him your-self, Lottie? He will never know the difference. He doesn't care two hoots for me, so what harm can it do?

Lottie took the letter and went back downstairs. She met her father as he emerged from his study. He was looking tired and worried and her heart caught with pain.

'Father—is something the matter?'

'Your sister has informed me once again that she will not marry the marquis and I'm damned if I know what to do. I suppose I shall have no choice but to sell the house.'

'Perhaps not…'

'What do you mean? Has she changed her mind?'

'You had better read this, Papa.' Lottie handed him her twin's letter. 'I have no idea where she has gone, but she has taken most of her things—including the silver that belonged to Mama.'

Sir Charles read it through and cursed. 'She is a thoughtless minx. Well, that settles it. I must sell—and if the marquis sues for breach of promise, I shall probably end up in the Fleet.'

'Papa! He wouldn't sue?'

'He might,' Sir Charles said. 'Rothsay will not take this well.'

'Supposing I did what Clarice suggested?'

He stared at her. 'Take her place, you mean?'

'Yes. She says the marquis doesn't love her.'

'They only met twice to my knowledge.' Lottie's father looked at her with dawning relief in his eyes. 'You wouldn't do it—would you?'

'Yes, I shall,' Lottie blurted unthinkingly, desperate not to see her father suffer any more distress. She almost denied it instantly, but the look of relief in her father's eyes prevented her from turning back. 'Clarice told me that all Rothsay wants from his wife is an heir—and that it was always to be more of a marriage of convenience.'

'Yes, he was clear that was all he wanted.' Sir Charles seemed to have shed ten years in an instant. 'If you could bear it, Lottie—it would be an end to my problems.'

'Yes, of course I can.' Lottie forced a smile. 'Most girls marry for money or position, so why shouldn't I?'

What else could she do in the circumstances? If she did not take her sister's place, Aunt Beth would be left homeless, her father might end in a debtor's prison; though he had given the family nothing but trouble over the years, Lottie remained devoted to her father. No, she couldn't bear for her family to suffer if there was something she could do to prevent it.

Chapter Two

'Are you certain you wish to go through with this, Lottie?' Her father reached for her hand, which was trembling slightly as the carriage horses began to slow to a steady walk. In another few minutes they would arrive at the marquis's country house and it would be too late to run back. 'I can tell him you are unwilling and ask him to give me time to pay.'

'How can you pay, Papa?' Lottie turned her lovely green eyes on him with a hint of reproach. 'I have thought long and hard about my decision. Clarice will not marry him. She's run away and we've none of us any idea where she is; besides, Aunt Beth is terrified of losing her home with you. How could she live on fifty pounds a year? I should have to find work to help support us both.'

'I am ashamed to have brought you to this,' Sir Charles said. 'I know well that your sister is selfish,' he added and looked rueful. 'She takes after me, while you have your mother's giving nature. I would not have minded that devil being married to Clarice, for I know she would have given as good as she got—but you may be hurt, Lottie.'

'I am stronger than you imagine, and, as I've said, there is no choice.' Lottie smiled at him. 'Now, Papa, you must be careful when calling me Lottie.'

'Rothsay knows nothing of you. He will merely think it a pet name, which of course it is, Charlotte.'

'Well, we must be careful all the same.' Lottie took his hand. 'As I told you, Papa—I shall see if his lordship will release us from the debt without marriage, but if he will not I shall become his wife. It is perhaps my only chance of marriage and I know I should like to have children, so it will not be so very hard for me.'

'Will it not, truly?'

Lottie dropped her eyes. She did not wish her father to know that it was the end of her naïve dreams of finding love and happiness. Clarice had told her the marquis was a terrible rake. Clearly, she could not expect to find happiness with her husband, but at least her aunt would have a home—and she might find content in her children.

'No, Father. I believe I shall be quite content—unless the marquis is good enough to relent.'

'I do not think he is likely to change his mind,' her father said and sighed. 'I fear you will just have to make up your mind to marry him.'

Lottie did not reply. The carriage had just now drawn to a halt before a grand and imposing house built at some time in the last century, and her heart was beating so fast that she could not have spoken if her life depended on it.

'The gentleman and young lady have arrived, sir.' Nicolas turned his head as his butler spoke. 'I have shown them into the green drawing room, as you requested. Shall I ask Mrs Mann to take in some refreshment?'

'Yes, you may bring it in ten minutes,' Nicolas said. 'I shall greet my guests.'

He was unsmiling as he walked briskly towards the green drawing room at the back of the house. He had waited for some protest, some inkling that the lady wished to withdraw, but none had been forthcoming. He could only hope that the young woman might give him some reason to request an end to this impossible arrangement.

'Yes, Father, it is very beautiful,' he heard the young woman's clear voice as he stood outside the door. 'I was just thinking how much Aunt Beth would love to live here. I wonder—'

The young woman broke off, turning to look at him with wide eyes as he entered, a faint flush in her cheeks. She was wearing a bonnet of chip straw tied with emerald ribbons, her carriage gown skilfully fashioned of velvet of a similar hue, and he was surprised. In Paris she had worn a gown that was, to say the least, bold, but this morning she looked a modest and very respectable young lady.

How dared she present herself as a demure country miss? Did she imagine he had such a short memory? His lips curled in scorn as his gaze swept over her. He thought the colour in her cheeks deepened. Was she remembering the night in Paris when he had caught her going through Ralph's pockets?

'Miss Stanton,' he said and took two strides towards her, inclining his head. 'Welcome to Rothsay Park. Sir Charles, how do you do, sir?'

'Middling.' Sir Charles looked hesitantly at his daughter. 'I understand you plan to give a ball to announce your engagement to…my daughter?'

'You would have preferred to give it yourself?'

The scorn in Nicolas's voice assaulted his own ears. He was being rude to a guest and, as his father would have told him, that was unforgivable. In his father's day it would have resulted in a beating and no supper. He added hastily to cover up his bluntness, 'I thought it would be easier here for I have a deuced many relatives, and I fear they will descend in droves once the announcement is made.'

'Ah, yes, well…' Sir Charles floundered unhappily.

'I am sure it will be much better held here, sir,' Lottie said and smiled as she removed her bonnet, revealing hair dressed in waves back from her face and drawn into a secure double knot at the nape. In Paris her hair had been loose, tumbling on to her shoulders, as if she had just risen from bed—which she had. 'I know my aunt will be very happy to visit. I do hope you will not mind my inviting her for the ball? There is no one else I truly wish to invite.'

'Indeed? You have no relatives?'

'Mama had one sister, who is now a widow and has no children. Papa has no family at all.'

'Well, there is Cousin Agatha, Lottie,' Sir Charles said. 'You know what a tongue she has on her. If I do not invite her, she will never stop complaining.'

'I think that perhaps I would rather not ask Cousin Agatha,' she replied. 'You should really call me by my name, Papa. The marquis will think my pet name unsuitable for the lady he intends to make his wife.'

'Lottie?' Nicolas raised his brows. 'Is that not more usually given to those with the name of Charlotte?'

'Mama liked the name. It was hers and it is also one of my names—everyone at home calls me Lottie.'

'Do they? I wonder why. I thought Clarice eminently suitable for the young woman I met in Paris. It has rather more sophistication, I think?'

'Yes, I am certain it has,' Lottie agreed. 'I am perfectly happy for you to address me as you please, sir.'

'Are you indeed? Thank you, Miss Stanton. I shall give the matter some thought.' He turned as the housekeeper entered with another maid bearing silver trays. 'Ah, here is Mrs Mann with your tea—and something stronger for you, Sir Charles. If you'll excuse me I have some business to attend to. Mrs Mann will take you up to your rooms when you have refreshed yourselves. I shall see you this evening before dinner.'

'Thank you, sir. We are much obliged,' Sir Charles said and nodded to the housekeeper as she indicated the Madeira wine. 'Yes, ma'am, that will do nicely, I thank you.'

'Miss Stanton, you will excuse me.' Nicolas nodded to her abruptly and left the room.

'Sir.' She bobbed a curtsy, but not before he had seen a flash of anger in her eyes. He felt a flicker of satisfaction; that was better, he was getting to the real Clarice now.

Nicolas frowned as he strode from the house. His business with his agent would have kept, but he was not sure he could have controlled his temper much longer. How dared the lady look as if butter would not melt in her mouth?

Her smile had reminded him sharply of Elizabeth when they first met. She had seemed charming and innocent—but when he offered her his heart, she had laughed and told him she was looking for more than he could offer.

Clarice—or Lottie, as she seemed to prefer—was not Elizabeth, but Nicolas was no longer a green youth. If Lottie imagined he had forgotten that scene in the bedroom in Paris, she would soon learn otherwise.

He would not be rude to her in front of her father, but when they were alone, he would ask her what game she was playing.

Clarice was so right! Lottie's hands curled into tight balls at her sides. What a rude, arrogant, cold, beastly man he was! She would have liked to give him a set down, for he had no reason to be so insufferably condescending. Papa had, it was true, lost more money than he could afford, but Rothsay could have insisted on being paid. He had accepted Papa's offer of his own free will. The least he could do was to treat both Papa and her with respect.

He deserved all he got. During the journey, Lottie's conscience had pricked her for practising this deceit on the unsuspecting marquis. She had feared that he was in love with Clarice and would spot the difference immediately, but he clearly hadn't. Indeed, apart from that scornful glance he had bestowed on her at the start, he had hardly seemed to notice her.

Lottie had hoped that the marquis might relent and release them from the outrageous contract he and her father had made between them. He was everything her sister had claimed and Lottie would not marry him.

Lottie's indignation drained away almost as soon as it flared into being. With no offer of a withdrawal the contract would still stand; if she were to break the terms then it would be her family that suffered. It might not be so bad, she consoled herself, the marquis had a beautiful home and it would be pleasant to live here, especially if, as she suspected, her husband-to-be preferred London life. It was large enough for her aunt to stay on an almost permanent basis, for Lottie had no illusions about her papa's promises of reform. He might be feeling chastened and sorry now, but within weeks he would become bored and once again the gaming tables would draw him like a moth to the flame.

It was a sickness, like Mama's weak chest, which fortunately neither of her daughters had inherited. Lottie loved her family, even her selfish sister, and she knew that if she went through with this marriage she would probably be in a position to help them over the years. Her husband would have provided her with a small income in the marriage contract and she had a frugal nature.

She reasoned that if all the marquis required was an heir he would not wish to spend much time in her company. Perhaps she could bear to accept a certain amount of intimacy with him for the sake of her family—and she would like children of her own.

'Shall I take you upstairs now, Miss Stanton?'

'Oh…yes, thank you, Mrs Mann.'

Lottie recalled her wandering thoughts. She was here and there was no getting out of the bargain her father had made, so she might as well make the most of things and enjoy her surroundings.

'I shall see you later,' Sir Charles said as she prepared to follow the housekeeper. 'Is everything all right, Lottie?'

'Yes…' Lottie raised her head. Her father was relying on her to solve his problems, as was her aunt. She could not let them down. If the marquis had not been such an arrogant brute, she might have felt bad about deceiving him, but he deserved no consideration from her. 'Everything is perfectly all right, Papa. I shall not keep Mrs Mann waiting.'

Following the housekeeper from the small but elegant parlour, Lottie walked up the wide main staircase, marvelling at the spacious beauty of her surroundings, the ornate ceilings and exquisite furnishings. The family that had built and maintained this house must be vastly rich. It had an air of wealth and security, of being the home of important men, like its present owner.

Why would a man like Rothsay choose to take a bride as payment for a gambling debt? There must be any number of eligible young ladies who would be delighted to marry him—unless his rakish reputation had made him an outcast as far as the matchmaking mamas were concerned?

Lottie's thoughts were confused, churning round in her mind and becoming no clearer. Had the marquis been a little warmer at their first meeting, she thought she might have liked the idea of her marriage very well.

Did she have a choice? What would happen if she changed her mind and withdrew at the last moment?

Oh, fiddlesticks! He was an impossible man and she

was being torn two ways. A part of her wanted to run away while she still had the chance—yet in her head a small secret voice wanted to make a fight of it. Rothsay was rude and arrogant. It would give her some satisfaction to prick his pride if she could.

Lottie changed out of her travelling gown, which was fairly new, into one of the more comfortable dresses she wore at home when walking to the village or the vicarage. She had decided to spend the afternoon walking round the gardens and what she reasonably could of the estate.

From her windows she had seen a large park, and in the distance a lake. Being fond of water and wildlife, she was torn between the park, which looked to consist of many beautiful old trees, and the lake, which was, she was sure, newer and man-made. As the sun was shining brightly, she thought the lake might be within distance and set out for it without reference to anyone.

It was a lovely day for walking; the peaceful surroundings soothed nerves that had become ruffled by her dilemma. She still did not know what she ought to do for the best. Being a sensible girl, she had made up her mind to take things as they came. If the chance presented itself, she might raise the question of a postponement or a cancellation of the contract, but if it did not, then she would simply have to marry him.

Enjoying the beauty of her surroundings, Lottie knew that being the wife of a man who took himself off to town for most of the time could not be a hardship for a girl such as herself. There were many young women who married for the sake of a comfortable home and a position in Society. Her marriage would be convenient to her in many ways, though the thought of how the heirs must be produced was a little daunting.

Could she really lie with a man as cold and arrogant as the marquis? A man she didn't even love?

'Oh, bother,' she said aloud and sighed. 'I shall not allow him to upset me.'

It was too nice a day for such anxious thoughts and staying at this wonderful place, even for a short time, was a treat.

Arriving at the lake, she stood admiring the excellence of the landscaping and how well the rock pools and greenery looked. A flock of black swans sailed majestically towards her, clearly expecting to be fed.

'I am so sorry, my lords and ladies,' Lottie said, feeling that royalty deserved the proper address. 'Had I known you were in residence, I should have brought some food for you.'

'They are magnificent, are they not? I've told Rothsay he is lucky to have found such specimens. We have the white variety, but the black species are something special.'

Lottie whirled round, startled by the man's voice. She had had no idea that anyone else was near by.

'Oh…I spoke aloud believing I was alone,' Lottie said, staring at the young man who had come up on her unawares. 'Yet they do command respect, do they not?'

'I was enchanted,' he said and offered his hand. 'Bertie Fisher. I am a neighbour of Rothsay and came to see him on business. He said that his fiancée had arrived earlier. Do I have the pleasure of addressing Miss Clarice Stanton?'

'Yes…though my friends call me Lottie,' she said and then blushed, for it was very forward of her to invite him to use her name. It was perhaps that he was attractive, his smile warm and friendly, and his manner not in the least arrogant. 'I am pleased to meet you, Mr Fisher.'

'It's Sir Bertram or just plain Bertie to my friends,' he replied and grinned as she offered her hand and he took it in a firm cool clasp. 'I hope we shall be friends, Miss Lottie. As neighbours we are bound to see something of each other. I was just telling Rothsay that I shall be leaving for London at the end of the week. I shall naturally return for your engagement dance.'

'Yes, I am certain we shall become friends,' Lottie answered warmly, then wondered if she would be here many days. 'I am looking forward to exploring the estate, and managed the walk to the lake, though I must return now or I may be late for tea.'

'Will you allow me to walk with you, Miss Lottie? I have something I must tell Rothsay, and we may as well walk together.'

'Yes, certainly,' she said and took the arm he offered. Sir Bertie was certainly a pleasant gentleman and if his wife was of the same nature she would have a friend— should she stay long enough to make friends. 'Have you known the marquis long?'

'Oh, all my life. My grandfather bought the estate and my mother still lives here for some of the time, though Mama likes to travel abroad for the sun in the winter. Sometimes I accompany her, though I do enjoy shooting and hunting in the autumn, and she has her friends, you know.'

'And your wife?'

'I am unmarried as yet—though it has been in my mind to marry. I am a few years younger than Rothsay, of course.'

'Yes…'

'I have to say that you are a marvel, Miss Lottie. We had all given up on the idea of Rothsay settling down. I dare say you know his reputation, but they say reformed rakes make the best husbands. No doubt you will soon have him curled about your little finger.'

'Why should Rothsay's marriage be such a surprise?'

'Oh, well, I suppose he has told you about Elizabeth. Everyone thought it was a match made in heaven. She was the toast of the Season, beautiful, clever and an heiress. Rothsay was head over heels; at least, we all thought so. An announcement of their engagement was expected but then he went off abroad and stayed in Paris for months.'

'He gave no explanation for letting her down?'

'It was all brushed under the carpet. She married a man several years older while Rothsay was in Paris, and now has three sons.'

Rothsay had clearly broken the beauty's heart, which resulted in her marriage to an older man. It just showed what kind of a man he was, leading her on and then deserting her without making an offer. Lottie fumed inwardly. No wonder he hadn't bothered to court Clarice. All he wanted was an heir and he had bought himself a wife for the price of a gambling debt. He must be a cold calculating devil and if Lottie's father had not been so desperate she would tell him what he might do with his offer and go home immediately.

Lottie would have asked more questions of her obliging new acquaintance, but for the fact that she had seen the marquis coming to meet them. She stiffened, her hand tightening on her companion's arm. He glanced at her, but made no comment, and Lottie lifted her head. Surely the marquis would not be rude to her in front of a neighbour.

'I thought you had left, Bertie,' he said, lifting his brows. 'Did you forget something?'

'Yes, as a matter of fact I did. I was walking home past the lake and happened to discover Miss Lottie making friends with the swans. It was then that I recalled what I wanted to ask, Rothsay. I decided to walk back with Miss Lottie.'

'And I was going to ask if you would like to stay for tea,' Lottie said, noticing the way the marquis's pupils took on a silver glow when he was intent. He was a very handsome man, she decided. He had a strong face with a square chin and a little cleft, which was rather appealing. His grey eyes could be very cold, but at the moment they seemed enquiring.

'Well, Bertie, since my fiancée has asked, I think we should all take tea together, and afterwards we can repair to the study and you can tell me what was so important that you felt compelled to return.'

'Certainly, my dear fellow,' Bertie replied amiably. 'It is nothing very much, you know—but it is a grand day for walking in the sunshine, especially in the company of a beautiful lady.'

'I dare say,' the marquis replied and glanced at Lottie, as if wondering whether his friend's remark was justified. 'It is, as you say, a glorious afternoon.'

'Do you allow others to feed your swans?' Lottie asked. His comment could be taken for silent consent that she was a beautiful lady, or a snub. She would ignore it for the moment. 'I should have brought food had I known how tame they are.'

'You should not be fooled by their docile appearance. They hoped to be fed, but swans can be vicious at times. One of my keepers had his arm broken by a male swan guarding its mate—and one of the pairs on the lake have young. However, if you insist on feeding them yourself, please give them the special pellets we use rather than bread. My bailiff will show you where the supply is stored—or one of the footmen will fetch it for you.'

'Thank you. I shall be careful to do nothing to alarm them,' Lottie replied. She was still walking with her hand on Sir Bertie's arm, but the marquis was at her right hand. 'Do you have deer in the park, my lord?'

'I believe there may be a few. I rarely visit Rothsay Manor, Lottie. I prefer to live in London for most of the year. Unlike Bertie, I do not enjoy either hunting or shooting, though my keepers encourage the pheasants and we have a regular supply for the table in season.'

'There are certainly deer in my park,' Sir Bertie told her. 'Do you ride, Miss Lottie?'

'I should—had I a suitable mount,' Lottie replied, turning to look at him. 'At home a neighbour sometimes takes pity on me. My father keeps only one hunter and his carriage horses.'

'I should be happy to provide you with a suitable

mount,' Sir Bertie said. 'My mother occasionally rides and I keep a horse for her—but I have another I believe might suit you. You can stable Heavenly here and then, should you wish, ride over to Greenacres with Rothsay or a groom.'

'That is extremely generous of you, sir. It would depend on Lord Rothsay's immediate plans, I imagine.'

'I dare say we have a horse that may suit you,' the marquis said, his tone sharp, causing her to turn her head and look at him once more. 'Your offer was well intended, Bertie, but I assure you I shall see that my bride has all she needs. I dare say she may care to ride over with me in the carriage and meet your mama—perhaps for tea tomorrow?'

'Certainly. Mama would be honoured.'

Lottie wondered if she imagined it, but she felt a slight squeeze of her arm and Sir Bertie's eyelid flickered.

At that moment she let go of his arm, walking into the house in front of the gentlemen. She heard the murmur of their voices behind her, then Mrs Mann came forward to greet her.

'Ah, Miss Stanton,' she said. 'Your father was anxious about you. I think he feared something might have happened to you. You were not in your room and no one knew where you had gone.'

'I went for a walk to the lake,' Lottie replied with a little frown. 'Forgive me if anyone was worried. I am not in the habit of informing anyone when I go out—though I do sometimes tell my aunt.'

'When are we to expect your aunt, Miss Stanton?' The marquis's stern question caught Lottie by surprise.

'I believe she will come for the ball,' Lottie said. 'I

am certain she would have liked to come with us—but I was not sure…'

'You must write to…I am not sure of the lady's name?'

Lottie met the marquis's eyes without a flicker of emotion. Two could play at this game!

'Lady Hoskins. My Aunt Beth. She came to look after…me, when my mother died. I am very fond of her.'

'You should have brought her with you. This is to be your home, Lottie. You must feel free to invite whomever you wish.'

'You are kind, my lord—but there is only my aunt, and perhaps Cousin Agatha. I do not particularly wish to invite her, but she may come if she hears of our engagement…'

'Indeed? A lady of some determination, then?' For a moment a gleam of amusement showed in the marquis's eyes and Lottie found herself smiling along with him, despite herself.

'Yes, most certainly. Both Papa and…Aunt Beth go in fear of her tongue.'

'You do not?' His brows rose.

'No, I have never feared her. She scolds me but I do not mind her. I am, you see, a very independent woman, my lord.'

'Should I take that as a warning?'

'Yes, I believe you should.'

Lottie preceded him into the drawing room that Mrs Mann had indicated. Her father was staring out of the window. He whirled round, relief in his eyes.

'Lottie! I thought you had done a bunk—' Seeing

that the marquis and a stranger followed her, Sir Charles checked himself and his neck turned the colour of brick. 'My daughter has a habit of wandering off alone for hours…'

Lottie was sure that neither of the gentlemen would believe his clumsy excuse. Sir Bertie would be imagining that she was being forced into an unwelcome marriage—and she had no idea what the marquis was thinking.

'Papa, anyone would think I was still your little girl. I assure you I am much too content here to run off without a word to anyone—which would be extremely rude of me. Had I known it would alarm you, I should have told you that I intended to go for a walk.'

'Well, you know how it is, a father will always be anxious for his daughters's safety.'

'Truly, Papa, you have no need to be anxious on my account. I am well accustomed to taking care of myself.'

'Yes, I dare say…' Sir Charles sat down, looking ill at ease as Lottie took a chair by the tea table. 'No tea for me, thank you. I would not say no to some more of that excellent Madeira, Rothsay.'

'I am certain it can be arranged,' he replied and flicked his coat tails as he sat on a chair near the fireplace. The large grate was empty because the room was pleasantly warm, lit by the afternoon sun. 'Bertie takes his tea with lemon, I believe—and I'll have the same.'

'Sir Bertie?' Lottie asked, directing her smile at him. 'Will you also take sugar?'

'No, I thank you, just the lemon. Rothsay knows my tastes well, Miss Lottie. Mama always has cream and sugar, but I prefer the lemon.'

Lottie poured the tea, handing it to a maid who stood waiting to pass it to the gentlemen.

'Would you care for anything more, Sir Bertie? Those almond comfits look tasty—or perhaps a sandwich? What do we have…I am not sure of your name?' She glanced at the young maid, who blushed.

'It is Rose, Miss Stanton. Rose Brown.'

'What kind of sandwiches are they, Rose?'

'Tomato and cucumber from our hothouses, Miss Stanton, also egg and cress…watercress, that is, from our own…'

'That will do, Brown,' Mrs Mann said after offering Sir Charles a glass of Madeira. 'If you would prefer chicken or salmon, I can have Cook make some very quickly, Miss Stanton.'

'I think I should like the cucumber,' Lottie said. 'What a treat. We seldom have it at home, for it is hardly ever to be found locally. You are very lucky to be able to grow your own, my lord.'

'I dare say. I had not considered it.'

'Rothsay takes everything for granted,' Sir Bertie said and grinned at his friend. 'He has been fed with a silver spoon since birth, Miss Lottie, and believes the world owes him the best of everything. It would do him the world of good to be denied something he truly wanted.'

'And I suppose you have had to work the skin from your fingers?' The marquis looked askance at his friend.

'I shall not deny that I too have been lucky to inherit a sizeable amount—but I do not take it all for granted, as you do, Rothsay. I know myself to be a fortunate fellow.'

His gaze dwelled on Lottie. 'Though not at this moment as fortunate as you…'

'It is a long time since we held a ball here,' the marquis said and frowned. 'My people are well able to cope but I feel we need a hostess. I shall ask my godmother to come and stay, but I wondered if your mama would care to help Countess Selby and Lottie compile a list of people who should be invited?'

'I imagine Mama would enjoy that very much—but you can ask her when you ride over for tea tomorrow. When exactly were you thinking of holding the ball?'

'In another two weeks,' the marquis replied, making Lottie catch her breath. 'I see no point in delay—and it will give us time to invite everyone and order whatever is needed from London.'

She had only two weeks to persuade him that she was not a suitable bride or accept her fate and marry him!

Lottie's hand trembled slightly as she sipped her tea. Everything seemed to be going so fast. The marquis had a note of decision in his voice when he gave the date of the ball. It was very strange, but Lottie had thought he might be regretting his decision to take her instead of the money her father owed him, but now she thought she detected a change.

There was, she believed, a gleam in his eyes that had not been there when they arrived.

Chapter Three

Sir Bertie and the marquis went off together after tea, leaving Lottie and her father together in the parlour.

'Well, Lottie, what do you think now you've met him?' Sir Charles asked in a low voice. 'Can you bear it?'

'Yes, I think so—unless the marquis were to relent and release you from the bargain and your debt, Papa.'

'You will certainly have all the luxuries that money can buy, m'dear—but if you should hate the idea I can tell him it won't do.'

'I believe we must be realistic. I am two and twenty and I have no fortune whatsoever. This may be my only chance to marry well. After all, most young women marry to oblige their families, do they not?'

'Your mother chose for herself,' Sir Charles said heavily. 'She made me promise that you and…'

'Papa,' Lottie warned with a glance over her shoulder, 'please say no more. I do not see that we have a choice. Besides, I believe I should be foolish to turn down the

chance of living in a house like this—and I have a fancy
to be the Marchioness of Rothsay…'

Anyone who knew her would have guessed immediately that she was merely funning, but the marquis, who
had returned from seeing his friend off, and stood outside the door heard only the last few words and thought
the worst.

His ears were still ringing with the congratulations
Bertie had heaped on him, and he had almost begun to
think himself more than fortunate to have found such a
lovely bride. However, catching the last few words and
hearing father and daughter laugh together aroused his
ire once more. The scoundrels! Did they imagine they
had found a soft nest for the two of them? He would send
them both packing and good riddance.

Nicolas was about to go in and have it out with the
pair of them when he heard a squealing sound, a murmur
of alarm and some very peculiar noises coming from
inside the parlour.

'Oh, you poor little thing. What a mess you have got
into…'

Intrigued by the new note in her voice, Nicolas walked
into the room and saw something that amazed him. The
woman he had just decided was a scoundrel was clutching a very sooty and disreputable animal he thought
might be a kitten. She was stroking it gently and he
could see that the beast did indeed look to be in a sorry
state. Glancing at the fireplace, he saw how much soot
the kitten had brought down and made a mental note to
have the chimneys swept before the winter.

'How in the world did that get here?'

'I imagine it must have gone up on the roof somehow

and fallen down. It feels so thin,' Lottie said and held the creature to her breast, stroking its filthy fur and getting soot all over her gown. 'We have some milk left from tea…' With one hand, she poured a little milk into one of the exquisite porcelain tea bowls. Still holding the kitten gently as she set both the bowl and the creature on the carpet, she allowed it to lap while supporting it with her hands. 'Oh, look how hungry it is. Do you think Cook would spare a little fish of some kind?'

'I imagine she might if you asked,' Nicolas said. 'You are, after all, to be the mistress here, are you not?'

'If it suits you,' Lottie replied without looking up. 'For the moment I am simply a guest. The milk has all gone. I must take Kitty to the kitchens. She needs a little wash, but it must be done carefully so as not to harm her, and she will need to be fed small amounts regularly. I think I shall keep her in my room…'

'She has already covered your gown and the carpet with soot.' Nicolas glared at her for no particular reason.

'Yes, I am sorry about your carpet, my lord. I know soot is difficult to get out. I will fetch a cloth later and see what I can do.'

'One of the servants will see to it. Good grief,' Nicolas said, feeling irritable without understanding what had changed his mood. 'Ring the bell and Mrs Mann will come. One of the footmen can deal with the wretched thing.'

Lottie looked up, her green eyes sparking with anger. 'It may be a wretched thing to you, my lord, but at the moment I believe it is to be pitied. I dare say it has been lost in your maze of chimneys for days, for I think it is near starving. I wish to care for it myself.'

He blinked and then lowered his gaze. 'I did not mean the thing was undeserving of pity. Merely that it would do well enough with the servants. If you wish to care for it, that is your own affair.'

'If you would kindly direct me to the kitchens.'

'I shall ring for Mrs Mann. She will assist you…' he said, but was saved the trouble by the arrival of the housekeeper and a maid to clear the tea things. 'Mrs Mann—a kitten seems to have got stuck up the chimney…'

'Yes, my lord. It is one of the kitchen cat's brood. We did think one was missing. Rose will take it for you, Miss Stanton.'

'Miss Stanton wishes to care for the kitten herself. If you will show her where she can clean it a little and also provide some food for the wretched beast.'

Mrs Mann glanced at him, but made no comment. She turned to Lottie with a smile.

'Rose will show you the kitchen and scullery, miss— if you are sure you wish for the trouble?'

'It won't be a trouble to Lottie,' Sir Charles put in. 'She always had a soft spot for any creature she found in trouble. Clar…uh, that is, *Clara* used to scream when she found wounded birds in the garden, but Lottie did her best to heal them if she could.'

'And who is Clara?' Nicolas asked. 'I thought your aunt was called Beth?'

'Oh, Clara is a just a friend,' Lottie replied, eyes wide and innocent. 'Excuse me, my lord. I must attend to the kitten—I think she has just wet herself.'

'And you, miss,' the housekeeper said. 'You will

have to house train the beast if you mean to make a pet of it.'

'Yes…' Lottie smiled. 'I shall have to teach her better manners, shall I not?'

Nicolas let his gaze follow her as she walked from the room. He had meant to send both her and her father packing. It would be simple enough to cancel the debt and pay a lump sum to ease the lady's pride. Yet the incident with the kitten had made him curious. He could not quite work out in his mind what was going on, but something did not ring true. Lottie had made nothing of the soot on her pretty afternoon gown or the kitten wetting her. How did the girl he had seen robbing his friend while he lay in a drunken stupor equate with the demure and compassionate young lady now staying in his house? She was like two different women!

She must be a consummate actress. Nicolas scowled, for he did not like the way she had played on his sympathies. Miss Stanton was not the only one to care for animals in distress. As a young lad he had rescued enough of them himself… Now what had made him recall his childhood? It was years since he had given it a thought, perhaps because painful memories had superseded the happier times.

He had, he supposed, been fortunate to live in a house like this and to have parents who cared for him, even if they spared him little enough of their time. His tutor and some of the grooms had been his companions, as he roamed the estate, fished with a net for frogs and newts in the streams and ponds, rode his pony and climbed trees. It was a very good place to bring up a family. The pity was that his mother had been a little fragile after his birth, and when she died from a putrid fever, the house had been plunged into mourning, from which it had never quite recovered. Nicolas's father had not remarried, spending most of his time away from the estate, working. Nicolas had been left alone with his grief.

Glancing around the parlour, Nicolas saw that although the furniture was good quality and made to the finest standards, the curtains and décor had become a trifle faded. He had spent only a few days at the house in the last years, and never in this particular parlour. If his wife intended to use it, he must have it refurbished for her.

His wife… Nicolas walked to the French windows and looked out. Was the reason he had been avoiding the subject of marriage down to his disappointment in love years before—or to the fear at the back of his mind that he might love too well, as his father had? Losing his mother at an early age had made Nicolas a little reserved and afraid of giving his affections. When the first woman he had believed himself in love with had also turned him down, he had put up a barrier to protect himself.

For a moment he thought about Elizabeth, the beautiful young lady who had been his first love. He had believed her nature as sweet as her face. The realisation that her gentle manner was false and covered a spiteful character had swept the illusion of love from his mind. He had thought her a woman he could trust, but her dismissal of his declaration had been deliberately cruel and meant to wound, destroying his trust in women and convincing him that love was for fools.

His father had been a fool for love. As a child, Nicolas

had not truly understood why his father could not bear to be in the house after his wife died. Nicolas had imagined the fifth marquis was too busy to be interested in his only son, but as an adult he could guess that his father had simply shut himself off from everyone who mattered because it was too painful; because he was suffering from a broken heart. Perhaps he had grieved as much as Nicolas, but been unable to show it, which meant they might have been more alike than either of them had realised.

No woman was worth the pain love inflicted. Nicolas was determined that he would never again offer his heart to have it crushed beneath a woman's dainty foot.

'Foolish…' he muttered and went out of the French windows. Love was a waste of time. A marriage of convenience was much safer. It was best to keep his mind on practical matters. He would walk down to the stables and speak to the head groom to discover if there was a suitable horse in their stables for a lady to ride.

'Now you must be good, Kitty,' Lottie said and stroked the kitten's fur. It still felt a little spiky and rough but with good food and care she did not doubt it would recover in time. Now that that the soot had gone, she could see that the kitten was a pretty tortoiseshell in colour. 'If you must wet, use the sand tray as I showed you.'

'You talk to her just as if she can understand,' Rose said and laughed. 'She will learn to use the tray in time. My mother puts the cats out to teach them, but they still wet in the house until they get older. Are you sure you wouldn't like me to take her down to the kitchen?'

'I shall keep her here until she is better,' Lottie said. 'If you would pop in and look at her now and then…'

'I'll come before I help with the dishes, miss,' Rose said. 'Cats are loners, you know. I dare say she will wander off when you let her outside. My mother says dogs are the best companions for they give love in return, and cats don't.'

'My aunt has a large and fat tabby that she adores,' Lottie said and laughed. She had taken to the young maid and was pleased that Rose was to look after her. 'I must go down now for the gong sounded five minutes ago. I do not wish to keep the marquis waiting.'

She went out, leaving Rose to tidy up. It would take a little time to get used to the idea of a maid waiting on her. At home they had a cook and one maid of all work, also Muffet, who had come with Aunt Beth and would turn her hand to anything. This meant that Lottie was accustomed to doing dusting and kept her own room tidy. She often cleaned her aunt's room, too. Living here with so many servants to care for just her and the marquis would seem strange—though of course they would probably entertain friends much of the time.

Lottie realised that she was beginning to rather like the idea of living in this wonderful house. She wrinkled her brow, because if she went through with this deception it would mean living a lie for the rest of her life.

Was she cheating the marquis?

She could not help feeling a little guilty. When she had taken Clarice's place, Lottie had tried not to question her motives or admit that she was doing something underhand—and when the marquis first greeted her so arrogantly, he had made her angry and she had felt he deserved all he got. However, her conscience was beginning to nag her. Perhaps she ought to tell him the truth before things went too far?

She was wearing a gown of green silk that evening. It had a dipping neckline, but was not low enough to show the little mole just above her right breast. Lottie was very conscious of the fact that in the more revealing gowns that Clarice wore it would have been easy to see that she did not have such a blemish.

As she approached the bottom stair, she was aware that the marquis had come out of the room to the right of the hall and was gazing up at her.

'I was about to send someone in search of you, Lottie.'

'Oh…' She blushed. 'Forgive me. I did not mean to keep you waiting for your dinner. I was talking with Rose and forgot the time.'

'Talking with Rose…you mean the parlour maid?'

'She is looking after me. We were talking about cats and dogs. Rose's mother prefers dogs, but Aunt Beth loves her cat—' Lottie broke off and laughed. 'You will think the subject obsesses me. I am sure you are used to far more stimulating conversation in London. I fear I do not know any amusing tales of the Regent to tell you. I have never mixed much in society…' She realised that she had made a mistake. 'Apart from the trip to Paris with Papa, of course.'

'You seemed perfectly at home there.' His brows met in the middle. 'Tell me, Lottie—is this an act for my benefit? If so, you are wasting your time. I am not a fool and my memory works perfectly.'

'I would never think you a fool, my lord…' She sensed

there was a deeper meaning behind his words and wondered whether he had seen through her disguise. Clarice had sworn she had met him only once and that he would not know the difference between them, but was there something her sister wasn't telling her about her time with the marquis? She crossed her fingers behind her back. 'I am not sure I understand you?'

'No, then perhaps I should refresh—' He turned his head as the butler came into the hall. 'Yes, yes, Mann. We are coming now.' His eyes narrowed as he looked at Lottie once more. 'We shall speak of this another time. Dinner is ready and Cook will not be best pleased if we keep her waiting.'

'No, that would not do at all,' Lottie said and laid her fingers tentatively on the arm he offered. 'I think it would be best if we talked soon, my lord. I believe there is something I ought to—'

A loud knocking at the door interrupted Lottie. The footman opened it and a lady entered, accompanied by several servants and a small King Charles spaniel, which barked noisily and jumped from her arms to rush towards Nicolas. He bent down and stroked it behind the ears, looking at the new arrival with rueful amusement.

'Henri! You can hardly have had my letter more than a day. I intended to invite you to stay, of course, but this is a surprise.'

'A pleasant one, I hope?' The diminutive lady laughed confidently up at him. 'I decided this morning I would visit you and here I am—and this young lady must be your intended bride?' The lady bustled towards Lottie, exuding lavender and a warmth that seemed to envelop all she touched. 'You are Miss Stanton? I am delighted to meet you. I have waited for this day too long.' She laughed and seized Lottie's hand, kissing her on both cheeks. 'You are wondering who the devil I am, of course. This wretched godson of mine has not thought to introduce us—Henrietta, Countess of Selby. You may call me Henrietta.'

'Ma'am…' Lottie made a slight curtsy. 'I am very pleased to meet you.'

'And I you, though I really know very little about you my dear, not even your name?'

'It's Clarice, but everyone calls me Lottie.'

'Well, it suits you, though I did not think your name was Charlotte?'

'Clarice's second name is Charlotte, which is why she often goes by Lottie. Anyway, enough chatter, Henri. We are late for dinner. Will you join us—or shall I have something sent up to you on a tray in half an hour or so?'

'I shall rest this evening and will take a little soup in my room,' she replied. 'You may come in and see me for a few moments before you retire, Lottie—if it will be no trouble to you?'

'No trouble at all, ma'am.'

'Then I shall not keep you longer. Nicolas has a decent cook. You will not wish to lose her…' She looked behind her, summoning a woman who looked as if she might be her companion. 'Give me your arm, Millicent. That staircase looks daunting after a day spent travelling.'

'You will become used to her,' Nicolas said as his godmother began her colourful ascent of the stairs, her servants fluttering around her, the spaniel bounding ahead up the stairs. 'Henri usually takes over the house when she arrives—though she has not stayed here often since…' He shook his head. 'Dinner awaits and we are now very late. We shall talk later.'

'You must be very fond of her?'

'I have many relations, but she is the only one I care for.'

'I see…' Lottie wondered what he had been going to say before his godmother arrived, but no doubt he would tell her later.

As it happened, Lottie did not learn what had been in the marquis's mind that evening. Dinner had been served in what was more usually the breakfast room because, as he explained, there were so few of them.

'Tomorrow evening I shall invite some of our neighbours,' he said as they all rose at the end of the meal. 'I had intended a period of quiet time for us to get to know one another, Lottie—but now that the countess has seen fit to join us we must entertain.'

'Please do stay and enjoy some port,' Lottie said. 'You need not accompany me to the drawing room. I think I shall visit your godmother and then go to bed. If I want a drink, I am sure Mrs Mann will have a tray sent up.'

'As you wish.' Nicolas frowned. 'I had thought we might talk?'

'Tomorrow morning if you wish,' Lottie said. 'I am a little tired myself and would wish to retire after I have visited the countess.'

'Very well,' he replied, inclining his head.

Lottie sensed that he was not best pleased. She was not sure why she was putting off the evil moment, because she could surely not delay it much longer.

It would be embarrassing, but there was really no alternative. Lottie had been feeling guilty enough about deceiving the marquis himself, even though he did deserve it in a way, but to deceive the lady who had just arrived would be unforgivable.

She would simply go in for a few minutes and explain that she was too tired to talk this evening. It was clear that the countess expected an intimate heart to heart, but that could not happen. Not until Lottie had told the marquis the truth.

If he truly had no preference for her sister, he might be satisfied with her in Clarice's place—but he must be given the choice.

Nicolas frowned over his brandy. He had offered to give Sir Charles a game of billiards but his future father-in-law had declined. They had talked in a desultory fashion of the King's madness, which had resulted in the prince being called on to become the Regent once more, then discussed the price of corn and the weather. Then, after smoking a cigar, Sir Charles had excused himself and gone to his room.

Nicolas sat on alone in his library. He was not sure why his thoughts were so disordered. The day had not gone as he expected at all and he was still undecided what to do about the situation he had created.

He should, of course, have spoken to Sir Charles as soon as he realised what a fool he had been, made some settlement and withdrawn. It was clearly too late now. Bertie would have spread the news all over the neighbourhood—besides, Henrietta had rushed here as soon as she had his letter. The delight on her face when she saw his fiancée had struck him to the heart.

Lottie gave the appearance of being a modest charming woman, exactly the kind of person who would grace his home and make his relatives welcome. He knew that at heart she was a scheming adventuress, but for the moment she seemed determined to play the part of an innocent—why? What could she hope to gain?

His fingers drummed against the arm of his comfortable wing chair. What a dilemma! And he had only himself to blame. He frowned as he recalled the laughing words he had overheard outside the parlour—so she had a fancy to become the next marchioness, had she?

Well, would it be so bad? He had considered she would do before he had witnessed the theft of those guineas. It was that that rankled, he admitted—and the suspicion that she had been making love with—or at least been prepared to be seduced by—Ralph.

The thing was that he found he did not dislike Lottie. He was not sure he could trust her—and he would have to send her father packing after the wedding. Yet he did need a wife and if Henrietta liked her…he supposed she would do.

Nicolas groaned. He was such an idiot to have become embroiled with a pair of adventurers.

Why did he have the feeling that Lottie was playing a part? Had she decided to reform her ways now that she had a chance to move up in society?

Nicolas knew that he would not find it difficult to play his part in this strange marriage. It would be no hardship to make love to her—and her morals could be no worse than some of the ladies he had made his mistresses in the past. His last mistress had been grasping and self-ish, which was why he had felt no remorse in finishing his arrangement with her. He would at least start his marriage without a clandestine attachment. He would certainly not tolerate being played false by *his wife*. If she imagined he would turn a blind eye to any future indiscretions, she would soon discover her mistake!

'Damn it!' he muttered and stood up. He would not find the answer in the bottom of a brandy bottle.

In the morning he would make it clear that, if they went through with this marriage, he would expect Lottie to be faithful—at least until she had given him a son or two.

Feeling unaccountably tired, he realised that for the first time in a while he would sleep as soon as his head touched the pillow.

It must be the country air.

Lottie rose early, as was her custom. She sat up and looked over at the kitten lying on her bed. She had left it in the basket that Rose had provided for her, but it seemed that Kitty had other ideas. Reaching out, she picked the tiny creature up and stroked it, kissed its head and then climbed out of bed and placed it back in the basket.

'That is your place, little one. You must not form bad habits, for I might roll on you in the night and suffocate you.'

Lottie found some water left over from the previous evening and washed her face and hands. She would have a proper wash before breakfast, but she wanted to go for a walk first.

Going downstairs, she surprised a maid already hard at work polishing the furniture.

'I beg your pardon, miss. We did not know you were awake. Do you wish for something?'

'Not until I return. I am going for a walk. I shall be back in time to dress properly for breakfast.'

A sleepy footman opened the door as she approached. She flashed a smile at him and went out into the early morning air. The dew was still on the grass and silky cobwebs hung between the perennials in the mixed border.

Walking across the lawns in the direction of the park, Lottie felt a sense of peace. The marquis's estate was a lovely place to stay and she would have liked to live here, but she had decided that she must tell him the truth this morning.

She entered the park, reflecting that some of the trees here must be very ancient. One particular oak tree had grown so large that she thought it must have stood here for well over a hundred years. Lost in thought, she was startled by the sound of a shot somewhere to her right. Whilst it had come nowhere near her, she was concerned—she was certain that the marquis had said he did not hunt or shoot. Who could be shooting on his lands?

Without consideration, she turned towards the sound and a moment or two later came upon an unpleasant scene. A man had been shot in the leg. He was clutching at his wound, and the blood was trickling through his fingers. He lay on the ground and looked up at the man with the gun standing over him.

'What is going on here?' Lottie asked, walking up to them. 'Why has this man been shot?'

'He was poaching on his lordship's land,' the man who she instantly realised was a gamekeeper said, and touched his hat. 'We do not allow poaching here, miss.'

'My wife is starving. I only wanted a rabbit for the pot…' the poacher whined looking at her hopefully. 'Tell him it ain't right, miss. There's more than enough game in these parts—and his lordship ain't never 'ere to want it.'

'Poaching is illegal and must be stopped,' Lottie said. 'For one thing it is cruel to trap things. You should have come to the house and asked for help. However…' She fixed the gamekeeper with a reproachful look. 'It was not necessary to shoot the poor man in the leg, sir. You will take him to the house, where I shall bind his leg— and then we shall give him some food for his family.'

'I don't know about that, miss. His lordship don't hold with poachers.'

'I dare say he does not, but I do not hold with what you have done, sir. If you will not help him, I shall do so myself.' She looked down at the poacher. 'Can you stand?'

'If he gives me a hand up.'

'I'll carry him over me shoulder,' the gamekeeper said grudgingly. 'You had best take me gun, miss. It ain't loaded now so it can't hurt you.'

'I should not fear it if it were loaded,' Lottie replied. 'My father shoots occasionally. I am used to guns in the house.' She checked that it was indeed harmless and slung the strap over her shoulder, following the men up to the house, round the back to the kitchen. 'Bring him into the scullery. Cook will not want him bleeding over her kitchen floor.'

'Miss Stanton…' Rose came out to them as they reached the scullery door. 'What is going on?'

'This poacher has been shot. He was stealing a rabbit because his wife is starving, or so he says. We shall give him some food to take home—but in future he must work for his wage. I dare say he can be found some kind of work on the estate?'

'That's Sam Blake,' Rose said. 'He has never done a decent day's work in his life.'

'Then it is time he started,' Lottie told her. 'He must obviously rest his leg for a while, but as soon as he can walk, he must be given a job cleaning out the stables.'

'I'll tell Mrs Mann you said to give him food, but you'll have to ask his lordship about giving him a job,' Rose said. 'Sit him down on that stool, Jeb Larkin, and I'll patch him up.'

'I was going to cleanse and bind his wound, Rose.'

'Best you let me, miss,' Rose told her firmly. 'He has a wound in his thigh and it wouldn't do for you to tend him, miss. Besides, I'll be sending your water up with one of the other maids. You'll be wanting your breakfast.'

'Yes, well, perhaps—but don't forget to give him some food.'

'I shan't forget, miss.'

Lottie left the maid to bind up the injured man and went upstairs. She bit her lip as she reflected that perhaps she had been rash to bring the poacher to the house. His story had touched her, but if he was a rogue his wife's plight might be his fault rather than anyone else's.

She hurried upstairs. Her walk had made her hungry, though she would have gone further afield had she not chanced on the poacher.

Lottie was at the breakfast table alone when the ring of booted feet on tiles told her that someone was about to enter. Her hand trembled a little as she sipped her tea. The unpleasant incident had put the thought of her confession from her mind, but it must be made this morning without fail.

'So you are here. What the hell do you mean by interfering in the way I run my estate? You are not mistress here yet.'

Lottie looked up and saw the anger in the marquis's face. He was speaking of the wounded poacher, of course. She rose to her feet, feeling the nerves knot in her stomach.

'Forgive me. The man was hurt. I thought your gamekeeper might have fired in the air as a warning.'

'And so Larkin might had the rogue not been warned a hundred times before. Blake is a thief and a scoundrel. You may feel that taking what belongs to others is acceptable but I think you will discover that others do not. Far from giving him work in my stables, I have called the constable. Blake will see how he likes a few months in prison.'

'That is harsh, is it not? His wife is starving…'

'He has only himself to blame. Besides, his wife never sees any of the game; he sells what he steals to the inn in the village and gets a few drinks in return, I've no doubt. He will be lucky if he does not hang.'

'Oh…I am sorry,' Lottie clasped her hands in front of her. 'And I do not condone stealing. I was just moved to pity for his wife.'

'You do not condone stealing?' He spluttered incredulously. His eyes narrowed dangerously. 'Then pray tell me whether you think taking gold coins from a man's pocket when he is in a drunken stupor is theft? Not to mention going to a bedroom alone with a man in that state.'

'What..?' Lottie felt the blood drain from her face. She was stunned, her mind reeling as she tried to take in what he was saying. 'She… I would never… Where did this happen?'

'You know full well where we were, at that gaming house in Paris. You were going through my friend's pockets as he lay senseless.' Nicolas stared at her intently. She looked so shocked and distressed that it suddenly dawned on him that it could not have been her. What an idiot he was! He should have seen it instantly. 'Who the devil are you? You're not her, are you? I thought from the start that something was different. You've been lying, trying to make a fool of me…'

'No, it wasn't to make a fool of you,' Lottie hastened to reassure him. 'I meant to tell you yesterday…to ask if you would let Papa repay the debt over a period of years. Clarice is my twin. She refused to marry you and—'

'You thought you would take her place. How noble of you—or was it just a clever move to trick me into marriage, because you had a fancy to be the next marchioness yourself?'

'No, of course not.' Lottie's cheeks were burning. 'If you heard me say that to Papa, it was just in fun…to set his mind at rest. I was going to tell you the truth. I realised last night that I could not deceive the countess. She was so kind and—'

'You would have deceived me happily enough, I suppose?'

'At first I thought you deserved it. You have been exceedingly rude to Papa, to Clarice—and to me.' Lottie raised her head, too angry now to care about what he thought.

'Do you think you have deserved my concern?'

'Mere politeness was all that was required. Well, you may set your mind at rest. I do not wish to marry you. Papa will just have to find the money to pay you what he owes. I dare say I shall find somewhere for Aunt Beth and I to live.'

'So you will renege on the bargain you made?'

'I made no bargain. And nor for that matter did Clarice. You made that deal with our father. Foolish Papa thought he could persuade Clarice to go along with your plans with the promise of wealth, but she dislikes you and—' She broke off feeling embarrassed. 'No, that is rude. I shall not be rude to you no matter what you have said to me.'

'Your manners do you credit, Miss Charlotte,' he sneered. 'If only I could believe in that innocent outrage.'

'Believe what you wish. Thank you for your hospitality, sir, but I am leaving.'

'No, you are not.' Nicolas grabbed her wrist as she would have passed him. 'You will not make a fool of me in front of my neighbours and my godmother. Your father signed the contract. He owes me fifteen thousand pounds. If you refuse to marry me, I shall press for payment—and I shall tell the world that your sister is a thief.'

'You would not…' Lottie stared at him in horror. 'How could you threaten to destroy my family? You are as cold and heartless as Clarice said you were. I do not know what happened in Paris, but she must have had good reason for what she did.'

'Perhaps I am heartless,' Nicolas said, his expression set in harsh lines. 'However, when I make a bargain I stick to it—and you will oblige me by keeping your part.'

'You are a devil! To think I felt guilty—almost liked you…'

'Perhaps you may come to find my presence bearable,' Nicolas said. 'I shall endeavour to put my own disgust to one side and we shall muddle through.'

'Why do you wish to continue? Surely you cannot wish to marry the sister of a woman you have named a thief? You clearly have no respect for Papa or me. Release me from the contract and I will make certain Papa pays you every penny from the estate.'

'No. Jilt me and you will be ruined, your father and sister with you.'

'But why?' Lottie was puzzled.

'Because I need an heir. One woman is as good as another in the dark. Your father owes me and you chose to deceive me. You will keep your part of the bargain whether you wish it or not.'

Tears were stinging behind her eyes, but Lottie refused to let them fall.

'Very well, sir. You can compel me to honour my father's bargain—but you will have no joy of your despicable behaviour.' She raised her head, looking him in the eyes. 'I shall be everything your bride ought to be in public. I will give you the heir you desire, but in my heart I shall always hate you.'

'I never expected you to love me. Why should you? Love is a myth and ever was. I dare say you will be content in your role as my marchioness—and I need an heir or two, perhaps, just to be certain. Do your duty and we shall go along well enough.'

'Have it your own way, sir. You hold all the cards, it seems, but you may come to regret this…' She walked past him and this time he let her go.

Chapter Four

'I was sorry not to spend more time with you last evening,' Lottie said when Henrietta came down to nuncheon. 'I felt a little tired, as I told you, but this morning I am much better.'

'Are you, my dear?' Henrietta looked at her speculatively. 'Well, we shall have them put chairs for us beneath the shade of the chestnut trees after nuncheon. We may sit and enjoy the pleasant weather for an hour and talk as much as we like.'

'You mean the stand of trees to the right of the house?' Henrietta nodded. 'I went for a walk in the park early this morning. A poacher had been shot. I fear Lord Rothsay was not best pleased because I had the keeper bring him back to the house to be patched up and gave him food for his family. He says that the man deserves to be in prison.'

'Ah, I thought there was something,' Henrietta nodded wisely. 'Gentlemen do not care for interference in the management of their estates. We ladies are expected to smile and plead for anything we think needs changing rather than dictate.'

'Papa's estate is small, for he has but one farm left, but he leaves what management there is to me—or he did before we came here. He has no interest in the land or the house. I am not sure what he will do once I am married.'

'I dare say the arrangement suited your papa—but it will not do for Rothsay. As I believe you have discovered, he has a temper and these days his manner seems stern. He can be the sweetest man—but I dare say you know that, Lottie?'

'Can he?' Lottie hesitated and then decided to be honest with the woman she had liked from the first. 'You must know this is not a love match, ma'am. The marquis offered for me because he needs an heir. I agreed because my father's circumstances demand that I should make a good marriage.'

'Oh…' Henrietta sighed. 'I suppose I should have known what Rothsay would do. I am sorry. I had hoped to see him deep in love.'

'I fear I am unable to help you, ma'am.'

'I am not so sure. I am certain he feels something for you. As a child, Nicolas adored his parents. He felt it deeply when his mama died and his father neglected him. I dare say he would not care to show his feelings openly. There was also that young woman—Elizabeth. Rothsay allowed me to believe he did not come up to scratch, but I think she broke his heart. He reacted by taking a string of mistresses and has resisted all the matchmaking mamas for years. I know he wishes to oblige me by setting up his nursery, but I think he would not have offered for you if there were not something between you.'

Lottie did not wish to disappoint her further, so she kept the fact of her father's debt and the marquis's brutal demands to herself.

If Rothsay had been as cold and brutal with Elizabeth, Lottie could not blame her for refusing him. Yet if she had truly broken his heart, it would explain his aversion to the idea of being in love.

No, she did not believe that Rothsay had a heart to break. He was the most arrogant, heartless man she had ever met! His behaviour that morning had been abominable. If her situation was not so desperate, she would have liked to give him a piece of her mind. However, she kept her thoughts to herself and let the countess talk happily about the wedding and the benefits Rothsay would gain from having a wife.

At two o'clock she left her companion and went up to change into a pretty peach afternoon gown. Henrietta had refused to accompany them to Lady Fisher's for tea. She preferred to sit on in the shade and have the butler bring her a cool drink.

'I shall see you this evening, Lottie dear. I believe Rothsay has invited Colonel Brand and his wife, the vicar and the Fishers to dine with us. I dare say I shall rest for an hour before I change.'

'I shall look forward to knowing you better, ma'am,' Lottie said.

When she came down at precisely half past the hour,

the marquis was waiting for her. He hesitated, then inclined his head to her.

'I approve of punctuality in a lady, Lottie. I think I owe you an apology. My manner this morning over the issue of the poaching was brusque and I believe I treated you to a show of temper—but you caused quite a stir.'

'There is no need for an apology, sir,' Lottie replied with a cool nod. So he was not going to refer to their argument over her deception? Her anger had cooled, because, being honest, she understood that she had in part deserved his censure, both for tricking him with her identity and rushing headlong into matters on his estate. Still, if the marquis didn't want to address the second issue she would play along, for now.

'I interfered in a matter that did not concern me. I have been used to ordering things for the comfort of my aunt and myself. Papa takes no interest in his estate and I acted as I would have at home. I ought to have remembered that this is not my home.'

'It will be your home, however, and I am sorry that in this instance I was forced to override your instructions. As for the matter of the food, that has been sent to the family in question—but the man has been arrested. If you wished to help the family further, I should not object. I believe the wife to be a decent enough woman. She takes in sewing and there would be nothing wrong in your employing her—should you wish it.'

Lottie turned her gaze on him. His expression gave nothing away, but there was a tiny pulse flicking in his throat and she understood that he was making her a handsome apology by his standards.

'Yes, I think I shall. If she is competent with her

needle, I shall need someone to help me sew my wedding gown. I was not perfectly sure before we came here, sir. I had a new ball gown made by a local seamstress very quickly, but I shall need something for the wedding.'

His eyes narrowed, darkened, as he regarded her seriously. 'Are you always this calm and controlled? I thought you might have demanded that your father take you home after our row today?'

If only he knew how much it was costing her to keep her temper in check! Lottie kept her expression bland, though she was unable to smile.

'My father owes you a debt. I am here to pay that debt, my lord. You made it plain that you would not release us, therefore I have no choice. I believe that such arrangements are common enough.'

'Yes, they are.' Rothsay looked uncertain for the first time. 'Yet I believe there is usually some liking or at least respect on both sides.'

'Indeed?' She raised her sparkling eyes to his. 'Should I like you, sir? Mayhap you will earn my respect in time. Your apology has been accepted. I believe I can behave in a civilised manner—if you can, too.'

'Then you are determined to go through with it?'

'Do I have a choice?'

'Neither of us does, Lottie,' he commented darkly.

Then his mood seemed to lift.

'Besides, I know it is my dear Henri's greatest wish to see me married, and I would do anything to oblige her. So, now that we are agreed…' Nicolas took her hand to help her into his curricle '…you will not have cause to complain of my temper again. I can at least be civilised.'

'I am certain you can.' Lottie smiled suddenly, her anger evaporating. His devotion to his godmother must surely reflect some level of compassion in his character. 'We must try to get along for the sake of our families, sir.'

Lady Fisher turned out to be a pleasant woman, if a little fussy in her manner. She welcomed the idea of a new mistress at Rothsay Manor.

'It is years since Rothsay bothered to entertain much. When he comes down for his brief visits he brings friends from London, but seldom gives a dinner for his neighbours. His father used to give the most wonderful Christmas parties. The whole house was decked with greenery and smelled of spices and pines—but that, of course, was when the late Lady Rothsay was alive.'

'Perhaps we shall be able to continue the custom in the future,' Lottie said. 'I believe I shall be living here most of the time. I shall certainly want to entertain often, for I love company, and you will always be welcome to call for tea—or a morning visit. I am an early riser.'

'My son tells me you like to walk and you enjoy the wildlife. We have red deer in our park and in winter they often come close to the house for the food I have put out.'

'That must be pleasant to see.' Lottie looked up as Sir Bertie approached. 'Lady Fisher was just telling me about the deer.'

'We cull them now and then for the venison, but Mama would make them pets if she could. I tell her that the farmers think them a nuisance if they overrun their fields—but if we did not take our share the damned poachers would have the lot.'

'Oh…' Lottie's gaze flew towards Rothsay but he seemed not to notice. 'I dare say poachers can be a trouble to you?'

'Sam Blake has been one of the worst, but Rothsay tells me that his keeper has dealt with the blighter. If they brought him up before me, I should be inclined to hang the fellow, but I dare say Rothsay will be the presiding magistrate as he is in the county. He says Blake will go to prison for a year. Too moderate by half for my liking, I can tell you.'

'Is the theft of a few rabbits really a hanging offence, sir?'

'I know you ladies have tender hearts,' Bertie said with an indulgent smile. 'But you have to make an example of these fellows, m'dear. Let them get away with it and there will soon be no law for anyone.'

'Well, I expect you know best,' Lottie said, deciding on diplomacy.

'That's it.' Bertie nodded and looked pleased. 'Leave all this unpleasant stuff to us. You have enough to think of with the wedding in three weeks. All those bonnets and furbelows. You will need to go shopping in London, I dare say—or shall you be satisfied with what is to be found in Northampton?'

'Three weeks…' Lottie was shocked—it was the first time the actual date of the wedding had been mentioned. Her gaze flew to the marquis but he was frowning and staring at a picture on the wall, apparently far away in his thoughts.

'There are some very good milliners in Northampton,'

Lady Fisher said. 'I dare say they are not up to London standards, but I know of a seamstress I could recommend—and the draper has a good stock of silk just now. I should be pleased to take you in, in my carriage.'

'Thank you. I believe I may need to purchase a few silks and perhaps a new bonnet.'

'You must have far more than that—must she not, Rothsay? Your bride needs a wardrobe to suit her position in society, does she not? I dare say you have plans to take her to Paris, and the local seamstress cannot compare to the elegance of a French gown—but she will need a wardrobe for the journey.'

'What? Yes, I am sure Lottie will need a great many clothes. Countess Selby is sure to advise her, ma'am. I intend to pay a fleeting visit to town myself almost at once. I can order anything necessary while I am there.'

'I think perhaps I would rather see what is to be found in Northampton,' Lottie said. 'Later, I may order what I need from town.'

'Your clothes are important, Lottie.' Nicolas focused on her. 'We have much to talk about. I shall certainly place some orders in town. You should discuss your needs with Henrietta.'

'Oh, yes,' Lady Fisher agreed. 'The countess has wonderful taste and is known everywhere. If she vouches for you, the best seamstresses will fall over themselves to work for you.'

Lottie thanked her, but made no further remark. She did not wish to argue with Rothsay in front of his friends, but she could not see that she would have the least need for a huge wardrobe.

Rothsay gave her a speculative look as they left but said nothing further until they had been driving for some minutes.

'She means well, you know.'

'I have no fault to find with Lady Fisher's advice, sir. Yet I do not think I shall need a huge wardrobe. As I understand it, I am to live here in the country, while you continue your own life in London—is that not what you require from a complaisant wife?'

'Well, yes,' he said and frowned. 'Once we have an heir, you will be free to live where you please—perhaps in Bath? You will have an allowance naturally, to spend as you please.'

'How generous.' Lottie's tone was perfectly pleasant, but she saw a faint flush in his cheeks. 'I think I shall probably be quite content to live at Rothsay with my children—and Aunt Beth, of course.'

'Yes, of course. Your aunt. Have you written to her yet?'

'I thought the invitation should come from you?'

'I shall attend to it immediately.'

'Thank you—that would be kind. I am sure she is anxious to know…to see us wed.'

'Yes, I dare say she may be.'

'What does that mean, pray? My aunt is a woman of good character and…'

What was he implying? Lottie gave him a fulminating glance and was about to launch into more scathing words when the shot rang out. It whistled harmlessly by their heads but the horses bolted and Nicolas was forced to give all his attention to bringing them under control. He was beginning to slow them when the curricle hit a bump in the road and Lottie was thrown to the ground.

For a moment or two she lay winded, her eyes closed. As a man loomed over her, she opened her eyes and stared up at him. For a moment she blinked foolishly and then her senses cleared.

'Are you badly hurt? Damn it, I am so sorry. I thought I had the horses in hand, but the shot took me by surprise.'

Lottie sat up slowly. As her breath came back, she realised that she felt bruised and shaken, but there were no sharp pains.

'I think I could get up if you gave me your hand.'

'Forgive me. I was so shocked. I thought you might be seriously harmed…or dead.'

'No, thank you, I believe I am just a little shocked and bruised.'

'Thank God for it!' He sounded and looked distressed and when she rose to her feet, he put his arms about her and held her until she placed her hands against his chest, giving him a little push. He released her instantly.

'I have never been so shocked in my life. Had you been badly injured I could never have forgiven myself. You are under my protection and this is outrageous.'

'Do you suppose they were shooting at us—or do you think it a random shot intended to scare the horses? Of course, it might have been that someone misfired.'

'In either case the result might have been the same.' He looked at her in a very odd way. 'Do you not realise that you have come very close to death, Lottie?'

She took a deep breath, refusing to give way to hysterics. 'Well, yes, I realise there might have been terrible consequences, but neither of us is much harmed. I think we should concentrate our thoughts on who might have done this, do you not agree? Is it more likely to have been a stray shot from a gamekeeper or a poacher?'

'Do you feel able to continue?' he asked and gave her his hand as she inclined her head. 'My keepers would not fire across the road. It must have been a poacher—or someone who intended me harm.'

'Do you have enemies, sir?' Lottie looked at him in shock, discovering that her chest felt very tight of a sudden. She imagined the consequences if the shot had found its mark and her heart jerked. Rothsay might have died. The thought of that left a hollow feeling in her heart; things were far from easy between them but still she would hate the thought of losing the man who would be her husband. 'I had thought it must have been an accident but…who would hate you enough to do such a thing? You have Sam Blake safely locked up?'

'Yes, though there may be others I have sent to prison before this. I do not often sit in court, but there were some trials last summer that I was asked to give judgement on. A gang of violent poachers was broken up and most went to prison, though I believe one escaped punishment. I do not recall his name.'

'Then the shot might well have been meant for you, though it might have just been a keeper's shot gone astray. We were not travelling at speed and a pistol aimed at you would surely have hit its target?'

'Perhaps.' He frowned. 'My keepers do their duty, Lottie. You must not take them in dislike because of what happened this morning.'

'I assure you I have not, but accidents will happen.'

'I shall make enquiries. If a man was that careless I should not continue to employ him. You might have been riding here alone.'

'I dare say you are right and it was someone with a grudge against you. Forgive me, I should not interfere in your business. I must remember to keep my opinions to myself.'

'That would be a pity.' He smiled at her. 'You were extremely brave, Lottie. I do not think I know another young lady who would have taken this in her stride as you did.'

Lottie felt her cheeks heat. She turned her face aside, as she said, 'I am not hurt. Pray say nothing of this to the countess. I would not have her anxious over your safety or mine.'

'No, indeed, you are very right. We shall keep this incident to ourselves.' He glanced at her before taking up the reins. 'I hope you will forgive me for not taking better care of you?'

'There is nothing to forgive, sir. Pray do not mention it again.'

'Very well.' He gave her a look that she found difficult to interpret. 'You continue to surprise me. I am beginning to think I have not made such a bad bargain after all.'

Lottie did not answer. Her cheeks burned, for his words had been more revealing than he perhaps realised. Had he been regretting his bargain? If so, why had he not simply released her immediately she and her father arrived? No one would have been any the wiser and he could have made whatever excuse he pleased, leaving him free to find a wife more to his liking.

* * *

Had Lottie been privileged to read Nicolas's thoughts, she would have known that they had been very similar at one time. Nicolas had wondered several times why he had not settled with Sir Charles at the start. However, at this moment his feelings had undergone a sudden and startling change.

When he saw her lying with her eyes closed, Nicolas had at first thought she might be dead. The feeling that swept over him at that moment had been one of utter desolation. Relief had followed so quickly that he had had no time to examine his reaction or to understand why he had felt such a sense of loss.

She had retired into dignified silence, which left him time to consider his reactions. How could it matter to him whether this young woman lived or died? Except that he would feel distress at causing harm to any young woman of his acquaintance.

Was that it—just a natural concern for a young life?

Nicolas was nothing if not honest and he faced the truth without flinching. Lottie had somehow managed to get partly beneath the barrier he kept in place. At first he had thought her a beautiful scoundrel, a hardened adventuress—but Lottie was not her twin sister. He believed she was neither a thief nor a light-skirt, though her sister might very well be both.

He frowned, for it might prove inconvenient to have Lottie's twin as a close relation in the future. He would have to try to make some arrangement that protected his wife and his name from Clarice's misbehaviour—but that was for the future.

In the meantime he needed to sort out his feelings for

this beautiful, brave and spirited young woman sitting silently beside him. He had begun to find her company stimulating, though sometimes uncomfortable as she challenged him openly.

The look in her eyes as she spoke of the lines he had drawn for their marriage had struck him more deeply than he liked. Of course he could not expect her to stay always in the country, hidden away as if he were ashamed of her. He would not want to live with her in town, of course—but she might have her own establishment in Bath if she chose.

He could visit her there or here in the country if he felt the need, but she must be able to entertain and live a proper sort of life. Yes, he decided, that would do very well—and yet somehow it was not quite what he wanted.

As she changed for dinner that evening, Lottie examined her arms and legs, discovering some nasty bruises that were just about to come out. She did feel rather battered and shaken, but had not wanted to make a fuss. She would, however, need to wear a stole this evening to cover some of the marks.

She was thoughtful as Rose brushed and styled her hair for her. The look of horror in the marquis's eyes as he'd looked down at her had been rather satisfying. It was good that he had some concern for her, because she was beginning to like him more than she had expected. He was stern and she had evidence of his temper, but he could be pleasant company when he chose. She hoped that they might come to an understanding as they became more comfortable with one another.

He was not in love with her. She would be foolish to look for romance in her marriage, but if they could perhaps become fond of one another it might be an ideal arrangement.

Lottie sighed as she went downstairs. She was to meet more of her neighbours that evening and must manage to give an impression of a happy young woman about to be married.

The marquis had spoken of going up to town for a flying visit. Lottie would have preferred it if he had stayed so that they could get to know one another, but three weeks was a short enough time to prepare her wedding gown. She would hardly have time to miss him.

'Well, I do not see why you must leave us to amuse ourselves here alone,' Henrietta commented, giving her godson a sharp look after the guests had left that evening. 'Surely there is nothing so important that it cannot wait for a few weeks?'

'I have some business I must see to with my lawyers,' Nicolas told her. 'Besides, Lottie will need some new clothes. If she will supply me with her measurements, and you will advise me on what seamstresses I should employ, I shall endeavour to supply the lack.'

'I intend to take care of my own wedding gown,' Lottie said. 'I should like one or two afternoon gowns and perhaps a new bonnet—but you may safely leave that to me.'

'You need not fear to trust him,' Henrietta said. 'Rothsay has excellent taste. I shall give him a note to my own seamstress and she will provide you with what you need for your honeymoon. If you go to Paris you may buy more there, of course.'

Nicolas frowned. 'If you will give me what I require, I shall do my best to please you, Lottie. We shall discuss what else you need on my return.'

Lottie inclined her head, but said nothing. Henrietta looked from one to the other and shook her head. It was clear to her that once again they had had some kind of disagreement.

'Well, I shall do it now for I know you like to start early in the morning. While you are in town, you may ask my doctor for some more of the excellent mixture he makes for my indigestion.'

'Of course,' he said. 'Are you ready for bed, Lottie, or shall you take a turn in the garden with me?'

'I shall take the air with you, if you wish,' Lottie said. 'It is a pleasant evening.'

Nicolas offered his arm and she took it, her hand so light that he hardly knew it was there.

'I wanted to make sure that you had all you need for the moment,' he said as they went out into the garden. 'I had not intended to leave before the wedding but there is something I must attend to—will you be all right here? Your aunt should arrive in a day or so and you have Henrietta for company, as well as your father.'

'Please do not concern yourself, my lord. I have plenty to keep me busy. The invitations are not yet written and I have a gown to make.'

'I could have the gown made in town.'

'It will not be necessary. I have always made my gowns and I like my own style.'

'Your gowns become you, but you might wish to have something a little more…'

'Stylish?' Lottie laughed. 'I shall not be offended if you speak your mind to me. If I intended a Season in town I should certainly seek the help of a seamstress—but I think that is unlikely.'

'It may not be in the future. You may visit town occasionally, I dare say. I am hoping we shall at least be tolerably good friends, Lottie.'

'Yes, I am certain we shall,' she said. 'I am prepared to forgive and forget—if you are?'

'Can you forgive?'

'I think it only sensible to put the past behind us. We shall begin again, my lord.'

'Shall we, Lottie?' He turned, looking down at her in the moonlight.

She was beautiful. Even when he despised her as Clarice, the adventuress, he had known that she stirred his senses. Without knowing why he did it, he reached out and drew her to him, his head bending to reach hers. He kissed her tenderly and then hungrily as he felt her response. Her body was soft and yielding, the scent of her intoxicating, filling him with an urgent need for something he did not understand. For a few moments he held her crushed against him, feeling the burn of desire in his loins. He was tempted to sweep her into his arms and take her somewhere he could make love to her right away, but he controlled his urges.

'A kiss to seal the bargain,' he said, trying for lightness. 'Goodnight, Lottie. I shall be gone only a few days—and then we shall entertain our neighbours in earnest. Henrietta will set you right if you ask her.'

'Goodnight, Rothsay,' Lottie said, sounding so calm that he was irritated by her lack of emotion. 'Do not concern yourself. I am quite able to amuse myself while you are gone.'

Lottie pressed her fingers to her lips. She could still feel the impression of his lips, the burn of his kiss. Had she wondered if it would be difficult to do her duty and provide the heir? One kiss in the moonlight had shown her it would be only too easy. She had wanted him to go on kissing her for ever, but she was foolish to let herself hope for more than she knew he was willing to give.

The marquis would be a skilled and passionate lover. She had been told that he had indulged himself with a string of mistresses after his attachment to Elizabeth was broken. Lottie frowned as she wondered what the woman he had wished to make his wife looked like. Her curiosity was aroused, but it would be most improper to ask Nicolas about his former love.

Lottie put the slight irritation from her mind. Nicolas had made it clear that she could not look for love or romance in their marriage. His kiss was merely to seal their bargain but it had shown her that she felt more for him than she had expected or wanted. She knew that she would enjoy the intimate side of marriage. She would be neither embarrassed or reluctant when he came to her bed—but she was not sure how she would feel when he left it.

If she allowed herself to like him too much, she might find that her heart was broken. The one thing Lottie must never forget was that this was a marriage of convenience.

Nicolas wanted an heir. He had decided to be generous and considerate to her, which was an improvement on his manner at the start.

Was it enough? It had to be, because she did not think she had the strength to break off their engagement now.

Alone in her room, she bent down to stroke Kitty and laughed ruefully.

'Am I a fool? Should I flee now while I can?'

Kitty purred and Lottie nodded.

'You are right. It is already far too late.'

Chapter Five

Lottie awoke to a sense of loss, though it took her a few moments to realise why. Was it only three days since Rothsay had gone to London? It seemed an age. She had begun to miss the sound of his voice and the ring of his boots on tiled floors. Oh, how ridiculous! She did not really know the man at all and she certainly could not spend the rest of her life moping when he was not here.

She threw back the covers with determination. She had done as she'd thought and arranged with Mrs Blake to come to the house and help her to sew her wedding gown, and this morning she was going into Northampton with Lady Fisher to choose some silks. The invitations had gone out for the ball and the wedding. There was more than enough to keep her busy, because the servants awaited their instructions and it could not all be left to Henrietta, who, Lottie was aware, was far from well.

She washed her hands and face in cool water and

dressed. Rose would bring warm water up later and she would change, but first she would go for a walk to the lake. She had got into the habit of feeding the swans. It had become her first task of the morning and gave her something to do before breakfast. After the incident with the poacher she had stayed clear of the park in the early hours, preferring to walk only as far as the lake before breakfast.

It was so beautiful out at this hour. The peace of her surroundings was taking away the small ache she had experienced on waking. She would see Rothsay very soon for he was sure to return before the ball.

Lottie thoroughly enjoyed her trip to Northampton with Lady Fisher and bought some yards of a deep cream silk shot through with gold. Trimmed with some old lace that her mother had given her before she died, it would make a perfect gown for Lottie's wedding and could afterwards be worn for special dinners. Brides often wore their wedding gown in the first year of marriage; Lottie could see herself making good use of hers. She knew exactly what she wanted, the bodice tight with a dipping neckline trimmed with lace, and three-quarter-length sleeves frilled at the elbows with the same lace. She would not wear a bonnet, but an arrangement of fresh flowers from Rothsay's hothouses in her hair.

Her head filled with plans for the wedding, she thanked Lady Fisher when she was set down outside the house later that afternoon.

'Will you come in for some refreshment, ma'am?'

'Thank you, Lottie. Another time, perhaps? I am

expecting visitors this evening and must be there to greet them.'

'Oh, that will be pleasant for you.'

'I am not sure. I find Hunter a difficult guest but he is my late husband's nephew so I must oblige him sometimes. I wish that Bertie was at home, but as you know he left for London this morning.'

'Yes, Sir Bertie said adieu to me yesterday,' Lottie said. 'You must miss him when he is away, ma'am?'

'A little, but I have many friends. Please call whenever you have time, Lottie.'

Lottie thanked her and waved as the carriage was driven away. She was feeling pleased as she went into the house, because now that she had the silk she needed, she would be fully occupied with the making of her gown.

'Did you enjoy your trip, Miss Stanton?' the house-keeper asked.

'Yes, thank you. I have several parcels. Perhaps they could be taken upstairs?'

'Yes, of course, miss. You have a visitor waiting in the front parlour with the countess. I took her some tea. Would you like me to bring fresh?'

'Aunt Beth has arrived?' Lottie's face lit up. 'That is excellent news, thank you. Yes, I should like some tea, please.'

She walked hastily to the small front parlour, hearing the sound of laughter. It sounded as if Aunt Beth and Henrietta had hit it off already, and, as she entered, she saw that they were perfectly at home together.

'Lottie, my dearest one.' Beth stood up, her face wreathed in smiles as Lottie went to embrace her. 'How are you, my love?'

'Perfectly well, thank you,' Lottie said and kissed her on both cheeks. 'I am so pleased to have you here. I see you are already acquainted with Lady Selby.'

'It is the most fortunate thing,' Henrietta said. 'We were acquainted as girls. Beth is some years my junior but we met in Bath when I was first married and she had just come out.'

'So many moons ago,' Beth laughed softly. 'I had no idea that Rothsay was your godson, Henrietta.'

'I was great friends with his mama,' Henrietta said. 'He was such a charming boy, you know. I confess he won my heart when he was no more than five or six, and I have loved him as the son I never had.'

'It is a pity he had to leave on business,' Beth said, her eyes thoughtful as her gaze rested on Lottie. 'You need to get to know one another, Lottie.'

'We have the rest of our lives,' Lottie dismissed her suggestion, as if unconcerned even though it echoed her own feelings. 'There is so much to do in a house like this, dearest Aunt. I refuse to give Henrietta all the trouble of this wedding, though her advice is invaluable for I should not have known how to start.'

'Well, I am here now to help, too,' her aunt said. 'Have you settled the menus? They are most important—your guests will expect only the best in a house like this, Lottie.'

'We made a start last night, did we not, Henrietta? However, no one understands food better than you, Aunt. You must look at my suggestions and tell me if they can be improved.'

'Yes, I shall certainly do so. Your cook has a light

hand with pastry, Lottie. However, there might be some improvements I can make without giving offence.'

Lottie could tell that her aunt was looking forward to ordering the kitchens and hoped that Rothsay would have no objection. She had always left the menus to her aunt, for her own time was taken up with other things. Aunt Beth would be a great help to her when she was mistress here—and if Rothsay had some fault to find he could tell her when he came.

She glanced at the countess. 'I suppose there has been no word from Rothsay?'

'No, he is very provoking, is he not?' Henrietta gave her a gentle smile. 'It is so much more comfortable when the gentlemen aren't here to give their opinion—though I think he will not interfere with your arrangements in the house, Lottie.'

Lottie stifled the faint irritation she felt at her fiancé's absence. 'I dare say his business is important. He will return as soon as he is able no doubt.'

'Excuse me, Miss Stanton…Lady Selby…' The house-keeper had entered the room and looked from one to the other, as if uncertain who to address. 'There is a problem. I am not sure what ought to be done…'

'What is it, Mrs Mann?' Lottie asked. 'May I be of assistance?'

'Perhaps we could speak in private, miss?'

Lottie followed her from the room into the hall. It was obvious the housekeeper was ill at ease, uncertain what to do about something.

'Is there a problem with one of the servants?'

'No, miss. I should not have troubled you with that, for I am able to deal with domestic problems. It is just that Sam Blake was seen in the village. Apparently, he was talking wildly about getting even with his lordship. Mr Barton, that's his lordship's bailiff, was wondering whether to set more men on to patrol the grounds.'

'Has Blake escaped, then? I am certain Rothsay told me he had been sent to prison.'

'He must have escaped, miss. Barton wanted to speak to the countess, but I thought you might be the best person in the circumstances. I did not wish to alarm Lady Selby. To tell you the truth, she don't seem quite like her old self, miss.'

'No, I think she tires easily.' Lottie frowned, because Rothsay had told her not to interfere in estate matters, but she did not see how she could avoid doing so. 'Please tell Mr Barton to set more men on at once. If his lordship should return and be caught unawares he might meet with an accident.' Remembering the shot that had caused her fall, she was anxious. 'A message should be sent to the marquis in London, making him aware of the situation. I shall write the note myself and Mr Mann may send it on.' She smiled at the housekeeper. 'You were very right not to trouble the countess. You may always come to me if you are in doubt on any account.'

'Yes, miss. I thought I might.' Mrs Mann looked relieved. 'I shall speak to Mr Barton immediately—and you will keep this to yourself?'

'Yes, I would not alarm either Lady Selby or Lady Hoskins. They do not need to know about this. I shall tell them it was just a little hitch with the wedding arrangements.'

'Yes, miss. That is very sensible of you.'

The housekeeper departed and Lottie returned to the

parlour. She told her curious friends that it was just a problem with the supply of fresh salmon for the wedding, which had been easily resolved.

'Well, I do not know why Mrs Mann should be concerned with that,' Henrietta said. 'Rothsay will have it sent down from his estate in Scotland, as usual.'

'Yes, I am sure you are right,' Lottie said, but did not enlighten her further. 'Now, I must tell you that I chose the silk for my wedding gown today and it is beautiful. Rose took it up to my room. You must both come and see. I shall begin work on cutting the pattern tomorrow. I asked Mrs Blake if she would come at ten and help me.'

Lottie wondered if the woman would still come after what had been reported. If her husband was on the run from the law, she might be afraid of her reception. It might be best to send Rose with a message first thing in the morning.

Lottie broke the seal of the letter that had just been brought up to her. She frowned as she saw it was from her sister. What could Clarice have to say to her? She scanned the letter, lingering over one particular paragraph.

How clever of you to snare him, Lottie, Clarice had written. *I know you must have agreed for Papa's sake and to give Aunt Beth a home. I am a selfish wretch, but I am in love—and it couldn't matter to you. You will have money and a home, and you can thank me for stepping back and letting you become the marchioness. I may visit you one of these days—and I shan't stop you*

*if you want to show your appreciation for my generosity.
After all, you are supposed to be me—aren't you?*

Clarice went on to describe some of the places she
was visiting in Paris, as if she had not made what might
be a veiled threat of blackmail.

She frowned, because although Clarice had always
been selfish, she seemed to have touched new depths.
Sighing, Lottie put the letter to one side. She was not
sure what Clarice expected, but she would face it when
the time came. In the meantime, she had more pressing
problems.

What ought she to do about Lily Blake after that dis-
turbing news about her husband?

'I wasn't sure you would want me to come after what
everyone was saying.' Lily Blake made a slight curtsy.
'But Rose told me you still needed my help…'

'Yes, I do,' Lottie said. 'Come and sit down, Mrs
Blake. I do not think we need to concern ourselves with
the gossip or your husband's intentions for the moment.
You need to earn some shillings for your work and I
need help.'

Lily looked at her for a moment, then, 'It weren't my
Sam spreading threats about the village,' she blurted
out, her cheeks hot with colour. 'I know he done wrong,
Miss Stanton, and I ain't trying to defend him—but it
were his cousin Dickon what put him up to the poaching.
They look a bit alike but Sam is still where his lordship
put him and cursing the day he got in with a pack of
rogues. It were Dickon as were shouting his mouth off
at the inn.'

'Sam's cousin, you say?'

'Yes. Dickon were alus a bad lot. He lost Sam his first job and after that my husband couldn't get work. No one would give him a chance, miss, and Dickon plagued him to help him with the traps. We've three children all under the age of five and he didn't want to see us starve.'

'Yes, I understand it must have been hard,' Lottie said. 'In future I shall employ you—and when your husband is released from prison I will see what I can do for him, though I promise nothing in his case.'

Lily's eyes brimmed with tears. 'Sam told me you would've helped him, miss. He reckons you be too good fer the likes of his lordship.'

'You must not say such things to me,' Lottie said and smiled. 'Now, I have heard you have some skill with your needle—can you also cut a pattern?'

'Oh yes, miss.' Lily brightened and brushed her tears away. 'Afore I was wed I worked for a high-class seamstress. She had a smart shop in Northampton and I worked in the back room.'

'Then I am sure we can create something special between us, Lily.'

'Yes, miss. With your figure it will be easy. What did you have in mind?'

Lottie explained, bringing a look of admiration to the other woman's eyes. 'It is a style I know suits me and I have made similar gowns for myself and others before.'

'It will suit you, miss—but perhaps we could change a few things here and there. After all, it is your wedding gown.'

'Yes.' Lottie was thoughtful as she watched Lily spread the silk on the floor and explain what she meant about getting the full potential from the hang of the material. Lily was clearly a talented seamstress and she deserved her chance, regardless of her husband's foolish behaviour.

After she was married, she would have a good think about the possibilities for Lily Blake's future.

In the meantime, she was trying not to worry about the orders she had given for Mr Barton to increase the patrols both on the estate and the roads leading to it. Rothsay might not be best pleased when he returned, but he should have been here and then he could have made the decision himself.

Nicolas glanced at the letter that had just been delivered from Rothsay Manor. He did not recognise the handwriting and looked for the signature before reading the contents. Why would Lottie have sent it to him urgently?

He frowned as he read what had happened and the orders she had given to protect the estate and his person should the rogue try to kill him on his return. He had wondered if Blake were behind the shot that had almost resulted in injury for Lottie, but to his best knowledge the man was still locked up in a prison in Northampton. He could, of course, have escaped in the meantime, but it was more likely to have been his cousin. Dickon Blake had served a year for his own misdemeanours and would have been released recently. The pair were similar in looks and could be confused on a dark night, though, unlike Sam, Dickon was violent and dangerous.

Sighing, Nicolas crushed the letter in his hand, tossing it to one side. He supposed he ought to return and sort this mess out. His business had been finished in an hour for it had merely been an addition to his will. Lottie must be provided for in the event of his death. He had visited various merchants, giving them instructions for the wardrobe Lottie would need as the new marchioness. There was no need for him to wait on their delivery, for the clothes and other things would be sent direct to Rothsay—so why had he delayed?

Walking to gaze out of the window, Nicolas faced the dilemma he had created for himself. Lottie was expecting a marriage of convenience. She had agreed for the sake of her family—in truth, he had given her no choice. What he had done was despicable from start to finish. He should have set her free the moment he realised who she was…or, rather, who she wasn't.

He had despised the woman he had seen rifling his friend's pocket in Paris, but he had formed a deep admiration for Lottie. She was different in every way from her sister.

The trouble was he was in danger of liking her too much. Long ago, he had discovered that unrequited love hurt. Even his mother's gentle but detached way of loving her son had been painful, and his father had ignored him after her death—apart from an occasional pat on the head or an instruction to work hard for his tutors.

It was quite ridiculous to hope that Lottie could ever care for him after the way he had treated her. He was in any case not sure that he wanted to love or be loved. He would do much better to continue as he had started, but that was easier from a distance than if he were with her.

That kiss in the moonlight had shocked him. It had

been a mere experiment, just to accustom her to what it felt like to be kissed—but he was very much afraid that he was the one who had been most affected. Lottie had taken it in her stride. Yes, she had seemed to melt into him while he held her, responding so sweetly that he had wanted to make love to her instantly. Yet afterwards, she had behaved in that calm, composed manner that seemed to suggest it meant nothing at all.

Damn it! He wanted more than a complaisant wife. He wanted to know that, when he made love to her, she would want him as much as he wanted her.

He turned with a grim smile on his mouth. He couldn't hide for ever. The ball was in five days and he must be there in time to make sure that everything was in order.

'Lottie, do come and see all the packages that have arrived for you,' Aunt Beth cried as she entered the house that morning after her customary walk to the lake. 'I have never seen so many all at one time. Whatever can be in them?'

'Rothsay said he would order a few things for me in London.' Lottie frowned. 'I told him not to be extravagant—I shall not need a huge wardrobe here. Besides, Lily Blake has made me such a wonderful wedding gown that I think I shall ask her to make all my clothes in future.'

'Yes, she has created something of a miracle,' Beth said. 'Far more stylish than we ever managed alone, dearest. I think she is wasted as the wife of that rogue.'

'Lily loves him, Aunt.'

'Yes…' Beth shook her head. 'We women are such

fools where men are concerned. My poor sister was much let down by your father. I do not know where he has got to these past few days.'

'He went home,' Lottie said. 'He promised to return for the ball.'

'We must hope he does not let us down.' Beth frowned. 'Rothsay has been a long time. I would have thought he would be here by now. If he is not here for—' She broke off, for there was the sound of the knocker and a footman sprang to attention to open the door.

Lottie turned, heart pounding as she saw the tall figure of the marquis enter. She had forgotten how handsome he was, how strong and masculine. Her heart caught as her eyes absorbed every detail of his appearance; it looked as if his dark hair had recently been cut short in a new style and it suited him.

'Rothsay, you are home,' she said and went forwards to greet him, offering her hand. 'I am glad to see you back. My aunt tells me several packages have arrived for me. I have not yet had time to examine the contents, but I think I should scold you for extravagance.'

'My wife must do me credit, Lottie. I cannot have the gossips saying I have a dowdy marchioness.' He took her hand, held it briefly to his lips. His eyes went beyond her to Aunt Beth. 'Lady Hoskins, I presume. Forgive me for not being here to welcome you to my home, ma'am. I am sure Lottie has made you comfortable. You are, of course, welcome to stay here for as long as you choose— though while in London I have instructed my agent on the purchase of a house for Lottie's benefit in Bath, and you may prefer to visit the spa together sometimes.'

'Really, Rothsay—did I not tell you I was perfectly content here?' Lottie's eyes sparked.

'Well, you must do as you choose,' he said easily.

'Thank you, sir,' Beth said. 'I like Bath very much. I am certain Lottie will enjoy visiting the town when she desires a change.'

'Just as you say, ma'am. I see you are a lady of good sense. Lottie, my love—may I speak to you in private for a moment?'

'Yes, of course.'

'In my library, if you please.'

Lottie followed as he strode through various apartments to the large room in the east wing. She had visited it but once in his absence; it was clearly his own preserve and he had left books lying out on the table, as if he wished to return to them without having to hunt. Brandy and glasses were waiting on a side table for his convenience. Mrs Mann had asked if she ought to tidy them away. Lottie had told her to leave all as it was until he returned.

She stood waiting just inside the door as he gazed out of the long windows at the view of the gardens.

'This business of Blake is unpleasant. I am sorry you had to be troubled with it while I was gone.'

'It was not a trouble, my lord. I was merely concerned that I must give orders to increase the patrols. I know that you do not consider I should interfere in your business, but—'

'Good grief, Lottie! What else could you have done in the circumstances? You said you had not told Henrietta or your aunt?'

'Neither of them will be tempted to go beyond the

immediate gardens. They do not need to know of any unpleasantness.' She looked at him as he turned to face her at last. 'You were not attacked as you travelled home?'

'No, not at all. I dare say it is all a lot of fuss for nothing—but you did exactly as you ought. I should have thought of it before I left, but I was not thinking too clearly.'

'You could not have known that Dickon Blake would decide to take revenge for his cousin's imprisonment. Lily told me Sam is still in prison, as no doubt you have learned.'

'It is not only Sam's incarceration that has angered Dickon. He has only recently been released from prison himself. I sentenced him to a year and he must have been freed just over a month back.'

'So it could have been he who fired at you?'

'Most probably. I shall have someone look into it. Extra keepers are all very well, but we must seek the cause and discover what is in his mind. I do not want to leave you alone until this business is resolved, Lottie. I shall hope to have it sorted before the wedding, but in the meantime the patrols will keep you safe.'

'I am certain of it. I have been far too busy to walk further than the lake and I have not yet ridden out—I was not perfectly sure which horse you would wish me to use.'

'I fear I have not treated you well, Lottie. I should have returned sooner. It was wrong to just leave every-thing to you. If you wish, we could ride out together tomorrow morning.'

'I should like that very much,' she replied. 'I am glad

you are not annoyed because I was forced to take charge. Henrietta could not have dealt with that kind of unpleasantness, you know.'

'Yet you take it in your stride?'

'I am accustomed to managing my father's estate. Very little distresses me,' she replied, a smile on her mouth. 'I believe we have covered everything we could. You were warned not to travel alone and the keepers have increased their patrols.'

'You are an unusual woman, Lottie. My mother would have screamed or fainted had she been asked to deal with such a decision.'

'I doubt it. Most ladies are capable of far more than gentlemen imagine. We are not, as we are so often termed, the weaker sex—though at times we may acquiesce to being thought so.'

'Is that so?' She looked at him in surprise for there was a new teasing note in his voice that she had not heard before. 'I believe I have a lot to learn about the fair sex, Lottie. I am but a man and cannot expect to understand the workings of the female mind. Besides, I think *you* are the exception and not the rule. I stand ready to receive instruction.'

'Now you are being provoking.' A laugh escaped her. 'Henrietta is right. You are the most provoking man.'

'I dare say I am—but perhaps you can teach me better manners?'

'Perhaps…' Lottie's heart raced. In this new mood her fiancé was very attractive. She must keep a tight rein on her feelings or she would end by falling head over heels in love with him. 'We have a great many gifts from your friends and relatives, Rothsay. Aunt Beth and Henrietta have been enjoying themselves going through them. All the cards are displayed with the gifts on a table in the long gallery. You may care to glance at them later.'

'I shall certainly do so. I dare say Great-Uncle Freddie has sent a silver tea-and-coffee service? It is his usual gift. I believe we may have upwards of four already, but I shall thank him with the proper gratitude.'

'You mean Lord Freddie, I suppose,' Lottie said. 'He sent me a very kind letter and a long string of beautiful coral and pearls, and a pair of duelling pistols for you. His letter said he thought you might appreciate them more than silver.'

'Indeed? How perceptive of him. I have always admired his pistols, which I know he once used in a duel with a rival.' Rothsay laughed. 'I am very surprised.'

'Well, I believe he may just have known that you had quite a bit of silver here at Rothsay. However, Lady Botham has sent us a silver service with both tea and coffee jugs so the tradition has been preserved.'

He chuckled. 'You see the amusing side of it, Lottie. I should have been just as happy to receive cards of congratulations, as expensive gifts, but it is a tradition, I suppose, and we must not offend anyone. We should send thank-you cards to everyone.'

'I have already replied to most,' Lottie said. 'I thought it best to attend to the replies once so many gifts began to arrive, otherwise it is easy to forget something and that is offensive, do you not agree?'

His right eyebrow arched in what she could only think a quizzical manner. 'I find myself agreeing with everything you say. You will make an admirable marchioness, Lottie.'

His words were those of praise, but something in his tone made her look at him sharply. He was not smiling and she sensed a change of mood.

'Have I done something to annoy you, Rothsay?'

'What could you have done? You have everything well under control, do you not, Lottie?'

'I have tried to do what I thought would earn your approval.'

'Indeed? Then you have succeeded. I have no fault to find, Lottie. You are everything you ought to be. Excuse me, I dare say you have much to keep you busy—and I must speak to my bailiff.'

Lottie frowned as he turned and walked from the room. He was angry or annoyed about something and for the life of her she could not think why.

Chapter Six

Nicolas had no idea why Lottie's efficiency had made him suddenly angry. It was foolish to resent the fact that she seemed to have the servants hanging on her every whim in just a few days. She was displaying all the right qualities necessary for the next marchioness, managing perfectly well, it seemed, without his help.

Was this how it would be when they were married? He would take himself off to London for a few weeks and return to a calm, smiling wife who could cope perfectly well without him?

Surely he had been fortunate beyond any expectation. He had chosen his bride so carelessly and he might have been hoisted with an adventuress who cared for nothing but spending his money. Lottie seemed more interested in scolding him for extravagance and caring for his estate in way that had been sadly lacking these past years. The perfect wife—except that she showed no sign of having missed him.

Nicolas laughed at himself. He was the one who had shunned love or anything like it for years. He was the one who had set the terms for their relationship—yet now he found himself wanting more.

He had noticed a new atmosphere in the house as soon as he entered; there was life and purpose, where before it had merely been a cold empty place waiting for someone. It appeared to have been Lottie everyone was waiting for. She had certainly made the place her own. She looked confident, composed and had smiled in welcome when he arrived—why, then, did he wish she had run to him, wanting to be caught in his arms and kissed?

She had asked him if she should like him after his abusive words to her, the threat that had made her his prisoner as much as his wife. Nicolas wished he could recall those bitter words. He knew now that she had not deserved them.

He had erected an invisible barrier between them. It was up to him to remove it brick by brick. Perhaps then she might come to like him, if not to love him.

Lottie frowned as she checked her lists, making small changes, adding little things to the tasks she must complete in the following week. The ball was the next evening, and everything was in place for the lavish supper, which would be served at ten o'clock. Henrietta had insisted champagne must flow like water all evening, and there were other wines for those who did not like the sparkling variety. The servants had worked hard to prepare the various delicacies and clean the house from top to bottom. However, there were still things to be settled for the wedding.

Because so many flowers would be used for the ball, the hothouses might not be able to supply all those needed for the wedding itself. Henrietta had mentioned a nursery run by a Northampton firm and she had sent to them to ask what would be available. The fresh salmon was coming from Scotland, more supplies of champagne would be sent from the marquis's extensive cellars in town, and would arrive on the morning before the wedding. Everything else would be supplied from the estate itself since they were almost self-sufficient. Even some of the candles they used were made locally with wax from their own hives.

Over the past weeks, Lottie had discovered the little cottage industries that relied mainly on supplying the big house and its villagers. Carpenters, a blacksmith, masons, farmers, a small brewery, a potter and an elderly lady, who made the most beautiful lace, were just a few of those depending on the marquis and his household to some degree.

It was a big responsibility and she wondered if that was the reason Rothsay disliked spending time at his home. For Lottie it was rapidly becoming the most beautiful place in the world. She enjoyed her work and her leisure, taking rambling walks when she had nothing more pressing to do. It was during her walks that she had met many of the marquis's tenants and was pleasantly surprised by the friendliness shown to her. Everyone was pleased she had come, they told her, for the master needed a wife to look after his interests.

If anyone had asked her what she would like best in

life, Lottie would have told them it was to live with her loving husband in a beautiful place where she could be useful. Here she had all she could possibly desire— except for one thing.

She could see no sign that Rothsay cared about her. He was on his best behaviour now, polite and complimentary of her efforts on his behalf. However, the distance between them was still there. It seemed he had not forgotten that he had been cheated, though he had accepted her in her sister's place.

It would not do to dwell on what was missing from her life. Lottie had faced the world as it was since her mother had died of a broken heart, and her father continued his downward slide. Rothsay would never love her, but, if she continued to show good sense and make no demands, he might in time come to feel affection for her.

She was about to go in search of her aunt and Henrietta, for it was nearly time for tea, when she heard a querulous voice seconds before the door of her private parlour was flung open. Everyone knew that this was the room she chose when she was busy working or wanted a few moments of reflection and it was by unspoken agreement that she was left alone here. Only this particular lady would ignore that and enter so abruptly.

'Cousin Agatha,' she said and rose to her feet with a smile. 'How nice that you could come.'

'No thanks to that father of yours, Lottie. I particularly asked that he should come and escort me, but I've seen nothing of him and I was forced to travel with just my servants.'

'I am sure they took good care of you, Cousin.'

'That is not the point…but there, I should not fuss at

you. Your father is a wastrel and nothing will change that, Lottie. You must make sure that he doesn't try to scrounge from you once you are married. I doubt Rothsay will put up with it. He is a bit of a cold fish I hear? I suppose you took him for the title and the money?'

'If you suppose that you are wrong,' Lottie said. 'As it happens, I have great respect and regard for Rothsay. I was just about to go in search of Aunt Beth and the countess. If you will accompany me, we shall have tea.'

'Henrietta Selby, I suppose.' Cousin Agatha's thin mouth twisted wryly. 'I know her of old. She at least is a decent sort. Don't tell me it's a love match. You've only known him a short time—besides, Clarice told me the whole story.'

'Did she? Perhaps Clarice does not know the whole story.'

'Humph…like that, is it? Well, if you care for him I shan't say another word about it. Clarice is a fool—she will end up in worse trouble if she is not careful. She came to me for money before she went off to Paris. I gave her a hundred guineas and told her not to expect more. She will run through that in five minutes, I dare say. She knows better than to come to me again, so you may expect a visit before too long.'

'Please, Cousin Agatha, may I ask you not to be so outspoken here? I do know how thoughtless Clarice is but I would prefer that others did not know of her foolish ways.'

'Foolish ways, is it? I should put another interpretation on it, but I won't pull caps with you, Lottie. I've always thought you the best of the bunch, my girl. You've a chance to make something of yourself now. See that you make the most of it.'

'Yes, I shall.' Lottie smiled at her. 'I truly will, Cousin—and I am happy you have come to stay.'

'I'd be a fool to turn down a chance like this,' Cousin Agatha said and laughed. 'Whatever you might think of me, Lottie, you know I ain't that.'

Nicolas paused outside the drawing-room door. He could hear the sound of feminine laughter and several voices. It was a long time since he had come into the house and heard something as pleasant. He walked in and his eyes sought Lottie. She looked very at home as she passed tea to the young maid. He noticed it was not Rose, but knew already that Lottie had promoted her to be her own personal maid. For a moment he almost felt a stranger in his own house, and then Lottie noticed he was there and her face lit with a smile of such warmth that he felt as if something had punched him in the stomach.

'Rothsay, please come in. We are all ladies, as you see, but the gentlemen will start to arrive later. Lord Freddie expects to be here for dinner this evening. He waited for your cousin Marcus to come home so that they could travel together—and your cousin Raymond will be here later this evening.'

He was drawn into her charmed circle immediately and walked to the fireplace, standing to get an overview of the room.

'I see we have a new guest, Lottie.'

'This is Cousin Agatha,' Lottie said. 'Lady Fox is my father's cousin, but I have always addressed her as cousin.'

'Indeed? Then perhaps I may also,' Nicolas said and inclined his head to the rather stout lady, who looked to be just a few years younger than Lottie's aunt. 'You are very welcome here, ma'am. I hope you will enjoy your visit.'

'Humph…you ain't quite the cold fish I was led to believe, Rothsay. I wondered if you were good enough for Lottie, but you may just do.'

'Thank you, ma'am.' A little quiver at the corner of his mouth told Lottie he was amused and not angry at the lady's outspokenness. 'Lottie, where is your father? I have something to discuss with him.'

'He went off for a few days. I dare say he will be back for the ball and the wedding.'

'Yes, I see.' Nicolas frowned. He could hardly blame his future father-in-law when he had done much the same thing. 'No doubt my relations will descend in force tomorrow. May we expect any more of your family, Lottie?'

'No, I think not,' she said. 'We are all here apart from Papa.' A faint flush stained her cheeks. 'I believe my sister will not come.'

'Clarice is still in Paris, as far as any of us know,' Cousin Agatha put in. 'She has friends there, I dare say. Besides, it might be awkward if she came, Lottie. You are better off without her.'

'Yes, perhaps.'

Nicolas saw that she was embarrassed. He looked at his godmother and saw the speculation in her eyes. There was no use in denying it, he must put the record straight now.

'I fear I have not been entirely honest with you from

the start, my dear Henri. Though I was engaged to be married to Clarice, Lottie is actually that lady's twin sister. For reasons I'd rather not go into, it was Lottie who turned up to deliver the news that Clarice had reconsidered our betrothal. But it was fortunate indeed for me; by changing her mind Clarice has given me the gift of being free to propose to her sister—and I have been luckier than I deserve in finding such a lovely bride.'

Cousin Agatha gave a derisory snort, but said nothing more. Henrietta looked from one to the other and smiled.

'Yes, I believe I understand, Nicolas. You must tell me more another time. Do sit and have some tea, dearest. It makes my neck ache to look up to you.'

Nicolas sat. Lottie shot him a grateful look and poured his tea just as he liked it. He understood why Lottie had not particularly wanted to invite Cousin Agatha. The woman was a liability, but he would have a word with her in private. He did not wish Lottie to be embarrassed in front of strangers—and Lady Fox must be quite certain of his support for his future wife.

'Lottie—may I speak to you alone please?' Nicolas caught her as she was leaving to change for the evening. 'I should like a few words in private—before the hordes arrive. I fear we shall not have a moment to spare once that happens.'

'Of course. Do you wish to go to the library?'

He led the way and she followed, then turned as he closed the door behind them, an apology on her lips.

'I am sorry, but Cousin Agatha has always spoken her mind. My sister borrowed some money from her, to pay for her trip to Paris, I must presume. Agatha does not approve of Clarice.'

'No, I dare say not. She seems to approve of you, however?'

'Yes, for I stood up to her when Mama died and she wished Clarice and I to leave Papa and go to her.'

'Well, we all have relations who cause us some unquiet moments. You will meet my cousin Raymond this evening.' Nicolas hesitated. 'I wanted to tell you that I have had my lawyer draw up a new contract for our marriage, which I should like you to sign. Your father must also when he returns. To neglect this might have led to complications if anything should happen to me. In order that your jointure is protected and our sons' inheritance secure I have made the changes necessary.'

'I see…' Lottie understood the reasons for his visit to town. 'Yes, it should be done properly. I shall sign—and Papa will do whatever you tell him when he returns.'

'Had it not been so important I should not have left you here to cope alone.' He produced a document from his pocket and placed it on the table with pen and ink. 'Please take a moment or two to read it, Lottie.'

'I am sure you have been impeccable,' Lottie said, looking up at him. 'Does this mean the other contract has been destroyed?'

'I thought it best to start again. Your father has his copy, of course, but no doubt he will accept the new one in its place. I believe the terms are more favourable than before.'

'I hope you have not given Papa anything more than the release of his debts. He will waste the money at the gaming tables.'

'He is to have an allowance, but in return must be discreet. Your own settlement has been increased. I do not wish you to go short of anything, Lottie.'

'I am certain you have been too generous, Rothsay. I have not yet had time to look at all the gifts you sent me from town, but I think you were extravagant, sir.'

'Not sir, please, Lottie. Rothsay or Nicolas, if you prefer.' He watched as she signed. 'You did not wish to read the contract?'

'I do not think it necessary. As I told you before, I shall be content here. Really, the estate is a perfect place to live. We have almost all we need here, you know. Yes, we do have to send to Northampton or London for luxuries, but most of what we require comes from the farms and the hothouses—or the local businesses and craftsmen.'

'Is that so?' He looked at her thoughtfully. 'I have left the management of this estate to others, except for brief visits. You seem to have learned a lot in a brief time, Lottie. I hope you have not found it too onerous a task preparing for the wedding?'

'It was a delight and a pleasure. I shall enjoy entertaining our neighbours, Rothsay—especially when you are at home, though I intend to hold small soirées when you are not.'

'You have it all settled in your mind? I had wondered if you might have suffered a change of heart whilst I was gone?'

'No, not at all. I think I shall do very well in this life you have chosen for us, Rothsay. If there is anything that needs your attention, I shall write as I did concerning the keepers, but otherwise I shall manage well enough.'

'In that case, it is time I gave you this,' he said with a wry twist of his lips. 'Allow me to take your hand, Lottie.' She rose to her feet and he slipped a magnificent ring on to her left hand. 'I had this made for you in town. It took a day or two longer than I hoped, but I am pleased with it.'

Lottie looked at the exquisite square emerald surrounded by white diamonds so pure that they took her breath.

'It is beautiful, Rothsay. I am overwhelmed.'

'It is worthy of you, I think. I have asked for the Rothsay heirlooms to be sent here in time for the wedding. You may take your choice of them and the rest will return to the bank. I think most of them too heavy and old fashioned, but anything you like could be refurbished. I have bought you a wedding gift, naturally. A bride should have her own jewels, though the heirlooms must be preserved for the future.'

'Thank you so much for my ring.' Lottie moved towards him impulsively. She reached up to kiss his cheek, then found herself crushed against his chest.

Rothsay's mouth was soft and yet demanding, drawing a sweet response from her. She could not keep the barrier in place and felt herself melt into him as the heat of desire swirled inside her. A little moan left her lips and she longed for something she had never known— the joining of a man and woman as one, flesh to flesh. Gazing into his eyes, she saw a hungry yearning and knew that he desired her as much as she wanted him.

He *desired* her. He did not love her, though she believed he was coming to respect her and perhaps like her. Happiness pooled inside her, bringing a smile to her lips and her eyes, had she known it.

'You are everything a man has a right to expect in his wife,' he murmured huskily. 'I should not delay you further, Lottie, or you will be late for dinner—but I wanted you to have the ring and to be aware of changes to the contract.'

'Thank you.' He seemed to have withdrawn again, yet Lottie was feeling happier as she went upstairs. Hers was perhaps a strange marriage, but she thought it might do well enough. The anger and resentment she had felt at the beginning had all gone and she was anticipating her wedding with pleasure.

How right Rothsay was to say there would be no time to talk once his relatives began to arrive. Uncle Freddie and his son Marcus were amongst the first. Lottie had appreciated his gift and thanked him for it with a shy smile and a kiss on the cheek. She liked him and his rather handsome son immediately and felt that the feeling was returned. Cousin Raymond was a disappointment. His clothes proclaimed him a macaroni and he strutted like a peacock, showing off his finery, seeming to have no interest in anything but his appearance and the latest *on-dit* in town.

After that, in quick succession, three families arrived that had not been expected until the following day. However, their rooms were prepared and since they had dined on the way and required only a light supper Cook was not much put out.

Lottie might have struggled to remember them all

had not Henrietta grounded her well concerning the family.

'The Cottrells are second cousins but Nicolas rather likes Sir James and his wife. Lady Tilda was the wife of Rothsay's cousin Rupert. She is a widow but her son Robert is the heir to the title for that branch of the family, though not yet of age. Nicolas oversees her affairs, I dare say, as head of the family. Lord William Stowe is a cousin on his mother's side, and his wife, Jane, is a silly little thing, but sweet and docile. They have two small children. There are any number of distant cousins, who will no doubt seize the chance to stay at Rothsay Manor, but most of them will be satisfied with a nod and a smile. In time you will know them all by name—that is, if you choose to ask them to visit, my dear.'

Supper was a lively affair in the drawing room, though Henrietta retired soon after the tea tray was brought in. Some of the gentlemen were in a jovial mood and seemed prepared to stay up all night, and at eleven o'clock the ladies decided to leave them to their wine and cigars.

Lottie smiled at Rothsay as she bid him goodnight. He took her hand and kissed it, bringing a little flush to her cheeks, but earning approval from his male relatives.

'I am sure I wondered if Rothsay would ever marry,' Lady Cottrell said as she walked upstairs with Lottie. 'He seemed so set in his ways, but they say reformed rakes make good husbands. I know he is meticulous in matters of honour. I dare say he will give up his mistress and settle down once you are married. They say she is quite beautiful but then, you are lovely yourself, my dear. Besides, we must forgive the gentlemen their little peccadilloes, must we not?'

Lottie could not look at her as she murmured something appropriate and escaped to her room. She was sure that the lady had not meant to be malicious, but until this moment Lottie had not thought about Rothsay's life in London. Of course he must still have a mistress. Was that lady the real cause of Rothsay's sudden departure for town?

Lottie supposed that he must have been with her in London all this time…yet the kiss he had given her in the library had seemed so full of passion…

Tears stung her eyes and caught at the back of her throat. How lowering it was to think that she had responded so eagerly to his kiss. She must remember that Rothsay wanted a marriage of convenience. He required complaisance in his wife, but nothing more. If she showed her feelings too plainly, he might feel uncomfortable—or even disgusted.

He had not seemed disgusted when he kissed her, but how could he care for her when he had a mistress he continued to visit?

Lottie had hoped that he might come to feel some affection for her, but now she realised that she had allowed herself to hope for too much. Rothsay was generous and meticulous in matters of business and honour. In having the contract changed to her name, he had safeguarded her from any bother in the future—and there might have been had her sister's name remained in the contract. Lottie had not even considered the legal side, but Rothsay had left nothing to chance. However, he had given her no reason to think his feelings had undergone a major change.

He might respect her more than he did her sister, but

that was not love. He was not in love with her—he might even be in love with his beautiful mistress.

Lottie's eyes sparkled with tears as she picked Kitty up and kissed her. The kitten was growing swiftly, its fur much softer now that it was well fed and groomed. Rose had been training the pet for her and there were less puddles than at the start.

Lifting her head, Lottie banished her tears. She would not give way to emotion. She had agreed to this arrangement and she would not renege on her bargain.

It struck her then that had she wished to, she could have refused to sign the new contract. At the time the possibility had not even occurred to her—nor would she have refused if it had.

Lottie wanted to live here and be Rothsay's wife. She just wanted him to be a little bit fond of her.

Oh dear, was she being foolish again? Lottie made a determined effort and succeeded in laughing at herself. She had been through this a hundred times in her mind. She must and would be satisfied with her life in this beautiful place—even if Rothsay's careless manner caused her pain at times.

What she would not do was to let him guess that she was falling in love with him. She had begun to develop feelings for him perhaps from the very first moment she saw him—and if not then, certainly when he held her close after the accident.

She frowned for a moment as she went to bed. Rothsay had said little about the threat to his life. She supposed that he had keepers watching for Dickon Blake. He would have made his own arrangements now that he was back.

* * *

'Poachers, you say?' Uncle Freddie looked at him hard. 'If they come before me I hang 'em or send 'em off to the colonies. Scum, that's what they are and deserve all they get.'

'In the case of Dickon Blake I would agree. I think he misled his cousin. If it would not appear weakness, I should be inclined to let Sam Blake off after a couple of months. His wife is an honest woman and, if he were given some employment, he might reform.'

'Not with his cousin Dickon about,' Uncle Freddie said. 'If the man is the rogue you describe, you will not be free of him until you either hang or transport him. All this liberal talk about giving the deserving poor a chance in life is a load of nonsense in my opinion. The deserving poor know their place and cause no trouble— the others are rogues and need to be kept in line.'

'Yes, that was my father's opinion,' Nicolas agreed. 'I suppose I should give Blake twelve months and have done with it.'

'Don't give it another thought, my boy. Still, it is best not to tell the ladies anything about these matters. They have soft hearts, but they may ease their minds by delivering succour to those who behave themselves.'

'Yes…' Nicolas smiled inwardly. Somehow he did not see Lottie agreeing with such sentiments. She might not say it to his uncle's face, but he believed she would have no scruples in giving him her opinion.

The devil of it was he had begun to wish for Lottie's good opinion. It was unfortunate that the case should come up on the morning of the ball. If he handed down the heavier sentence, he hoped she would not be too upset to enjoy the evening. Yet his uncle was right. It would be foolish to show weakness. Sam Blake had broken the law and ought to serve his proper sentence.

Nicolas would have to try to keep the news from her, until after the wedding if possible. He would visit Mrs Blake, reassure her that she was safe in her cottage, and ask her not to tell Lottie until after the wedding day. The woman was honest enough and he might give her something to tide her over while her husband was in prison—but the man must serve his time.

His decision was made and he would not change his mind, but it did not sit easily with his conscience. He would have been lenient if he could, but weakness would encourage others to think they could trap game in his woods with impunity and that would not do. Especially as he was thinking of bringing in a herd of deer and some exotic game birds.

'Lottie...' Hearing the sibilant whisper behind her, Lottie turned, looking for the source. She was in the shrubbery searching for greenery that she could use to decorate the house and did not at first see the young woman crouching out of sight. 'I'm here, but I didn't want anyone else to see me.'

'Clarice!' Lottie's heart pumped madly as she glanced round. 'What are you doing here?'

'Do not worry, I haven't come to demand that you step aside for me,' Clarice told her. 'Come here so that I can stand properly without being seen. We returned from Paris three days ago and I've been trying to get you alone ever since.'

Lottie's heart sank as she saw her sister's face and

understood why she had come. 'What do you want, Clarice? If you have come to ask for money, I have very little to give you.'

'Don't be so mean, Lottie. You have all this—and it should have been mine.'

'You ran off and left Papa in the lurch,' Lottie said. 'Besides, the estate belongs to Rothsay, not me. As yet I have only a small allowance. I could give you twenty guineas, but that is all I can spare.'

'I never thought you would be so tight-fisted,' Clarice said and looked sulky. 'I suppose it will have to do for the moment—but I shall expect more when you're married. It wouldn't look too good if I told everyone what you had done, would it?'

'Wait here and I will fetch your money, Clarice. I do not mind giving you something when I have money to spare, but do not expect me to give you large sums. Rothsay will give me an allowance, but he will not pay your debts, so do not think I have a never-ending purse.'

'If I had known how mean you would be, I should have married him myself,' Clarice said. 'Make it fifty guineas, Lottie—or I might tell him the truth.'

'He already knows,' Lottie said. 'You cannot blackmail me, Clarice. I will give you twenty guineas now—and, occasionally, I might give you similar sums, but Rothsay is under no illusions and he is satisfied with his bargain.'

Seeing the flicker of annoyance in her sister's face, Lottie returned to the house to fetch the money. She did not grudge her sister a few guineas, but she was afraid that Clarice's demands would not end here.

Chapter Seven

Lottie put the unpleasant incident with her sister to the back of her mind. The wedding was approaching so fast that she did not have time to dwell on Clarice's threats. On the morning of the ball, she was so busy that she hardly noticed Rothsay had disappeared for several hours. She had received so many small tributes from friends and neighbours that she seemed to be opening gifts and admiring bouquets the whole time. Having guests in the house meant that she must be concerned for their comfort and could not go for her usual walk.

'I never expected all this,' she said to Henrietta when that lady gave her a pretty little box that contained a diamond pin. 'You have already given us that lovely painting of Venice and those exquisite lace tablecloths.'

'This is just for you, because I love you,' Henrietta said and kissed her. 'I am so glad Nicolas has you in his life, dear Lottie. I was beginning to think he would turn into a miserable old man and be entirely alone in his later years.'

'No, how could you?' Lottie laughed. 'He has so many friends and relatives. He need never be alone.'

'One can be all alone in the midst of a crowd,' Henrietta said. 'Rothsay was lonely, but he isn't now. Everyone has been telling me what a change they see in him—and I have seen it from the first. I believe he loves you, Lottie. Truly and with his whole heart, as I had hoped.'

'Oh…I do hope you are right,' Lottie said and pressed her hand. Her throat felt tight, but she dismissed the urge to cry. Henrietta meant well, but Lottie knew the truth—her husband would never truly love her. 'Do you happen to know where he is?'

'I believe there may be a court session in Northampton,' Henrietta said. 'He didn't tell me, but someone mentioned it. Rothsay may have been asked to sit. No doubt he will tell you if you ask.'

Lottie nodded. She wasn't sure Rothsay would wish to discuss his business with her or that she ought to ask. They had been getting on so much better and she did not want him to be angry because he thought she was interfering. She hoped he would be lenient with Sam Blake, but she would not ask.

She was still determined not to ask awkward questions when Rothsay joined them after nuncheon. Chairs had been set out under the trees and some of the gentlemen were playing a game of quoits on the grass. Others had walked to the lake, while the ladies took their ease before changing for the evening.

'Is everything all right?' Lottie asked when Rothsay came up to her.

He nodded but she thought his expression strained, his

manner slightly reserved. Lottie decided that she would say nothing that might precipitate a quarrel that evening. Perhaps tomorrow when the ball was over, though it might be better to be discreet and not mention the fact that Henrietta had let slip about the court session.

It was, after all, none of her business what Rothsay chose to do in his position as a magistrate. She might privately wish that he had let Sam Blake go with a reprimand, but she could not expect her opinion to matter. Rothsay was not alone in his opinion that poaching was a crime that needed to be punished severely.

When it was time to go up to change for the ball, Lottie had managed only a few words alone with Rothsay. She held her curiosity in check. Lily Blake was coming that evening to help her dress, just in case any last-minute alterations needed to be done. No doubt she would tell her what sentence her husband had received that morning.

However, Rose brought the news that Lily was feeling unwell and could not come that evening.

'She has apologised and says she will definitely be here for the wedding, Miss Lottie, but she has a terrible headache and cannot come tonight.'

Lottie looked at her reflection in the mirror. 'Well, there is nothing for her to do so it does not matter. I hope she is not truly ill?'

'I think it was just a headache,' Rose said, but Lottie had an uncomfortable feeling that she was hiding something. 'You do look a proper treat, miss. That dress suits you well.'

'It is my usual style, but Lily made a few changes

that made all the difference. I do not think the stylist in Northampton would have done better.'

'No, miss, nor half so well in my opinion.'

Lottie smiled as the girl fastened Aunt Beth's pearls about her throat. She was just about to go downstairs when someone knocked the door. Rose answered it and gave a little squeak of apprehension.

'It is his lordship, miss.'

'Oh, please come in, Rothsay,' Lottie said and turned to face him as Rose escaped into the dressing room and shut the door. 'I was just about to come down.'

'I see you are wearing pearls. I thought you might like these…' He handed her a box, which, when opened, revealed a pair of pearl-and-gold bangles.

'How pretty! Thank you, yes, they will go well with Aunt Beth's pearls.' She slipped them over her long gloves and fastened them, smoothing out the skirts of her pale green gown. 'Shall I do, Rothsay?'

'You look beautiful, as I am certain you know.'

'I am well satisfied with my gown. Lily Blake helped me style it a little. She is very clever with her needle.'

'Yes, so I understand.' He offered his arm. 'Shall we go down? We must be the first so that we can welcome our guests.'

'Of course,' she said. 'Your gift was another lovely surprise. You will overwhelm me with presents, Rothsay. I assure you they are not necessary.'

'I wish my wife to have pretty things.'

Lottie was aware of how very handsome Rothsay was as he stood by her side to receive their guests. Tall, powerful and with clean-cut features that told of his noble lineage, he drew the eyes of all the young women. She saw envy and even jealousy show briefly in their faces, before their mamas drew them away. The more protective mothers might feel he was not good husband material, but as far as breeding, position and wealth was concerned he must be one of the matrimonial prizes of any Season.

Lottie felt both proud and happy to be wearing his ring, which was much admired by everyone. They opened the dancing together with a waltz, and his hand at her waist sent sensual tremors winging down her spine. She gazed up at him, at his mouth, which she knew could arouse such delicious feelings in her, and saw that it was set in a thin line.

'Is something troubling you, Rothsay?'

'Was I frowning?' He glanced down at her and smiled. 'Forgive me, my thoughts had strayed and that is unforgivable on a night like this. Did I tell you that I am very proud of my beautiful fiancée?'

'Proud?' She lifted her delicate eyebrows, her mouth pursued in a teasing smile that was, had she known it, both provocative and sensual. 'That is a great change, Rothsay? I believe it is not a month since you called me a damned adventuress.'

'I must beg your pardon for that, Lottie. I did not know you then. You know I mistook you for your sister.'

Lottie's cheeks felt warm. He already despised Clarice—what would he think if he knew that she had tried to blackmail her?

Realising he was waiting for an answer, she looked up at him. 'And you do know me now? Are you sure?'

'I am beginning to learn more,' he replied and laughed throatily as he saw the expression in her eyes. 'You are a minx, Lottie. If we were not entertaining I should punish you for that, but it would take too long and our guests would miss us.'

Lottie gurgled with laughter. Banter of this kind was amusing. She was very glad she had not brought up the subject of Sam Blake earlier in the day. It would have angered him and thrown a cloud over the evening. As it was, Rothsay seemed to be in a good humour, which meant she could relax and enjoy the ball.

After their dance, she was surrounded by young gentlemen asking her for a dance. Most of them had only been introduced to her that evening and showered her with compliments, asking ridiculous things like why they had not seen her first, and did she really wish to marry a scoundrel such as Rothsay? Since they were clearly his friends and the banter was all in good fun, she merely laughed and assured them that she was very happy with her choice.

It was not until much later in the evening that she danced with Sir Bertie Fisher.

'Are you settling in well, Miss Lottie?' he asked. 'Mama is delighted to have you as her close neighbour. She tells me she hears good things of you—and I believe you have been shopping together in Northampton?'

'Yes, we have, sir. I bought some beautiful silk for my wedding gown.'

'Ah, yes, the wedding is fast approaching. Tell me

where do you go on your honeymoon or has Rothsay kept it to himself?'

'I am not certain we shall go away,' Lottie replied and now her cheeks felt warm. He was not the first to mention the honeymoon and she was perfectly certain that Rothsay had no idea of it. The word had not crossed his lips and she would not dream of asking such a question when she knew very well the reality of her situation. 'I believe Rothsay has business and I have much to do here.'

He said nothing, but she sensed that he thought her answer odd, and perhaps it was. She was not perfectly certain what occurred when two people married for the sake of convenience—did they go through the motions of a honeymoon or simply got on with their independent lives?

At the end of the dance, she smiled at Bertie, then left him and went upstairs to freshen her gown and apply cool water to her cheeks. It had become very hot in the ballroom and she needed a moment to recover.

A lowering thought had occurred to her. The young women who had looked at her with envy this evening would very soon be laughing behind their fans when it was realised that Rothsay had little regard for his wife and meant to carry on exactly as before.

She had known it from the start. She just had not expected it to hurt this much.

Now she was being quite ridiculous. The ball had put a lot of people to a deal of trouble and she would be stupid to spoil it for them or herself. She must go back down and smile and laugh, as if she were the happiest woman in the world—which she would be if Rothsay loved her.

Returning to the ballroom, Lottie stood up with her partners for every dance. Rothsay escorted her into supper and their table was one of the largest in the room, everyone wishing to spend at least a few minutes with them. Lottie forgot her doubts as Rothsay teased her and accepted the teasing of his friends in good spirit.

'You are a dashed lucky dog,' Uncle Freddie said. 'Had I been twenty years younger, I should have cut you out, Rothsay.'

Lottie threw him a laughing glance. 'Had I seen you first, dear Uncle Freddie, it is quite possible that I would have taken you.'

'Sensible gel,' Uncle Freddie said and winked at her. 'Keep 'em guessing, that's the secret of a long and happy marriage. Not that he would be fool enough to stray now that he has found you, m'dear.'

'Thank you,' Lottie replied and glanced at Rothsay. She was shocked by the brooding expression in his eyes. What could he be thinking?

She wondered if he was thinking of his mistress and wished she could ask if he intended to keep a mistress after they were married, but that of course would be quite shocking. Wives and fiancées did not ask such awkward questions.

After supper Rothsay claimed his second dance of the evening. It was once again a waltz and as his hand pressed lightly at her waist, she felt as if she were melting with pleasure. The music was sweet and the air was filled with the perfume of the flowers that had been banked along the bottom of the dais. Overhead, the glittering chandeliers threw showers of light over the dancers and their jewels sparkled at throats and fingers. It was, Lottie thought, a scene of privilege and indulgence. Only the very wealthy could afford to give parties of this kind, and she found it sobering to think that the food left over from this evening could probably feed a village community for a week.

Well, why shouldn't it? Lottie decided that in the morning she would have some baskets of good food made up and taken to the poorer tenants. It was only right that they should share the delights of their lord's celebrations. She would speak to Mrs Mann about it in the morning.

'You are very thoughtful, Lottie?'

'Yes, my mind had drifted,' she said. 'It must have cost you a great deal for this evening—and a great deal more for the wedding.'

'It is no matter.' His gaze narrowed. 'Are you thinking of crying off at the last minute, Lottie?'

'No, of course not,' she replied. 'I have no intention of it. I was just thinking of all the people who would benefit from just a little of the money that we have spent this evening.'

'Well, as mistress of Rothsay I dare say you may dispense charity where you see fit in the future.'

'You will not mind if I send food to the tenants?'

'Why should I? My mother always did so, though the last few years I have seldom been here and these things may have been neglected.'

'Then I shall certainly do so. Forgive me, Rothsay. This is not the moment to speak of such things.'

'No, it is not,' he agreed. 'We must find time to discuss many subjects, Lottie, but I think we could put
serious matters out of our minds until after the wedding,
don't you?'

'Yes, certainly. This is a very special night, Rothsay.
Thank you for giving me something so wonderful. I am
not sure I deserve it.'

'Oh, yes,' he said and smiled oddly. 'I think you do,
Lottie. Besides, you had all the work of it—so I should
be the one thanking you.'

Their dance ended and Rothsay went off to do his duty,
dancing with a married woman, who seemed delighted
with his attention and flirted with him desperately.

Lottie tried not to mind that he appeared to enjoy her
efforts. She had been told that Rothsay had a mistress.
For all she knew, the woman might be amongst their
guests…might even be the lady he was even now escorting out to the terrace.

She fought an unworthy urge to follow and confront
them. Instead, she accepted the hand of her next partner,
resisting the temptation to look at the French window
through which Rothsay had disappeared with his beautiful partner.

However, he was back in the ballroom within a few
minutes and she saw him talking to Aunt Beth and
Henrietta, who were watching the proceedings, but not
dancing.

'I am past my dancing days,' Aunt Beth protested
when Lottie suggested she might care to indulge once
or twice.

She saw Rothsay escort Henrietta from the room and

knew that his godmother would have left the ball earlier than most because she could not stand late hours.

However, he had not returned within half an hour, and the lady who had flirted with him so wickedly was also missing.

Lottie felt her throat tighten and her smile became a little forced. Surely Rothsay would not have invited his mistress to his engagement ball? It would be a terrible insult, for everyone would know and pity her.

No, no, she would not deign to think such things. He was no doubt taking the chance of a cigar in the fresh air or perhaps talking with his godmother.

He returned shortly before the guests began to take their leave and joined her as she said goodbye to them. Most would be returning in a few days for the wedding, some were staying and simply went off to their rooms. When everyone had gone, Rothsay poured himself a glass of brandy from one of the decanters set out on a sideboard.

'Well, Lottie, I think we may say it was successful, don't you?'

'Oh, yes, I am sure of it,' she replied. 'I am glad you were satisfied with the arrangements, Rothsay. If you will excuse me, I shall go up now. I am a little tired. Goodnight.'

She left him without another glance. There was a pain in her chest, which she found difficult to bear. The urge to weep was very close, because she could only conclude that Rothsay had been gone so long because he had slipped away to snatch a little time with his mistress.

Once alone, Lottie allowed Rose to unhook her gown at the back and then sent her off to bed, after thanking her for sitting up so late.

'I can manage now, Rose. Thank you so much for looking after me. Goodnight.'

'Goodnight, miss. I hope as everything went well?'

'Yes, it was all delightful. I shall come to the servants' hall tomorrow to thank everyone. At the moment all I want to do is sleep.'

All she really wanted to do was to sleep. Her first rush of emotion resulted in hot bitter tears, but after a while she wiped them away. She was being so foolish. Rothsay did not wish for a clinging bride. He wanted a sensible woman who accepted the fact of his mistress. She could not fault his manner of late. He was polite, considerate, but uninterested in more than a comfortable arrangement.

She was the fool. She was the one who had gone into this with her eyes open. He had kept his part of the bargain in full and she must do the same. Many gentlemen kept mistresses and their wives turned a blind eye. She must do the same—but she had not expected it to hurt as much as it did.

For a moment she was overcome with anger and an urgent desire to weep and rage, but she conquered her feelings.

She must think of all the things that would bring her contentment and make her life worthwhile.

As Lady Rothsay she could do a great deal of good. Rothsay admitted that he had neglected the things that were so necessary for the well being of his tenants. She could repair much of that neglect. Her marriage would be good for her family. Aunt Beth was assured of a home here or in Bath when Lottie chose to visit, since a house there was one of Rothsay's wedding gifts. He had been extraordinarily generous, far more so than she could have expected after the way the business began.

She could not withdraw. She did not wish to withdraw. She had experienced a moment of weakness, but she would conquer it. In the morning, she would become the calm controlled woman the world saw and these needs and longings inside her would be banished to a distant part of her mind.

Nicolas smoked a last cigar in the gardens. He frowned as he wondered what lay behind the withdrawal he had sensed in Lottie. During their first dance, he had felt her happiness and the closeness between them, and had wished that he could whisk her off somewhere to be thoroughly kissed. However, she had seemed changed when they bid their guests goodnight. He wondered what had happened in his absence. Had she heard something that upset her?

After escorting Henrietta to her room, because she was too tired to remain longer, he had been called to attend to some business he would rather not have been troubled with on such a night.

His mouth tightened to a thin line. At the court sessions earlier that day, he had discovered that he was not down to try Sam Blake, but another set of rogues altogether. They were accused of murder and, since they had been caught in the act, the sentencing was easy. He had ordered them to be hung, but their sentences could be exchanged for transportation as a bond servant for seven years should they choose. Men invariably chose the latter and some of his fellow magistrates considered he had been too easy on the rogues.

It was only after the trial, which had taken some hours because he had listened to all the evidence, that he had learned Bertie Fisher had sat on the poaching case. He had sentenced Sam Blake to three years in the local prison, which was, in Nicolas's opinion, far too severe. He had remonstrated with Bertie afterwards, but his neighbour was adamant that poaching needed to be stamped on.

It was, of course, a serious crime, because many violent individuals became involved in the business, which was often linked to other more serious crimes. However, Nicolas had found himself wishing that he had let the man off with a warning in the first place. Especially in the light of what had happened this evening.

He had been given the news that three men had broken free when being taken back to the prison. Two of them were the murderers, who were to be transported—and the third was Sam Blake.

'The damned fool!' Nicolas had been frustrated to learn of Blake's escape. 'Had he accepted his sentence I might have been able to have it cut in a few months. Now he will be a wanted man and may be shot on sight—and he may well hang if he is taken.'

The news had unsettled Nicolas, making him disinclined to return to the dancing. He had, however, rejoined Lottie to say goodnight to his guests.

The point was—was her new mood down to what she had heard or was she merely cross with him for deserting her?

He threw the cigar into the shrubbery and went in, unaware that he had been watched for some minutes from the shadows.

Lottie rose a little after her usual time at nine o'clock. She washed in the water Rose had brought her and went down to the breakfast room. She was feeling rested and perfectly calm, her feelings under control. She did not know for certain that Nicolas had been with his mistress the previous evening. Perhaps she had been too hasty in her conclusions and ought to give Rothsay more credit, for he was a gentleman and such behaviour would not have been expected of a true gentleman. She had allowed her jealousy to mislead her.

A few of the men were already in the breakfast room but there was no sign of the ladies—and she was told Rothsay had been in an hour before her.

'You are an early riser, m'dear,' Uncle Freddie said and smiled at her approvingly.

'It has always been my habit,' she said. 'I do not much care for breakfast in bed, and I like to walk while the dew is still upon the grass.'

'If you go walking this morning, you should take a groom or your maid with you,' Uncle Freddie said with a frown. 'I hear there are some dangerous men in the area. I doubt they will come on to the estate, for Rothsay's keepers are armed and alert, but if you go to the village you should be careful.'

'I do not plan to walk this morning. There is bound to be a great deal of food left from last night, you know. I would not have it wasted. I intend to visit the kitchens after I have eaten and arrange for baskets of food to be taken to our tenants and the poor of the village.'

'That's the ticket. Don't approve of waste meself. We always send the food to the local orphanage, though I'm not sure the children see much of it. I dare say the governors take the best for themselves. Not much we can do about it.'

'Oh, I think one ought to try to improve things where one can,' Lottie said. 'At home I sometimes visited the workhouse. I think I was able to ease the condition of the poor by being elected to the board to see that the improvements I suggested were carried through. As Rothsay's wife I shall be able to do more.'

'Yes, you will if you care to,' he agreed. 'But all work and no play—you know the saying, m'dear. You must have some fun before you settle into the life here. Rothsay will want you to entertain for him in London, I dare say.'

Lottie wondered if that were true. She did not think it but would not tell his uncle. Instead, she chatted to him about the wedding and enquired what he wished to do with himself all day.

'Might take you for a drive this afternoon if you have time for it, m'dear. I was accounted a whip in me young days.'

'Would you drive me about the estate? I have never been much further than the lake or the park. I should like to see the village and some of the farms.'

'Delighted,' Uncle Freddie said, looking pleased with the idea. 'Rothsay should have done it at the start, but he is an odd fellow at times. I dare say he will wake up to his responsibilities once you are married.'

Uncle Freddie was a good trencherman and Lottie left him to the enjoyment of his breakfast, having partaken of a cup of tea and a buttered roll with honey herself.

She visited the kitchens and discussed what Cook felt could be spared from her larder.

'Most of the fancy stuff is finished, Miss Stanton, but there is quite a bit of ham and roast meat left over. It won't keep more than a day or two at most in this weather. We shall need some of it here, but I'll be cooking fresh this evening and a lot will waste if last night's spread isn't sent out. I had it in mind to send a bit to the tenants, but now that you've taken the trouble to consult me I shall send the meat pies and pasties to the village hall. There's a fête today for the children, miss, and they will find it useful.'

'That is excellent, Mrs Bent. In future you have my permission to send what is not needed here for the poor folk. We shall see if the children can be given a few treats during the year—perhaps a tea or supper at the village hall?'

'The marquis's mother used to hold a children's party here once a year, miss. I was wondering whether you might wish to start the tradition again?'

'That is an excellent idea,' Lottie said. 'I am glad you mentioned it to me. I should like to know of anything that I can do to help make our people happy, Mrs Bent. Now I must go, for we have guests and I ought to see if they have all they want.'

Lottie walked from the room. Mrs Bent nodded her approval as the housekeeper entered.

'She will do for us, Mrs Mann. The marquis's fiancée is a real lady if you ask me.'

'Yes, she is,' the housekeeper replied. 'It was a little odd that her father was not here for the ball. We must hope that he turns up for the wedding.'

'Yes, that is a bit strange,' Mrs Bent said, 'but I dare say there is a reason for it.'

Unaware of the speculation in the servants' hall, Lottie carried on being a charming hostess for the rest of the morning. She did venture out into the garden for a stroll amongst the shrubbery when some of the ladies came down to join her, but did not venture further than the immediate gardens.

Catching sight of one of the keepers, Lottie remembered Uncle Freddie's warning and wondered just who the dangerous men were. She could not think that Sam Blake was one of them, for he had not seemed particularly violent to her—just a rather weak man who had let life push him down.

Before nuncheon, she wrote a note to Lily and asked her to call when she was feeling better and sent Rose with a basket of sweetmeats for the children.

In the afternoon, she went driving with Uncle Freddie. She was impressed with the fertile fields and the fat stock grazing in their meadows. Everywhere they went, men took off their hats to her and bowed their heads respectfully. One or two women came to the doors of their cottages and called out good wishes for her wedding—and she smiled to see a group of children playing happily around the maypole that had been set up on the village green with some other amusements.

However, on the way home, they passed a huddle of

very poor cottages that looked in bad repair. Lottie asked Uncle Freddie to stop, which he did reluctantly.

'You don't want to look there, Lottie. That's the Hollow. All the scum of the neighbourhood live there. Rothsay should pull it down. It is a blot on the landscape.'

Leaning over to look, Lottie caught an unpleasant smell, which, she guessed, came from an open ditch that ran through the middle of the cottages. She could see that the people here did not wave or smile, but looked at her with sullen indifference. One man came out to stare at them in a way that made Lottie shiver. He was tall and heavily built, but she saw the resemblance to Sam Blake instantly and realised it must be his cousin Dickon. His look was one of such malevolence that she sat back in her seat.

'I wouldn't come this way again if I were you,' Uncle Freddie said as he whipped up his horses. 'These people are not like the villagers. They resent interference and do nothing to help themselves.'

'It must be very unhealthy to live in such a place,' Lottie replied thoughtfully. 'Perhaps Rothsay would consider putting in a drain for that ditch and at least doing some repairs.'

'He did make some such suggestion once, but it was met with hostility. There are some folk you simply cannot help in this world, Lottie m'dear. Save your efforts for those that appreciate it.'

Lottie murmured something appropriate. She would like to see improvements made to the Hollow but again it was something that might annoy Rothsay and would be best left until after the wedding.

There were only a few days to go now. All she had to do was make the best of things and see her part of the bargain through. No doubt Rothsay would soon take himself off back to London and she would be able to do small things herself. He surely could not object if she spent her own allowance on improving things for the tenants of the Hollow just a little?

Chapter Eight

After that afternoon, Lottie seemed to have little time for thinking of the changes she would make once she was the mistress of Rothsay. More guests arrived for the wedding as the time grew nearer and most of her day was taken in entertaining them and making sure the arrangements for the wedding went well.

She and Aunt Beth, together with Rose and a footman to carry all the paraphernalia, visited the church the day before the wedding and decorated it with masses of beautiful flowers, mostly in white and pink.

'It all looks absolutely lovely,' Aunt Beth said when she had finished. 'Are you happy, dearest Lottie? You seem so busy and there are so many guests…I have hardly had time to speak with you alone for days.'

'Yes, of course I am happy,' Lottie told her. 'Who could not be when everything is so perfect? The house is filled with people who are all very kind, and I have never seen so many lovely things—all those beautiful gifts in the long gallery, valuable silver and jewels to say nothing of wonderful porcelain and all the other things we have been given.'

'I know you have everything in a material sense—but are you happy, Lottie? I thought at first you were, but just recently you have been very quiet.'

'Oh, I have been busy. Forgive me if I have neglected you, dearest. I knew you were quite happy helping with various little tasks, and I think Henrietta has come to rely on you very much.'

'The countess had been kind enough to say I have helped her, but anyone could have done as much. I was not complaining, Lottie. My concern is for your happiness.'

'I am perfectly happy. What more could I want?'

Aunt Beth shook her head. 'Well, if you are as happy as you say, then I am content. I love you dearly, Lottie, and I do not wish you to be miserable in the life you have chosen—not that you did choose it, really.'

'Oh, yes, I did,' Lottie corrected her. 'You must not think I was forced into it.' She frowned. 'I do hope Papa will return by this evening. I am not sure what we shall do if he does not.'

'He has behaved very badly,' her aunt said and frowned. 'I really do not know what has got into him. He knows he must be here for the wedding.'

Lottie nodded, feeling a little uneasy about her father's reasons for not joining the wedding party at Rothsay's before this.

However, when they returned from the church later that morning, she discovered her father sitting with Uncle Freddie and Rothsay, sharing a glass of wine.

'You have arrived, Papa. I was a little anxious.'

'Well, you know me. Not much of a one for all this fuss,' her father said and came to kiss her cheek. 'I had something to do, but I am here now. I couldn't miss my little girl's wedding, could I?'

Lottie smiled and allowed him to charm her, as he always had. He was thoughtless and careless, but he was her father and she loved him.

'Come and see all the wedding gifts,' she said and took his arm. She wanted a little time alone with him and it was a perfect excuse to draw him from the rest of the company. 'People have been so amazingly kind...'

Sir Charles looked at her uneasily as they entered the long gallery. 'Now don't scold me, Lottie. I did not intend to stay away so long, but I got caught up in something.'

'A card game, I suppose?'

'Yes, I cannot deny it—but it worked out very well for me. I won a small fortune, Lottie, and I offered to pay Rothsay my debt, but he has refused me. I signed the new contract, which is very generous for you as well as me.'

'Yes, I believe it has been changed from the original.'

'Did you not read it?'

'No, I had no wish to know what was in it.'

'You will be quite a wealthy young woman should anything happen to Rothsay—and your allowance is extremely generous. I dare say you may not spend the half of it.'

'I shall use some to help others.' She stopped and pointed to the table where so many valuable things had been laid out. 'Look at all these gifts. People have been so generous.'

Her father frowned. 'Do you not think it a risk to leave all this stuff lying around? That sapphire-and-diamond set must be worth a king's ransom.'

'Yes, I expect it is,' Lottie said. 'Rothsay's great-uncle gave us that. I asked Rothsay if it should be put away, but he said it was quite safe. The grounds are patrolled at night, you know—and I am sure neither the guests nor the servants would touch anything. After all, the house is full of treasures, is it not?'

'Yes, I suppose so. Just makes me a bit uneasy, that's all,' her father said. 'I'm in funds at the moment but I know I would find it tempting if I were short.'

'Papa!'

Sir Charles smiled oddly. 'I wouldn't touch anything of yours or Rothsay's. You must know that, Lottie—but I've known the time I might have felt tempted.'

Lottie looked at him. 'Have you heard from Clarice? She is back in England. She hid in the gardens the other day to speak to me.'

'After money, was she?' Sir Charles frowned. 'Do not give in to her blackmail, Lottie. She will spend it all on her lover.'

'Do you know who he is, Papa?'

'I dare say it is that rogue de Valmer. I think she may have married him,' Sir Charles said. 'I would not have allowed it had I been asked—but she is beyond me, Lottie. I have given up on her, to tell you the truth.'

'You must try to discover where she is after the wedding,' Lottie said, looking at him earnestly. 'Clarice is reckless and she behaves in a way she ought not—but

I would not have her fall into desperate trouble. Please see if she is all right, Papa.'

'Yes, well, if you ask it,' he said and sighed. 'Are you settled here, Lottie?'

'Yes, I am. Do not worry for me, Papa. It is Clarice you should be concerned for.'

'She will go her own way.' He fished in his pocket and brought out a small velvet box. 'I refuse to give Rothsay a penny, Lottie. He has more than any one man needs, including you—but I got this for you.'

He offered the box. She opened it to find a beautiful diamond star set in silver on gold and gave a little cry of pleasure.

'This is lovely, Papa. Thank you so very much. I shall treasure it.'

'Well, it is little enough for all you've done for me over the years.'

'It is perfect.' She reached up to kiss his cheek. 'I am so glad you are here. I was afraid you would not come.'

'I've let you down enough times, but I wouldn't let you down on your wedding day.' He smiled at her as they walked the length of the room. 'Tomorrow is your big day, Lottie—after that you will be Rothsay's wife.'

'Yes…' Lottie's stomach clenched with nerves. She had been so busy she had hardly thought about it, but tomorrow night she would be Rothsay's wife in truth. How would she react when he came to her bed? One part of her longed to be his, but a small voice told her that without love her marriage would be a hollow sham. 'It is almost time for nuncheon, Father. We must join the others.'

* * *

Lottie woke suddenly in the middle of the night. She sat up in bed wondering what had woken her, and then she heard the shouts and the sounds of running feet. Throwing back the bedcovers, she went to the window and looked out. Men with lanterns were everywhere and, as she watched, one of the keepers raised his gun and fired into the darkness. The sound shocked her. What on earth was happening?

She hastened to dress in a simple gown and went out on to the landing. Several of the gentlemen were already dressed and moving about the house with a look of purpose that made her call out and ask what was going on.

'Don't come down, Lottie.' Sir James came briskly up the stairs to where she was standing. 'I am sorry you were disturbed, m'dear. There is no real cause for alarm—just an attempt to break into the house. Fortunately, Rothsay had trebled the guards patrolling the ground because of—' he broke off and looked conscious, as if he were in danger of saying too much. 'I suppose some wretch thought to steal your wedding gifts.'

'Papa did say they might tempt rogues to steal from us, but Rothsay did not think it possible.'

'Well, it was not, as it turns out,' Sir James said. 'You should return to bed, Lottie. There is nothing you can do.'

'Very well. I do not wish to cause you more trouble.'

She went back to her room, but did not retire immediately, instead, she sat in the window embrasure and looked out. The activity was dying down now and she thought that the would-be thieves had been scared off. She was about to undress once more when someone knocked at her door. She went to open it and saw Rothsay. He had dressed hurriedly, his shirt open at the neck, his hair looking rumpled. For some reason the sight of him like that made her catch her breath and she felt a spiral of desire spread through her body. She wished that he would reach out and take her in his arms, kiss her until she melted into his body—but she could see that lovemaking was far from his mind.

Lottie moistened her lips. 'Has the rogue been caught?'

'No—may I come in, Lottie?'

'Yes…' Lottie stood back uncertainly, for it was hardly proper, but they were to be wed in the morning. It could not matter now. 'Of course.' She stood watching as he went to the window and fastened it. 'I was about to shut that, Rothsay.'

'I doubt anyone would climb up here, but it is best to be certain. I should not forgive myself if anything happened to you.'

'I think the intruder was after valuables, don't you?'

'Perhaps.' He frowned. 'They chose to try to break in at the back of the house and were spotted instantly. We chased them off and Larkin thinks he may have winged one of them.'

'Then they will surely not come back in a hurry.'

'I do not think it.' He frowned at her. 'I wanted to tell you that Larkin believes Sam Blake might have been one of them. I preferred you to hear that from me.'

'I thought he was in custody?'

'He was sentenced to three years' imprisonment a couple of days ago, but escaped with some others. They are dangerous fugitives, Lottie, because after this they will almost certainly hang.'

'No, surely not?' Lottie looked at him in distress. 'Surely imprisonment… Three years was too long for what he did. I am not surprised he chose to escape.'

'Blake has fallen in with murderous rogues. One of them fired a pistol at the keeper who raised the alarm. If Blake was one of them, I shall not be able to save him from the noose.'

'If…?' Her eyes met his. 'You have some doubts?'

'It may have been his cousin. They look much alike.'

'Yes, except that Dickon Blake is a bigger man—but facially, yes, the resemblance is there.'

'What do you know of Dickon Blake?'

'I think I saw him when Uncle Freddie took me driving the day after the ball.'

'You went to the Hollow?' His face darkened. 'How could he be such a fool as to take you to that hellhole? I have been meaning to have the whole place pulled down. It is a nest of rats and the sooner it has gone the better.'

'Could you not cover the ditch, drain it and make some repairs—for the sake of the women and children?'

Nicolas's brow furrowed. 'Do not interfere in what you do not understand, Lottie. You have a compassionate heart, but this is men's business. Please leave this to me.'

'Very well.' Lottie felt her eyes sting with tears. Nothing had changed between them. He was as harsh and determined to go his own way as he had been at the start. 'Forgive me for interfering. I thought that some gesture of goodwill might win hearts and minds—but you must do as you see fit.'

'Thank you.' There was a note of sarcasm in his voice. 'I am still master in my own house. Goodnight, Lottie. You had best get some sleep or you will be tired tomorrow.'

Lottie stood motionless as he went out. She did not cry or rage, but inside she felt as if she were being torn apart. He had made his feelings quite plain once more. She was nothing to him. Just a means to an end—as he had made plain from the start.

What a fool she was to care.

What had made him snap Lottie's head off that way? Nicolas cursed his hasty tongue as he returned to his room. He had gone to her because he was concerned for her safety and her peace of mind. Then she had told him she had seen the Hollow and touched some secret part of him that was ashamed. In his heart Nicolas knew that the hovels were a disgrace. They had been wretched enough in his father's time. As a young man he had thought he would pull them down and build new when he came into the estate, but then had come disillusion and the constant pursuit of pleasure that had kept him in town. The Hollow had been banished to a distant corner of his mind, though occasionally it pricked at his conscience.

He had avoided the place for years, because he knew that it was a disgrace—and because it had been the cause of his mother's death. For the most part he had been a good landlord; his tenants had no cause to complain of his treatment and his agents had orders to keep the labourers' cottages in good repair. While the village bordered his land, it was not actually part of his estate. He owned some of the houses and they were in perfect order. The church was another beneficiary—but he had ignored the Hollow and he was not quite sure why. It was one of those things that the longer you put off doing something, the harder it became to right the wrong.

The only way to deal with a slum of that order was to pull it down—but where would the occupants of those hovels live then?

Nicolas's brow furrowed because he knew the answer. Most of them would have to camp in the open until they gave in and moved into the workhouse or drifted away from the area. Many of his neighbours would think that a good thing. The petty crimes, which so annoyed the local gentry, could nearly all be traced to the nest of rogues that had settled there over the years. Freddie had told him it was time he tore the whole place down.

Nicolas scowled as he put the unpleasant matter from his mind. In a few hours he would be getting married… and he had sufficient concerns of his own without trying to work out a problem that had defeated his father all of his life.

He had let his damnable temper come between them once more. He could not expect Lottie to care for a man who overrode her every suggestion with what must seem like arrogance. Why hadn't he explained that he had previously considered the repairs she had suggested but found them inadequate? The cottages were so damp and unsanitary that there was only one way to deal with them, like it or not.

'Oh, damn,' he muttered. If he didn't get some sleep he would be like a bear in the morning. 'It would serve me right if she changed her mind…'

Why had she not changed her mind?

The only thing Nicolas could think of was that she was prepared to accept him with all his faults for the sake of a comfortable home and a life of ease—except that Lottie had made it plain she had no intention of sitting around while others worked. Freddie had told him that she was already planning to discover more about local charities and had asked his advice about setting up a school for the children of his tenants.

A rueful smile touched his mouth. Nicolas was beginning to understand that he might have got more than he bargained for when he demanded that Lottie pay her father's debts by marrying him.

'You are so beautiful,' Aunt Beth said, dabbing a lace kerchief to her eyes as Lottie twirled for her in her bedchamber. 'That dress is gorgeous, Lottie—the nicest you have ever had, I think.'

'That is all due to Lily,' Lottie said and smiled at the seamstress, who had kept her word and arrived that morning to help with dressing her and to make any last-minute adjustments. 'Thank you so much for my dress, Lily. My aunt is right. I've been thinking that you should have your own establishment in Northampton—or even London.'

'I should never dare to set up in London,' Lilly said, a flush of pleasure in her cheeks. 'I have thought I should like a little shop in Northampton, but that is not likely.

Especially now…' Her eyes darkened with unspoken sadness.

'Do not despair,' Lottie said and pressed her hand. 'If Sam keeps out of trouble, we may yet find a way to make things better for you both.'

'I know you mean well, Miss Lottie—but you have a soft heart. The magistrates are gentlemen of property and to them Sam is a wicked rogue. If he'd ever had a chance, he could have been a good man, but you know what they say—give a dog a bad name and you may as well hang it.'

'I promise I shall try to help him when the time comes, but if you see him tell him not to get involved in his cousin's misdeeds.'

'It weren't him last night, miss.' Lily said swiftly. 'He knows you've been good to me. Sam might not like his lordship, but he wouldn't lift a finger against you—or he would have me to answer to!'

'And I believe you.' Lottie laughed softly. 'Well, Lily, do your best to keep him out of trouble and I may yet arrange something.'

Lottie turned to her aunt, who was regarding her with anxious eyes. 'Do not look so worried, dearest. When all the guests have gone you and I will be alone here—and I dare say we can think of something. I kept Papa out of prison more than once. I dare say it may be possible to come up with an idea.'

'Rothsay may have something to say.'

'Well, he may not care to stay in the country for more than a few days or so,' Lottie said. She ignored the look of enquiry in her aunt's eyes. 'We had better go down or we shall be late for the church.'

* * *

The sun was very warm as Lottie got down from her father's carriage outside the church. She saw that several villagers were waiting outside to watch and wave as she entered the beautiful Norman church on her father's arm. They smiled and clapped as they saw her, calling out good wishes for her wedding. Lottie's hand trembled slightly on her father's arm, but she controlled the wave of nerves that had swept over her.

She had slept the previous night after Rothsay left her, though her dreams had been troubled. There was a tradition that it was bad luck to see the bridegroom the night before the wedding. Lottie had not given it a thought until she was drifting into sleep. The omens were anything but propitious and the prophets of doom would say that she was bound to feel nothing but disappointment in such an ill-conceived match—if they knew the truth, which they did not, of course. Everyone thought they were the perfect pair, and Rothsay's relations were thrilled with the prospect of an heir for the family.

Lottie's stomach tightened with a spasm of nerves as she saw Rothsay waiting for her in front of the altar. How tall and strong he was, and as he turned to look at her walk down the aisle, she was aware of his masculinity as never before. Tonight he would claim the privilege of a bridegroom. The thought made her lips part on a sigh and desire pooled low in her abdomen. She longed for the moment when she became his wife in truth, yet she was afraid that she would give herself away in a moment of passion. Whatever she did, she must say nothing that made him feel she expected more than he was willing to give.

She turned her head to look at him as she drew to a halt by his side, and her heart missed a beat. He had such a sensual mouth and he was almost too good looking, though at times he could look harsh, that generous mouth tight with anger. She did not understand him, because they hardly knew one another. They had spent so little time alone that it was impossible to form a true picture of his character. He seemed harsh and arrogant at times, but was there another man beneath the mask he showed to the world—or was she deceiving herself?

Lottie forced herself to concentrate on the service. Rothsay was word perfect when giving his vows, but she stumbled over the word obey and his head turned sharply towards her, one brow arching in enquiry. Lottie trembled as the vicar pronounced them man and wife and then Rothsay lifted her pretty veil to kiss her lightly on the lips.

After that it all became somewhat blurred as they left church to the sound of bells ringing joyfully. As they paused on the church steps, Lottie saw several armed men at the edge of the crowd and knew that Rothsay had left nothing to chance. She thought it unlikely that anyone would try to assassinate him in front of the whole village and all his tenants, but, after the previous night, it was best to be prepared.

Nothing untoward happened and they ran for their carriage as a shower of rose petals and rice was thrown over them. Once inside, Rothsay looked at her, an odd smile on her lips.

'So you did not run away despite my show of temper last night?'

Lottie smiled, because when he was the charming

man of fashion she liked so well she felt at ease in his company.

'Did you really imagine I would? I dare say I shall learn not to speak without thinking in time, Rothsay.'

'Shall you? I wonder if I shall learn to control my damnable temper?'

'I am not afraid of your temper, Rothsay.'

'No, I have discovered that for myself.' He looked at her quizzically. 'Do you think you could call me Nicolas now we are married, at least when we are alone together?'

Alone together.

Lottie felt the nerves in her stomach tighten. In a few hours they would be completely alone. His attentions in the marriage bed would not be unwelcome. Her problem was that she might show her pleasure too much and send him hurrying back to London to the arms of his mistress.

Nicolas did not want a clinging wife.

'I imagine I can do that quite easily, Nicolas,' she said and smiled as he leaned towards her, his mouth seeking hers. Her lips parted as his tongue probed and she felt her resolve melting. How could she hold back when she felt this surging desire, the longing to feel his flesh close to hers?

What a wanton she was! Lottie ruefully accepted the truth. Had Nicolas asked her to be his mistress at the start she would probably have accepted—but of course he wasn't interested so much in having her in his bed as the end result. She exercised control and sat back in her seat as he studied her face. Her instincts told her to throw her arms about him and kiss him back, but her mind told her to remember that she was to be no more than complaisant.

'You really are very lovely, Lottie. I am fortunate to have such a bride. My relatives are all enchanted with you—did you know that?'

'Uncle Freddie is a dear and Sir James is a true gentleman.'

'Even Cousin Raymond told me that I was a lucky dog,' Nicolas said and grinned at her. 'I suppose we must entertain them all this evening and slip away quietly in the morning.'

'Slip away?' she asked. 'I am sorry, Nicolas. I am not quite certain what you mean. I thought you would stay here for a few days and then return to London. I have not prepared a trousseau for a wedding trip.'

'I think you have enough for a short stay in the country, Lottie. I have a small hunting lodge in Hampshire. It has been made ready for us and will give us a little breathing space before we return to our own lives. My family would expect us to have a wedding trip and I did not wish to disappoint them. Henrietta thought Paris, but I believe we need to get to know one another in private—do you not agree?'

'Yes, I do,' Lottie said and smiled. 'That is thoughtful of you, R—Nicolas, thank you. It is exactly what I should wish.'

'It does not mean we shall never go to Paris—perhaps another time?'

'Yes, perhaps,' Lottie replied. 'You must do exactly as you please, Nicolas.'

'Must I?' he asked and such a very odd expression came to his eyes. 'Well, we shall see how we go on together, Lady Rothsay. I did not give much thought to the matter when choosing a bride, but I shall certainly pay more attention to my wife.'

Lottie's eyes strayed to her husband again and again during the evening. They had entertained their guests lavishly to a grand reception. There had been music, dancing, cards for those who chose, and then fireworks in the grounds as the night descended and another light supper was served for any that wished for it. Cook and her helpers had worked extremely hard and Lottie sent a message of congratulations and thanks to the kitchens.

The hour was growing late when Nicolas suggested that perhaps she would like to slip away to her rooms. The guests who had travelled only a short distance were leaving and the family members who were staying on for a while were gathering in small groups, preparing to seek their beds.

'I think everyone would excuse you if you went up now, Lottie,' Nicolas said. 'I shall join you in half an hour—if that is convenient?'

'Yes, thank you, of course.'

Lottie's stomach fluttered with nerves. He was so polite, almost a stranger again. Earlier in the day he had laughed and teased her as the toasts were made, but now he seemed to be brooding, keeping a distance between them.

Was he wondering if he could bear to do his duty? Lottie felt the pain slash though her at the thought. Perhaps he was thinking of his mistress and regretting that she would not be waiting for him that night?

She must not allow herself to think such lowering

thoughts. Lottie banished her desire to weep as she undressed and then sent Rose to bed. Alone, she sat at her dressing table and brushed her hair, thoughtful and nervous, but not afraid. She wanted to be Nicolas's wife—was excited by the prospect of being with him that night.

The time drifted by and she realised that he had been longer than he had promised. He must be gathering courage, perhaps having a drink to bolster his sense of purpose. She had noticed that he drank very little at the reception and during the evening.

As the door that led to the dressing room, which connected the master suite, opened slowly and Nicolas came through, Lottie rose to her feet. Her heart began to pound wildly, then she saw that though he had taken off his neckcloth and coat, he was still wearing his shirt, breeches and boots.

'Nicolas?' She was bewildered by his manner as he came to her. 'Is something the matter?'

'Nothing…' His eyes were serious as he met her anxious gaze. 'I came to say goodnight, Lottie. You are expecting to do your duty this evening, I believe, but I find I am reluctant to begin our marriage this way. We are almost strangers. I shall make no demands of you tonight. There will be time enough in the next week or so…when we are better acquainted.' He leaned towards her, gave her a chaste kiss on the cheek, then turned and left.

Lottie stared at the door as it closed behind him. She could feel the tightness in her chest and tears burned behind her eyes. She longed to throw herself down and weep but was afraid he might hear. Not knowing what to expect, she had imagined many things of her wedding night. What she had not even considered was that he would leave her to sleep alone.

Why? Why had he not taken her to bed? If an heir were all he wanted…surely she was not so ill favoured that he could not bring himself to make love to her?

He had called her lovely in the carriage. She was sure that at various times she had seen the hot glow of desire in his eyes when he looked at her. So why had he held back?

Frustration was a part of her suffering—her body cried out for his and she had anticipated his loving with some pleasure. Yet perhaps all was not lost. Perhaps there was reason for hope if he wished them to be on a better footing before he exerted his rights as a husband.

Nicolas's frustration was a hundred times stronger than Lottie's had she but known it. The sight of his new wife in that fetching lace bedgown, the scent of her perfume and the look of invitation in her eyes had all been sorely tempting.

The devil of it was that he knew she was ready to accept him into her bed. She would not lie cold and unresponsive, for he had felt the softness of her lips in the carriage. He could go to her, make her his own and she would accept him, perhaps even welcome him—but for some reason it was not enough.

He could not convince himself that her compliance was more than that, a willingness to make her duties as pleasant as possible for them both. Lottie was a remarkable woman. He would swear there was passion in her—but he had found passion in the arms of a dozen women and somehow it was not what he wanted or needed now.

Ridiculous as it was, he wanted Lottie to love him. He wanted her to be his wife in the true sense of the word, not only the mother of his children but his partner in life—the other half of his self.

What kind of a fool was he? Nicolas laughed at the thoughts chasing round in his head. It was merely lust. He should go back into his wife's room, make love to her and carry on as he had intended in the first place. A brief wedding trip, then bring her here, leave her with her aunt, and return to London to the life he enjoyed. Yet he was not a man to enjoy celibacy and he had vowed since becoming betrothed that he would stay faithful to his wife. It had been several weeks since he had bid his last mistress farewell.

Surely that was it. He had never been short of willing partners to share his bed. This self-imposed restraint was the cause of the burning need he was feeling. It wasn't love for Lottie that was making him ache with the need to hold her in his arms and feel her sweet surrender. No, he wouldn't be such a fool as to fall in love with his wife.

He would be bored with a clinging wife in a week. He enjoyed his freedom and the chase was all; it always had been so, for he seldom found much pleasure once the woman had given into his demands. No doubt it was a fault in him, but it was the main reason that he had not married—or so he told himself. At the moment, he fancied himself in love, but it would soon pass.

He would let Lottie sleep alone tonight and then

perhaps things would happen naturally when they were alone at the lodge, apart from a few servants who would keep well in the background.

Once he had tasted her delights a few times, he would certainly wish to be free once more. It was just so damned inconvenient to feel this wretched frustration...

Chapter Nine

Lottie glanced at the man sitting beside her with his eyes closed. He had ridden his horse for the first part of the journey, leaving her to travel in solitary state, but for the past hour he had been in the coach with her, his long strong legs stretched out in front of him, his eyes closed. She wondered if he were bored with her company.

'You do not need to go through with this if you would rather be in town,' she said and saw his eyes fly open. 'If you are bored, Nicolas, it might be best if we returned to Rothsay and you left me there.'

'Good grief, what makes you imagine I am bored?' His eyes went over her. 'If you must have it, I am a dashed bad traveller, which is why I rode for part of the way. Travelling in a carriage does not suit me—unless I drive the thing myself.'

'Then why don't you?' Her eyes challenged him. 'Are you not capable of driving a team of six horses?'

'Damn it, Lottie,' Nicolas's eyes gleamed suddenly.

'That is very provocative. You realise you have put me on my mettle, I suppose?'

'Well, can you drive six horses? Papa tried once for a bet, but I fear he lost his blunt. He could not manage them and had to be rescued by the coachman.'

'You are a wicked jade,' he said and laughed. Reaching up, he tapped the roof of the carriage with his silver-topped cane and brought it to a halt. Opening the door, he jumped out and called to the coachman.

Lottie listened to the one-sided conversation. She judged the coachman to be uneasy in allowing his master to drive the team of six spirited horses, which was a very different matter to the pair that Nicolas regularly drove about the estate.

'If you are sure, my lord...' he said reluctantly. 'They take some handling, sir—if you don't mind my saying so.'

'I do, damn it. Move over and leave them to me.'

Nicolas poked his head in at the door. 'Hang on, Lottie, for there's a good stretch of road ahead and I intend to let them go.'

'Are you sure?' She was doubtful now, half-wishing she had not challenged him.

'You'll see...' Nicolas grinned at her.

Lottie sat back in her seat and heard him climb up to the driving box. After some argument, the groom went to the back of the carriage and the coachman stayed in place—just in case he was needed.

Nicholas gave the order and the carriage started moving. For a few moments it travelled at a normal pace, then she felt the horses gather momentum and the carriage seemed to lurch forwards. She held on to the strap as it began to jolt and bump, throwing her forwards and then back as the horses raced down the country road. She looked out of the window. Trees, hedges and fields seemed to flash by at an alarming rate, but apart from some discomfort everything was going well.

Lottie did not see the obstruction ahead, but she heard Nicolas's shout of alarm and then felt his efforts to halt the carriage as he tried to stop the horses' headlong flight. She was thrown forwards violently and then just as violently back against her seat. It was uncomfortable but exciting, dispersing the tension that had been growing between her and Nicolas these past few hours. Above her head there was shouting and some argument, she fancied, and then the carriage halted; looking out of the window, she saw they were surrounded by sheep.

The next moment Nicolas jumped down and wrenched open the door. He glared at her and she could not help herself. She laughed at his annoyance.

'Stupid animals. I think we might have rounded that corner ahead if they hadn't blocked the road...'

'You were travelling too fast. I did not want you to kill us all, Nicolas, just to prove you could handle the team.'

'Well, I could until those wretched sheep appeared.' He looked cross. 'You had best get down. There is some bother with one of the wheels—and the sheep farmer is looking irate. I must settle with him for any distress to his beasts. I just hope the repair will not cause us much delay. We do not wish for another night on the road if we can avoid it.'

'Did you not appreciate the inn last night?'

'It was all very well for you, Lottie. I swear I booked

two rooms—you did not have to make do with a couple of chairs in the private parlour last night.'

'You could have shared my room, Nicolas. We are married. My reputation would not suffer.'

His eyes narrowed. 'I do not know what you are up to, Lottie—but be careful. My temper is wearing thin, even if this is supposed to be a wedding trip.'

Lottie smiled. She was not sure why she had provoked him, perhaps she had wanted a little revenge for his neglect of her. Pretending to be asleep when he was wide awake, indeed.

She gave him her hand and was assisted down. Shaking out the skirts of her dark-green travelling gown, she took a stroll up a small incline and looked down over the surrounding countryside. It was very beautiful, a pleasant place to stop. If she had brought a basket of food, they could have had a picnic. Turning as Nicolas came up to her, she said as much.

'I suppose it is pretty enough,' he said and smiled reluctantly. 'All right, I admit I needed help to halt them—but I shall master it, believe me. I am not a member of the four-in-hand club, though I have driven a team of four often enough. Six is rather more tricky. However, next time we travel this way I shall be able to drive them, I promise. If we cannot go on this evening, I shall hire a curricle and pair from the first hostelry we come to and drive us to my lodge. It is not above ten miles from here.'

'Good. I am hungry. I have not eaten much for a day or so.'

'Nor I...' He laughed suddenly. 'We are an odd pair, are we not? I do not know what got into me earlier.'

Nicolas knew very well what had made him pretend to be asleep. The scent of her sitting so close had stirred his senses, his arousal so strong that he had been hard put to keep his distance.

'Shall you forgive me, Lottie? Could we possibly be friends, do you think?'

'Friends?' Her heart leaped as she saw something deep in his eyes. 'Are you sure that is what you want, Nicolas?'

'Damn it, Lottie! I have been trying to be a gentleman and not rush you.' He reached out and drew her into his arms, crushing her against his chest, his mouth seeking hers hungrily. His lips were hard and demanding at first, then softened to a questing kiss that begged for her response. She gave it, unable to hold back as she felt the burn of his arousal when he pressed her closer still. 'I think I have been a fool, have I not?' His hand caressed her cheek, brushed against her sensitised breast, which peaked beneath the soft silk of her gown, bringing a gasp to her lips. A warm sweet sensation moved through her like thick honey and she spoke without thinking.

'You would have been more comfortable in my bed last night, Nicolas.'

'Should I? You hardly spoke to me after we left Rothsay. I thought you were angry.'

'Perhaps a little,' she admitted. 'You ignored me for most of the journey—yesterday and this morning.'

Nicolas laughed. 'So you are like other ladies sometimes? You do have a little vanity?'

'If I have, it has been sadly crushed. I did not think myself so ill favoured that you would leave me to sleep alone every night, Nicolas.'

'I see I have been wasting my time trying to spare you,' he said and laughed down at her. 'I shall make up for lost time this evening, madam.'

Lottie smiled. She did like him so very much sometimes.

'I believe Coachman is trying to attract your attention, my lord. I think we are ready to go on.'

'I believe I shall ride, if you do not mind, Lottie. We cannot be more than an hour or so from my house. I shall ride on ahead to make certain everything is ready.'

'Yes, of course,' she replied. 'You must do just as you please, Nicolas.'

'You keep saying that,' Nicolas said. 'One day you may regret having given me *carte blanche*.'

Lottie stared after him as he walked to the carriage. She allowed him to help her inside, then watched as he changed places with one of the grooms and set off on horseback.

Just what had he meant by that last remark? Did it mean that when he had had enough of her he would go to London and take up with his mistress where he had left off?

When Lottie arrived at the hunting lodge, which was a pretty country house, small by Rothsay's standards, but situated in a quiet park with a pleasant outlook and an approach through perfect countryside, she found the servants lined up waiting for her. There were far fewer than at Rothsay, and, apart from one maid who was to serve her, all the others were men.

Nicolas had suggested that she leave Rose at Rothsay, because, as he put it, he wished to be private with her.

She soon saw that the servants here were discreet and disappeared as soon as the meal had been served. Was it Nicolas's custom to bring ladies here? Lottie wondered. Had his mistress stayed here—or perhaps women of easy virtue that his friends had enjoyed?

Ladies did not have such improper thoughts, but Lottie could not help herself. She hated the little green imp of jealousy that had taken residence in her subconscious, for after all, Nicolas had never claimed to love her. Yet she could not quite squash the foolish thoughts.

However, he did not desert her that evening, but spent an hour reading poetry to her after dinner, before suggesting that she might retire.

Lottie went without a word. Would he simply visit and say goodnight, as he had on the two previous occasions?

She did not have long to wait; the maid had scarcely left her when Nicolas walked through the adjoining door and stood looking at her. He was wearing a long dark-blue silk robe and his feet were bare. Lottie's heart quickened, her pulses racing. She had been sitting at her dressing table. Now she stood up and waited uncertainly.

'I know you would not refuse me,' he said. 'It was a part of the arrangement and you have been meticulous— but may I hope there is some warmth in your heart? Is it just a duty, Lottie?'

'I know well that you do not want a clinging vine,' she replied with a smile, 'but I cannot deny that I shall find pleasure in our marriage, Nicolas.'

'Then it is all I can hope for and must think myself fortunate after the way I forced you to marry me.'

'It was not so very hard to bear once I had met you—and seen your house.' Her eyes sparkled and teased and he gave a shout of laughter as he drew her to him. 'There are compensations in being married to a marquis—even if his reputation as a rake is daunting.'

'You always give as good as you get, do you not?'

'I have found it is best to meet a challenge head on, Nicolas. Life was not easy with Papa, especially after Mama died. Had I not been prepared to fight for what was needed, we might have foundered long before that trip to Paris.'

'I think life has been unkind to you in the past, but I hope you will find it better in future.'

'I am sure I shall…' She tipped her head, her mouth slightly open as she invited his kiss. It was not long in coming. His lips demanded, his tongue explored and teased, while his hand stroked, down over her hip, cupping her buttocks as he pressed her closer.

Lottie could not doubt the strength of his arousal; with little between them she could feel the hard bulge and the heat of him.

'Come, it is time we began to know one another, Lottie,' Nicolas said and took her by the hand. He led her to the bed, reaching for the ties that fastened her nightrail. He untied them, then pulled the filmy garment over her head, revealing her slender hips, slim waist and full breasts. 'You are even more beautiful than I imagined…'

'Am I?' she asked her eyes on his face. She felt oddly shy as he stretched out a hand, stroking the line of her cheek, her throat and then her breast with a light touch that made her shiver.

'Lie down, Lottie,' he said huskily and divested himself of his robe. She saw that he was completely naked and her cheeks heated as she saw that he was fully aroused. 'I think this is your first time?'

'Yes…' she breathed out on a little gasp as he lay down beside her and half-turned to him. 'You are the first, Nicolas.'

'I knew it even when I called you those names, when I believed you to be Clarice.'

His breath was warm on her face as he began to kiss her with little feathery kisses on her brow, her nose and throat; then he took her lips in a much deeper demanding possession that made her sigh and wriggle closer.

Nicolas laughed throatily, his hand stroking the satin arch of her back, down over her buttocks. He pulled her close so that they lay flesh to flesh, silk to satin, looking into each other's eyes as he caressed her.

Lottie's breathing came quicker, her lips parting with sensual pleasure as he bent his head and his tongue caressed her nipple. She moaned and moved towards him urgently, her body seeking something she could not quite understand. Nicolas kissed her, rolled her over on to her back and then raised himself so that his eyes looked down into hers.

'You are so wet and warm. I think you are ready for me, Lottie. I shall try not to hurt you too much.'

His hand had been moving between her thighs, caressing her with a steady, almost languid movement, but now he parted her legs further as he lowered himself down to her. She felt the probe of his manhood, nudging at her, seeking entry into her moistness. She instinctively opened wider, inviting him to take her, though when he thrust deep into her silken sheath she could not prevent a gasp of pain. He stilled for a moment, allowing her to catch her breath.

'The first time it is always so,' he murmured against her throat. 'Forgive me, my darling.'

'It doesn't matter,' she whispered. 'Please do not stop. I want to be yours completely.'

He began to move again and at first it was a little painful for her, but then as she relaxed the pain seemed far away. She let her body follow his so that when his climax came she felt something too, a little cry escaping her as she clung to him and arched into him, her legs wrapping round him.

Nicolas nuzzled his face against her throat. 'It will be better next time,' he murmured. 'You were sweet and lovely, Lottie. Thank you.'

Lottie's hand touched his head. She stroked his hair, tears on her cheeks. So this was what it felt like to be a woman and to love a man. If she had hoped that she would be able to stop herself giving her whole heart, she knew now that it was a vain hope. Somewhere along the line she had given everything. Did he know that—and would he care?

Lottie did not know and she was too afraid to ask, because she did not wish to know the answer. She realised that Nicolas had fallen asleep as he lay by her side, his face buried in her hair. She moved it from his face, leaning up on her elbow to watch as he slept, thinking how peaceful he seemed…so much younger in sleep than he ever was awake.

She touched his cheek lightly so as not to wake him, her heart aching. He had loved her tenderly and she was grateful for his care of her, but was she more to him than a fleeting pleasure? He had wanted her badly but without love how long did physical attraction last?

She must not torture herself this way. Lottie snuggled closer to him, shutting her eyes. She must accept what he gave and not think of tomorrow.

In the days that followed, Lottie clung determinedly to the promise she had made herself. There was always a smile on her face when Nicolas looked at her or touched her. She took pleasure in everything they did: riding, walking, playing cards, reading aloud from their favourite books, and music. Lottie was proficient at playing the pianoforte, but Nicolas had a rare talent. When he played he became wrapped up in the music, an absorbed faraway look in his eyes, as though the music carried him to a world of his own.

'That was wonderful,' she said when he played for her the first time. It was evening and they had sat over their meal and wine until the light faded from the sky. 'I had no idea you were so talented. I have never heard you play before?'

'I seldom do—especially when anyone else is staying. When I am alone I sometimes play for an hour at a time. I do not subject others to a display of my indulgence.'

'I am sure they would take pleasure in your playing, as I do, Nicolas.'

'Would they?' His eyes had that strange haunted look she had seen before. 'I think you are different, Lottie. You are more generous and kinder than some ladies.'

Lottie had not known how to answer him. Had he

really no idea how talented he was? She merely smiled and shook her head.

She was painting a portrait of him. She had begun the sketch when they sat together in a wild meadow, and he lay back with his eyes closed, his face to the warmth of the sun. Since then she had made sketches of Nicolas in almost every pose and now she was painting a head-and-shoulders portrait that she thought she might frame and keep in her room.

'You paint very well,' Nicolas told her. 'You have made me too handsome, but I can find no other fault with your work.'

'Catching a likeness is a skill I do have,' she said, 'but I have much to learn about colour and texture. I do well enough for an amateur, which is all I aspire to be. I think you should have your portrait painted professionally for Rothsay, Nicolas.'

'We shall both have them done,' he said and frowned. 'I should like to stay here longer, Lottie—but I think we should go back. I never intended to stay more than a few days and we have been here nearly three weeks. There are things that need my attention…'

Lottie saw a brooding look in his eyes and her heart sank. Had he begun to be bored here with her? Did he miss his friends and the life he led in London—his mistress?

Their lovemaking had been very satisfactory to her, but her courses had started that morning, which meant the nightly visits must cease for a while.

Was Nicolas disappointed that she had not fallen for a child immediately? He had certainly loved her thoroughly these past days, sometimes three or four times a night, but she had failed to give him a swift result.

'I am sorry that I have not conceived, Nicolas.'

'In heaven's name, why should you be sorry? You are not a brood mare, Lottie. It will happen in time.'

'I thought you might be disappointed?'

'As it happens, I would prefer to have you to myself for a while longer.' He smiled at her. 'I am in no hurry, Lottie.'

She felt warmed by his smile. Their time here had been pleasant and she felt that she had begun to know him so much better. She had no right to ask for more. He had given all he had promised and more.

'So what are you thinking?'

'I was just thinking it had been very pleasant here, Nicolas.'

'Yes, it has, but it is not real. We should return to Rothsay and reality before it is too late.'

'I am not certain I understand you?'

'Why should you? I am not certain I understand myself.' He frowned. 'Do you love me at all, Lottie?'

'Yes, of course.' Her heart thumped because she was afraid of betraying herself and would not look at him. 'I am very fond of you, Nicolas. You are my husband.'

'Yes, I thought so,' he replied. 'I think I shall go for a long ride, Lottie. Do not expect me back to supper. There are some friends I wish to visit. Tell the servants to pack. We shall leave first thing in the morning.'

Lottie felt as if he had slapped her. What had caused him to suddenly withdraw from her? Had she showed her feelings too plainly? Tears stung her eyes. She had tried so hard not to impose conditions or strings—but to no avail. He had grown tired of her as she had expected, though she had hoped he might find contentment in their arrangement, as she had.

'Yes, of course,' she said. 'You are quite right, Nicolas. There is a great deal to do at home. This has been a pleasant interlude, but it is time to move on.'

He inclined his head and walked purposefully from the room, leaving Lottie to fight her tears.

Nicolas did not come in until the early hours of the morning. Lottie heard him moving around in his room. There was the sound of something falling, as if he had knocked over a stool or small table, and then he swore. She waited for a few minutes, then, as everything went quiet, took a candle and went into his bedchamber. Nicolas was lying on his bed, wearing his breeches, shirt and boots. His eyes were closed and he was snoring.

'Nicolas…is something the matter?'

He did not answer, but a little snore told her that he was fast asleep. She went closer and caught the smell of strong drink. He was drunk!

Lottie was shocked. She had never known Nicolas to drink too much and it made her feel very guilty. She had failed him and he had been driven to drink to get away from her. Or perhaps he had felt trapped because she had shown him too clearly that she was in love with him.

'I am sorry, dearest,' she said and went to remove his boots. They came off with a series of sharp tugs. He stirred once and muttered something but she continued to pull them off and then went to cover him with a light blanket. 'Forgive me…'

'Damn it, Elizabeth,' he muttered. 'You knew I adored you—why didn't you tell me? I suppose it doesn't matter if you break hearts…'

Lottie drew back, feeling as if he had thrust a dagger into her heart. Here at last was the key to that bleak look she saw sometimes in his eyes. He was still in love with Elizabeth—and she had obviously hurt him very badly when they parted. Lottie had been told right at the start by both Bertie and Henrietta that Nicolas had once been madly in love, but she had put it out of her mind. Now she felt as if she had been doused in cold water.

It was little wonder that he felt trapped by his marriage. He had wanted to marry Elizabeth, but she had broken his heart and he had sought comfort in the arms of various mistresses. He had married for the sake of an heir, but Elizabeth was the woman he dreamed of and regretted even now. Lottie would be a fool if she hoped that one day he would love her.

She went back into her own room and sat down on the edge of her bed. Her heart felt as if it were breaking, but she refused to cry. Nicolas had never promised to love her. She had mistaken his kindness for something more and that was her fault, not his.

She got into bed and shut her eyes. Tears were trickling down her cheeks. She could no longer control them. It was useless. Her honeymoon had been so very pleasant that she had been lulled into a false security, believing that Nicolas was ready to settle to marriage. Now she understood why he never could.

No wonder he had not cared who he married. He was still suffering from his blighted hopes and did not care who he took to wife.

All he wanted was an heir and Lottie had failed to provide him with that small thing. No wonder he wished to return to Rothsay. He would probably be off to London soon after they arrived.

Lottie was feeling tired when the carriage pulled up outside the house. Nicolas had ridden his horse for most of the time. She had hardly seen him other than the night they had spent at the inn or when they had stopped for refreshment. He was polite and concerned for her well being, but had made no attempt to kiss or touch her. Of course, there was no chance of making an heir while she had her courses. If she had needed confirmation of what she meant to him, this was it.

Lottie had cried herself to sleep for two nights, but now she felt numb. She had decided that the best defence was to keep her distance, be polite, as he was, but reserved. Inside, she was hurting, but she had no intention of letting Nicolas see that he had broken her heart.

She got down from the carriage with a sigh of relief. Now they were home they need not be forever in each other's company. Indeed, she thought it might be less painful if he took himself off to London. Every time she looked at him she was reminded of the way his lips felt on hers, or the touch of his hand, the feel of him inside her, giving her such pleasure.

'You will forgive me if I do not come in with you, Lottie,' Nicolas said. 'I must speak to the bailiff and I dare say you will enjoy an hour or so to chat with your aunt.'

'Yes, certainly I shall,' she said. 'Please, Nicolas, you

must do just as you wish. I am perfectly capable of finding something to do—especially now that we are home. I have it in mind to do something for the children of our tenants.'

'Freddie said something about a school,' Nicolas said and smiled for the first time in days. 'I approve of the idea, but hope you do not intend to teach them yourself?'

'Certainly not, though I might have enjoyed it had I not had other duties. I shall employ a young man to teach them. I am certain there must be suitable young men of good education in need of such work.'

'I am certain there must.' Nicolas laughed suddenly. 'I think I have been abominably rude to you these past two days, Lottie. Please forgive me, if you can?'

'There is nothing to forgive. I understand, Nicolas.'

'Do you?'

'I dare say you found a diet of my company tedious. You will wish to be off with your friends again soon. Do not imagine I expect you to dance attendance on me all the time.'

'Do you not?' He frowned. 'I see I have no need to apologise. I shall be late this evening, Lottie. Do not wait up for me.'

Now what had she said to upset him? Lottie was thoughtful as she went into the house. It seemed that there was no pleasing Nicolas in this mood.

Lottie spent a pleasant hour having tea with her aunt. She was told that the countess had gone home soon after they left for Rothsay's hunting lodge, but she had written to Aunt Beth telling her that she intended to visit London in the very near future and inviting her to stay.

'We got on very well,' Aunt Beth said. 'I am quite content here, Lottie—but should you wish to be private with Rothsay for a while I have a standing invitation from Lady Selby.'

'You must visit her if you wish,' Lottie said. 'I have no intention of being private with Rothsay and you will be of help to me here, but I shall not deny you the pleasure of a visit to town.'

'Well, I might go for a while later. The Season will be over by then, but I like to visit the theatre and too much racketing about is not for me—though of course there are always some hostesses who never entirely desert the capitol.'

'Yes, I suppose there must be.'

Aunt Beth hesitated, then, 'I had a visit from Clarice while you were away, Lottie.'

'She came here to the house?'

'She wore a hat with veiling. No one but I would have seen her face, Lottie. She asked me for money. I gave her ten pounds, but I think she hoped for far more.'

'Yes, I dare say she did. She asked me for money before the wedding. I gave her twenty guineas.'

'You must not make a habit of it, Lottie.'

'No, but she is my sister. I cannot forget that we were close once—and, if it were not for her, I should never have met Rothsay.'

'Well, I suppose there is that, but do not let her take advantage, dearest.'

'No, I promise I shall not.'

After her aunt went up to rest before dinner, Lottie

discovered that she was too restless to do the same and decided to go for a walk.

Clarice might be a problem in the future. She would never be satisfied with small handouts, but what else could Lottie do? The jewels she had been given were not truly hers to sell or give away—at least she would feel badly if she disposed of a wedding gift in order to pacify her sister. How could she look Uncle Freddie in the eye if she sold his necklace? Besides, even if she gave Clarice a thousand pounds, it was unlikely to be her last request.

Oh, bother, she would not let Clarice upset her!

She set out for the lake, enjoying the feel of the breeze in her hair. It was good to be home. She had come to think of Rothsay as her home and was content to spend her life here, though she might take Aunt Beth to visit Bath in the autumn for a few weeks.

Lottie stood staring at the opposite shore of the lake. There was an old summerhouse there, which Nicolas had told her had been shut up for years. Lottie wondered if it might be suitable for the school she was planning. The building looked sturdy enough. It was too far to explore further this evening, because she would be late changing for dinner, but in the morning she would see whether or not it would do. About to turn away, she thought she saw something at the window—a face or a flash of white.

She was certain Nicolas had told her the building was locked, because he had mentioned the key being in the bailiff's office, and she had planned to fetch it the next day. Perhaps it was just a trick of the light, and yet she could have sworn she had seen something.

She was thoughtful as she turned and walked back

to the house. It was as she reached the rose arbour that someone came up behind her. She turned and saw Lily, her instincts telling her immediately that the seamstress was in some distress.

'Lily—did you wish to speak to me?'

Lily hesitated, then, 'Yes, my lady. Forgive me—I was wondering if you would help me? I need some money…' She glanced over her shoulder, as if frightened of being overheard. 'It is for Sam…he needs to get away, Miss Lottie. They have put a price on his head. I've seen the posters up everywhere. His price is fifty guineas. People will give him away. It is a fortune to most folk.'

'Yes, of course, it must be,' Lottie said. 'He is hiding at the moment?'

'Yes…' Lily glanced back towards the lake and Lottie understood what she had seen earlier. Sam must be hiding out at the old summerhouse. He was in a very dangerous situation, because he could be discovered at any moment. 'There's someone who would help him get away to the coast. If he could find a ship and go to France he might be safe there.'

'What about you?'

'I shall stay here until he finds work and can send for me. I'll work for you for nothing until I have paid back anything you give me.'

'That would not be necessary…' Lottie thought quickly. If she gave Lily money knowing that it was intended for a fugitive, she would be breaking the law— but Sam Blake had been unfortunate. She did not think he deserved a price on his head for what he had done. 'Come to the house with me now, Lily. How much do you need?'

'Would twenty guineas be too much?' Lily looked doubtful. 'I know it is a lot to ask…'

'No, I can give you that quite easily,' Lottie said. 'You need not worry about paying me back, Lily. I had intended to make you a present for making my wedding gown so beautifully—and that will do very well. You may continue to work for me if you wish, but I had thought of helping you to set up a small establishment in Northampton, if you should like it?'

'You are so generous. If things had been otherwise it is just what I should have liked—but Sam will send for me soon. I shall take the children and follow him to France just as soon as he is settled there.'

'Then I can only wish you good luck. I am glad we returned in time to help you.'

Lily looked over her shoulder once more. 'I know I shouldn't have asked, but Sam is desperate. He says if they catch him he will hang for sure this time.'

'Yes, I know. I am so sorry, Lily. It isn't fair that he should be treated so harshly. I do not think his crime so very terrible.'

'You are a good woman, my lady. There's not many as care about folk like us. His lordship…' She shook her head. 'No, I shouldn't say, but Sam says he's a fool to trust that Larkin…'

'What makes you say that, Lily?'

'He's the one been selling game to the inn, my lady. My Sam only did it the once when he were desperate. He needed medicine for me when I had the last babe—but mostly it was just a rabbit for the pot.'

'Larkin is cheating my husband? Are you sure, Lily? And Sam can prove this?'

'It's only his word, miss. No one would listen to a convicted fugitive, would they?'

'No, they wouldn't. I am so sorry, Lily.' Lottie felt pity for the woman and her husband, but there was little she could do other than to give her some money. 'Come up to my room now and I shall give you the twenty guineas…'

Chapter Ten

Aunt Beth had gone to bed and Lottie was sitting in her favourite parlour reading when she heard the ring of hurried feet and then the door was flung open and Nicolas strode into the room. Raising her head to look at him, she saw that he was angry. She rose to her feet apprehensively.

'Is something wrong?'

'Do you know anything about this?' He threw down a purse of something that clinked. It landed on the floor at her feet with a little thud. 'Blake claims that you gave him the money—is it true?'

Lottie swallowed hard. 'Has he been caught? Why couldn't you have just let him go, Nicolas? He doesn't deserve to be hung for stealing a few rabbits.'

'It wasn't just my rabbits. Bertie has lost deer and the game birds have been disappearing too fast to be the work of just one man. There is a gang of the rascals at work in the area.'

'Sam Blake wasn't one of them. He sold game only once when Lily was ill.'

'I suppose she told you that?' Nicolas glared at her. 'And you believed her—and you gave her twenty guineas for Sam?'

'Yes, I did.' Lottie raised her head defiantly, meeting his furious gaze. 'She told me something else, too—but I dare say you would not listen if I told you who was behind this outbreak of poaching?'

'I would not believe anything Blake said—and you are a fool to believe his wife.'

'I gave Lily the money as a present, but I knew she intended it for her husband. He was going to France and she was to join him once he had found work there.'

'Very likely. The man was a lazy good-for-nothing and would never have done an honest day's work.'

'Was…' Lottie shivered. She felt sick as she looked at her husband's face. 'Are you saying…what happened to him? You didn't…?'

'Larkin shot him. He was searched, questioned and told he was being taken to prison—he knocked a man down and ran off,' Nicolas grated. A pulse flicked in his throat. 'I am sorry, Lottie. I know you like his wife and you had sympathy for the man—but he would have hanged had we caught him. He was seen leaving the area of the lake and some of the keepers went after him. He was warned several times, but he continued to run and he was shot. I am afraid he was killed outright.'

'No! How could you allow that?' Lottie stared at him in horror. 'I thought you had some compassion in you—how could you let your keeper murder a man just like that?'

'I was not present or I would have stopped it. However, Larkin acted within the law. Blake had a price on his head, which meant he could be shot on sight. Larkin says he intended to wing him, but…the shot killed him instantly. He couldn't have suffered.'

'Lily and their children will suffer terribly,' Lottie said. Her eyes stung with tears. 'Larkin is the man who is taking your game, Nicolas. Sam Blake knew the truth. Larkin killed him to cover his crimes.'

'That is ridiculous,' Nicolas said, his mouth set in a harsh line. 'You do not expect me to believe my own keeper is stealing from my neighbours and me?'

'No, Rothsay, I do not expect you to believe it,' Lottie said and raised her head proudly. 'Yet I believe it—and in time you may, too. I just hope that nothing happens that makes you wish you had listened.' She glanced down at the purse on the floor. 'That money belongs to Lily Blake. She will need it if her children are not to starve.'

Leaving it lying on the floor, she walked past him and from the room, going upstairs to her room. Once alone, she sat on the bed, trying not to give way to her emotions.

How could Nicolas have allowed his keeper to kill a man just for the crime of stealing a few rabbits? If he thought that justice, then he was not the man she had thought she loved.

'Damn you, Lottie.' Nicolas caught her as she reached her bedroom door, following her inside. 'I will not leave this there—nor shall I be made to feel in the wrong over this business with Blake. The man was a fool to fall in with hardened rogues—and Larkin was within the law to shoot him.'

'Be damned to the law,' Lottie said, rounding on him furiously. All caution was gone as her feelings reached boiling point. 'Have you no compassion at all? I believed you a man of honour, but now I begin to think I was mistaken. You are not the man I thought I was marrying.'

'Indeed?' Nicolas looked at her, his expression frosty. 'I hardly think you are in a position to preach to me of morals, Lottie. You were ready to deceive me—to allow me to think you your sister. You are as much a schemer as she—perhaps worse, for at least she refused to be part of the deal.'

'You forced me to keep the bargain.' Lottie's cheeks flamed with heat. She felt as if he had slapped her. 'I confessed and begged you to let me go.'

'You had chances enough to break it off. You need not have signed the contract. You knew I would have let you go then. Do not pretend otherwise.'

'I thought I liked you,' Lottie said. 'I knew it would never be a love match—but at least I thought you would deal fairly with me. Now I am not sure that I like you at all.'

'So, now we have the truth at last.' His expression was dangerous, his eyes glittering with anger. 'You married me because you had a fancy to be the marchioness, I suppose. I thought you very different from your sister, but it seems the difference is slight after all.'

'Damn you!' Lottie lashed out, striking him across the face with the palm of her hand. 'Why don't you go back to your mistress—or your precious Elizabeth? It is she you love, is it not?'

'Who told you about Elizabeth?' Nicolas's face was white apart from the red mark where she had struck him. He reached for her, catching her wrist as she would have turned away, his fingers clasping her like a ring of iron. 'Answer me, Lottie! Who has been feeding you these tales?'

She lifted her head proudly, refusing to let the tears fall. 'I know that you could never love me,' she said. 'Let me go, Nicolas. You can seek a separation or a divorce if you prefer—but let's stop this pretence now. You despise me and I—wish I had never met you.'

'You are my wife whether you wish it or not—and I have no intention of seeking a divorce. You made a bargain and you will stick to it.'

'You may force me to be your wife—but I shall never love you.'

Nicolas stared at her in silence for a moment, then turned and walked from the room, slamming the door behind him.

Lottie sank to her knees, covering her face with her hands as she wept.

Nicolas woke and groaned as he felt the pain in his head. He looked round and saw that he was the library, where he had gone to get drunk after the bitter quarrel with Lottie. He had said such things to her—but it was Lottie who had delivered the most telling blow.

She wished she had never met him.

Why had he gone after her and forced the quarrel on her?

He had been so angry when he discovered what she had done. Larkin had given him the money and reported what the man said, though pretending not to believe a word. Nicolas had been furious, though he could do nothing about the man's impertinence. Lottie was in the wrong. Had Blake told his tale to someone else, Lottie might have been in some trouble for helping a fugitive.

Nicolas regretted that Blake had been shot while trying to run away. He had remonstrated with Larkin, but the other keepers backed up the man's story. Blake had been warned and he had struck one of them before making his escape. Larkin's action was within the law. The posters offered the fifty guineas' reward dead or alive—and Larkin would no doubt share the blood money with the others.

Leaving the library, Nicolas felt the bad taste in his mouth. It was partly down to the drink he had taken after Lottie walked out on him earlier, but also the unpleasant feeling he had that someone was pulling the wool over his eyes.

Could Lottie be right about the keeper? He walked up the stairs into her sitting room and saw her curled up on the daybed, fast asleep. Why was she not in bed? Had she been frightened that he would enter her room and force her to do her duty?

His wicked, wicked temper! She must have thought that he was threatening her, telling her that she must do her duty as his wife and give him an heir. He had behaved in a disgusting manner—and the worst of it was he could not be certain that he would not give in to temptation if he continued to sleep in the next room. He knew that seeing her every day would drive him mad if he could not have her. The memory of her warm body close to his and her sweetness pricked at his heart.

She hated him now.

He must go away, remove his unwanted presence.

Lottie would not miss him. She had shown herself perfectly at home here, and after the way he had spoken to her the previous night, she would be glad to see him go.

'I am so sorry,' he said softly. 'I would beg you to forgive me, but I don't think I could bear to see the disgust in your eyes. You will be better off without me.'

By forcing her into a marriage she clearly regretted, he had ruined Lottie's life.

He walked into the dressing room and found some water, dipping his face in its coolness. He would leave as soon as it was light, taking only a few things with him. His town clothes were in London and the sooner he was gone the better. He would write to Lottie from London, tell her she could do pretty much as she pleased here, and he would instruct his agent before he left that Lottie was to have complete control. It was small recompense for what he had done to her, but he must hope she would forgive him in time. He could do little about Sam Blake—but he would make some enquiries about Larkin.

Nicolas's mouth drew into a thin line. He would send a couple of Bow Street Runners down here to keep an eye on the man—and someone to watch over Lottie. If the man *was* a rogue, he might try to harm her.

Nicolas hesitated. Should he stay here and try to make it up with her?

No. He shook his head. There was no point. She must hate him. To see scorn in her lovely eyes would destroy him. It would be best to end this now before he was in too deep. He would have Larkin investigated and make sure she was protected—but she need know nothing about it.

Lottie woke feeling stiff and with a neck ache. She sat up and looked about her, wondering why she had been sleeping on the uncomfortable sofa when she had a soft bed. As the memories flooded back, she frowned. She had sat here and cried herself to sleep, too miserable to seek the comfort of her bed.

She had had such a terrible quarrel with Nicolas. They had both said cruel things—and she regretted it bitterly. To argue with the man she loved over something that was not truly his fault was foolish.

Lottie hated the system that allowed men like Larkin to shoot another man with impunity just because he was a wanted fugitive. Sam Blake might have been a poacher, but he was a husband and the father of three children. What must his poor wife be thinking now?

She decided that the first thing she would do this morning was to visit Lily and apologise for what had happened. Lily might resent her because she was the wife of the man whose keeper had shot her husband, but in time perhaps she would forgive and accept Lottie's help.

She would ride over with one of the young grooms, and on the way back she would take another look at the Hollow. Lottie intended to ask Nicolas again if he would consider cleaning the place up—or at least give the occupants alternative accommodation before he tore down their homes.

She considered speaking to her husband first, but

thought that he might still be angry with her. Dressing in an old riding habit that she had owned long ago, she glanced at herself in the mirror and was satisfied with her appearance. It would be ridiculous to go to a place like the Hollow dressed in something that cost as much as a family might need to live on in a year.

Nicolas had been generous with her allowance. Lottie doubted that she would spend the half of it, which meant she could redirect it in other ways.

She left the house and walked down to the stables, making a brief inspection of the horses until she found one she thought looked a suitable mount.

'Would you saddle this one for me?' she asked a young groom who had tipped his cap to her and was watching curiously. 'And please saddle one for yourself. I want to visit Lily Blake's cottage—and the Hollow on the way back.'

The lad's mouth opened in surprise. She thought he was about to protest, but then he merely touched his greasy cap and set about saddling the mare she had selected. Lottie waited until he had his own mount ready, then led hers to a mounting block and mounted without assistance. Once her hands were on the reins she felt the mare's restiveness and knew she had chosen a spirited beast, which was what she had hoped for.

She glanced at the lad. 'What is your name, sir?'

'I be Willis, ma'am, and the mare be Red Ruth,' he said. 'That 'un ain't bin out fer a couple of days. She'll be a mite fresh.'

'Thank you, Willis. I can feel she wants her head, but she will have to behave. I have serious business this morning.' Lottie smiled at him. 'Now, can you show me the way to Mrs Blake's cottage?'

'Yes, ma'am,' Willis said and grinned. 'I reckon I can. I like Lily. She's a good 'un—too good fer the likes of that Sam Blake. Me pa alus did say it.'

Lottie nodded. The groom moved off and she followed him. They walked the horses until they were clear of the yard and then broke into a trot. She felt her horse pull, as if it wanted to gallop, but she held her reins steady and would not give into the mare's desire. On another day she might have done so, but she did not wish to take any risks this morning.

Lily was red eyed and had little to say when she saw Lottie at her door that morning. Her manner was angry and resentful and the look in her eyes cut Lottie to the heart.

'I don't blame you, miss,' she said. 'You've been good to me and I know you would have helped Sam if you could—but the rest of them don't give a damn.'

'I am sure that isn't true, Lily. Some people are harsh and poaching is a crime, whether we like it or not, but I am sure a lot of people will think what happened was very wrong. I know you are grieving and angry—but when you are ready, come to me. Let me help you set up your own business in Northampton.'

'Thank you, my lady—but I can't ask for more than you've done already, though I am still willing to sew for you to pay my debt.'

'I asked my husband to return the money that was taken from Sam. It is yours, Lily. Please do not be too proud to take it for the sake of your children.'

'I'll think about it—if it happens.'

Lottie left her cottage feeling saddened. She could not expect Lily to welcome her with open arms or to accept her apology. Lily's grief was sharp and it would take time for her to think of a future without the man she had loved.

The visit was something Lottie had had to do, and now there was something more she must see to—even though she expected an even more hostile reception at the Hollow.

'Are you sure you want to stop here, ma'am?' Willis asked as they approached the little cluster of hovels. 'They be a rough lot at the Hollow.'

'They do not have much chance to be otherwise,' Lottie said. 'That open ditch is unhealthy and it smells vile. Who would not resent living near to something like that?'

'Just be careful, ma'am. Not that they'll touch you while I'm around. They know my father and uncles would come back and thrash 'em.'

'Thank you, that makes me feel much better.' Lottie smiled at him. She did not know it, but her manner and her smile had won her a staunch friend that morning.

They dismounted at one end of the hamlet, because Lottie wished to see the true condition of the houses for herself. She lifted her long skirt, hanging it over her arm so that it did not drag in the filth. The smell was vile, but she bore it without flinching, though she was amused to see that Willis covered his nose and mouth.

As she walked the length of the street, people started to come out of the houses. Every now and then she stopped to look at a house. It seemed to Lottie that some of them could be restored, though some would need to be replaced. There was no doubt that it was not an easy project, but she thought it could be done with a little thought and management. The most obvious need was to have the ditch drained and covered.

Intent on her inspection, Lottie was not aware that the crowd had grown until Willis touched her arm and gave a little nod of his head. She turned and saw that they had all gathered at the end of the street, and one man stood at the front, as if intending to block her return to her horse.

Their mood was clearly hostile and she could hardly blame them after what had happened to Sam Blake. However, Lottie was in no mood to be intimidated.

'I have seen enough,' she told Willis. 'We shall leave now.' She saw the discomfort in his face and smiled. 'Do not worry, Willis. I know they are angry, but I do not think they will harm me.'

As they reached the small group at the end of the street, Lottie saw that Sam Blake's cousin Dickon was at their head.

'Good morning,' she said pleasantly in a voice that would carry. 'I dare say you are all wondering what I am doing here this morning?'

'You shouldn't 'ave come 'ere,' Dickon growled. 'Pokin' yer nose in where yer ain't wanted.'

'Unless someone comes, these houses will become nothing but ruins within a few years,' Lottie said. 'It is my intention to repair those that can be repaired. Some will have to be torn down, but they will be rebuilt—and we shall begin by putting in drains and covering over that awful ditch.'

'We don't want yer interference, missus. Clear orf and don't come back or I'll make yer sorry.'

'Speak for yerself, Dickon,' one of the other men said. 'My wife and baby suffer every winter with the damp; our first lad died of a fever on his lungs. If her ladyship means what she says, I'll give a hand with the ditch.'

'I intend to start the repairs at once,' Lottie announced. 'I shall use local labour if possible—so if any of you have building skills, please let me know.'

'I've been a builder,' one of the men said. 'And Sid Carne is a roofer. Most of us can use a spade or a hammer. We would have repaired the houses ourselves if we had the money.'

'Anyone who is willing to work should be here tomorrow morning. I shall be bringing my husband's agent at eight sharp and he will draw up a list of the houses to be repaired and what must be done—and he will pay those who work each day.'

'What about them houses you said 'ad ter come down?' Dickon asked. 'Where will the families go then?'

'I shall begin building a little further through the Hollow. As one house is finished, so one of the houses that cannot be saved will come down; we shall start with the worst and continue until the end, though that may take some time. I hope that you will be as patient as you can, for I cannot do it all at once.'

'Give 'er ladyship a chance, Dickon,' one of the other men said. 'No one but 'er 'as bothered about us fer years. Let 'er see what she can do.'

'I shall be here tomorrow,' Lottie said. 'Be prepared to work. I should prefer that you earned the money yourselves, but of course that is entirely up to you. I can bring in outside craftsmen if I have to.'

The crowd parted to let her through. Willis helped her to mount and they rode away.

'If you are serious about the building, my lady, my elder brother could do with some extra work. Tom can turn his hand to anything—and I reckon as there will be a few more glad of some extra money.'

'Tell him to be there, Willis,' Lottie said.

She could not help feeling a little nervous as she dismounted in the stables and walked into the house. Nicolas might well say that she was interfering in his affairs, and she was—but something had to be done. Lottie was prepared to pay for the repairs with her own money. She just hoped Nicolas would not be too angry with her.

'My husband has gone to London?' Lottie did not know how she managed to hide her surprise and disappointment when Mrs Mann told her why Nicolas had not come down to nuncheon. 'Ah, yes, I believe he did mention some business. I was not perfectly sure when he meant to leave.'

Her heart felt as if someone had taken a knife and stabbed her. So it was all over. He had soon tired of her company and after their quarrel he had decided to return to London—and his mistress, perhaps.

For a moment she recalled the look in his eyes when she had spoken of Elizabeth. He had looked stunned and then angry, as if enraged because she had dared to speak his beloved's name.

Grief and disappointment threatened to overwhelm

her. What was she to do with her life now? For a moment it seemed as if there was nothing left to live for—then she lifted her head as pride came to her aid.

She conquered her disappointment and decided to speak to her husband's agent after nuncheon. Lottie was a little apprehensive, for she imagined he might resist her ideas for the Hollow, but he listened in silence and then nodded his agreement.

'I told his lordship that some of the houses might be saved, but he was insistent it should all come down—perhaps because of things that happened in the past, my lady.'

'I am not sure I understand you, Mr Masters?'

'The late Lady Rothsay was like you, ma'am. She was forever trying to help people—she took a fever after a visit to the Hollow and died within two days. His lordship was but a lad at the time and I dare say he took it hard.'

'That is sad,' Lottie said. 'Surely the best way to prevent something of the sort happening again is to drain that awful ditch and cover it over.'

'I dare say it would help,' Simon Masters agreed. 'There will need to be a cesspool to dispose of the… I beg your pardon, my lady. I should not speak of these things to you.'

Lottie laughed. 'Who else should you tell, sir? I need to know everything that goes on, because I want the work to start immediately.'

'Then perhaps I should draw up a schedule of works for your approval?'

'Yes, of course. I am not sure how fast I can do

all the work, but I want to do as much as I can afford immediately, and then we'll see.'

'Naturally, the repairs will come from the estate revenue, my lady. His lordship left orders that you were to have a free hand—I am certain he would expect to pay himself for any repairs.'

'Nicolas said that I might have a free hand?'

Lottie was surprised and pleased. This was the last thing she had expected.

'Yes, my lady.'

'Very well, we shall begin first thing tomorrow and use as much local talent as we can for the labouring work. Some of the residents may be craftsmen and we must give them the chance, but I shall be guided by your experience in the matter.'

'You may safely leave it in my hands, my lady.'

'Oh, I intend to be there myself at the start,' Lottie said. 'I shall be keeping an eye on what happens—and do not let them cheat you, Mr Masters. I want to help them, but they must do a fair day's work for a fair day's pay.'

The agent smiled. 'Just so, my lady. May I say that I believe things will prosper now that you are here—and perhaps his lordship will take more interest?'

'We must hope so, sir.'

Lottie returned to the house. It was time to take tea with Aunt Beth. Perhaps by working hard every day and concentrating all her thoughts on the unfortunate people of the Hollow, she could forget that Nicolas had deserted her and that her heart felt as if it had split in two.

Chapter Eleven

'Lottie, look at the state of you,' Aunt Beth scolded some three weeks later. 'I approve of what you are doing for those people, naturally, but I did not expect you would actually work yourself.'

'I helped one of the younger women to move from her house into a cottage Mr Masters found for her on the estate. Once her new house is built she will move back to the Hollow,' Lottie said and laughed. 'She has three children and her house is the first to come down. I fear the baby has deposited the contents of his napkin all over my gown. It is just as well I was wearing an old one.'

'You should change before the countess sees you. She would be horrified. I fear you smell, Lottie.'

'Yes, it was my intention to go straight up before seeing anyone,' Lottie said and frowned. 'I thought the countess was in London?'

'She says she needs to speak to you, dearest—but please change before you see her.'

Lottie hurried to change. She knew that she must look terrible, but she had hardly sat still a moment these past weeks since Nicolas left. It would not be true to say that her heartache had eased, but she had little time to think of him, at least during the day. At night her loneliness was hard to bear, but bear it she must, for there was nothing else to be done. Nicolas did not want or need her and she must fill her life with good works.

Having changed into a clean gown and scraped her hair back into a knot at her nape, Lottie went down to the parlour. Henrietta was there alone, and her eyes went over Lottie with disapproval.

'It seems there is not much to choose between the two of you,' she exclaimed. 'I came down to tell you that my godson is on a course set straight for hell and will not long be for this world if something is not done. Now I find you in hardly better shape. You have lost weight, Lottie. What in the world has got into the pair of you?'

Lottie flushed—she knew she had not bothered with her appearance of late. 'Forgive me for not making more effort, Henrietta, but I have been working at the Hollow. I spent the day helping a young woman to move house and—'

'Surely you have servants enough without working yourself to the bone?' Henrietta frowned at her. 'I thought you might see sense, but it seems you are no less stubborn than my godson—did you hear what I said about Nicolas?'

Lottie frowned. 'I heard, but I did not understand you. Is Nicolas ill?'

'Not yet, but he mostly certainly will be if he continues this way. He has been drinking and gambling, and I've never known him to be so careless of his appearance. I called on him the other morning and he looked terrible.'

Lottie's heart contracted with pain. 'I am sorry to hear that, Henrietta, but I really do not see what I can do about it. Nicolas would take little notice of me.'

'You are his wife, Lottie. Do you not care what becomes of him? I have never seen him like this. I do not understand what has changed him—he is like a man possessed, driven to destruction. Indeed, he reminds me of his father just after the marchioness died.' Henrietta's eyes narrowed. 'Have you quarrelled with him, Lottie?'

'No…at least nothing that should upset him in the way you describe. I believe he may regret that he married me. He was not in love with me, Henrietta. There was someone else he cared for deeply.'

'Are you certain of that?' Henrietta looked puzzled. 'He was always moody, of course. Not when he was younger, but these past few years—but then he seemed much happier. I really thought you were the perfect wife for him.' She looked at Lottie intently. 'Do you care for him at all?'

'I love him with all my heart—but please do not tell him so. I fear I drove him away. He does not wish for a clinging wife.'

'Ridiculous! What Nicolas needs is to love and be

loved. If you cared for him, you would do something before it is too late.'

'Would you have me send for him? I doubt he would come—and if he did I could not keep him against his will.'

Henrietta was about to answer, but Aunt Beth entered the room and she thought better of it.

Lottie was thoughtful as she handed out tea and cake. Was Nicolas really behaving that badly? Could he be upset over their quarrel? She had not thought it would affect him—or perhaps he was simply being reckless because he felt trapped?

It was a problem, for she could not simply ignore Henrietta's appeal for help. Her mind was busy with all the alternatives as she went upstairs to change for the evening. If Nicolas wished to be free she would oblige him, but first he must be honest with her and tell her what he wanted from her.

Lottie did not think there was much point in sending for her husband. He would either ignore her or pay a flying visit that would do no one any good. For a while she could not think what she ought to do, but as she was dressing the idea came to her. She had not bothered to purchase many clothes, for she had thought she would have no need of them, but she had been invited to dine several times by her neighbours, and if she were to visit Bath with her aunt she would certainly need more fashionable clothes.

Her plan was bold and risky—Nicolas would be within his rights to be angry. She had agreed to his terms, which were that he would be free to go to London while she stayed here or visited the house in Bath. If she turned up at his London house on the pretext of needing to buy clothes, he would quite possibly be furious.

Well, if they had a row, it might clear the air. Lottie faced the prospect head on. If Nicolas wanted a separation he must tell her—otherwise he would simply have to put up with having her around.

'Go to London to buy clothes?' At dinner that evening, Henrietta looked at her in silence for a moment, then she smiled. 'I think that is an excellent idea, my love. We shall all stay at Nicolas's house while you refurbish your scanty wardrobe. If you will be guided by me, I think we can soon have you looking more the thing, Lottie.'

'I think I shall need your advice if I am to acquire a little town bronze, Henrietta. I do not expect to become the toast of the town, but I should like to be well received.'

'I see no reason why you should not be—and I know my friends will be happy to take you under their wings, my dear. People have been asking why you had not come up with Nicolas. I could not explain, for I had no idea.'

'That is simple—my aunt was poorly, but she is recovered now, are you not, Aunt Beth?'

'What are you up to, Lottie?' Aunt Beth said. 'If you do not mind, I shall stay here, dearest. I may pay your father a little visit, just for a week or two while you are away. He wrote to me and seems worried about your sister.'

'Yes, of course. Go to him if you feel he needs you,' Lottie said. 'But please come back to me soon, aunt.'

'I shall not desert you, Lottie,' Aunt Beth said. 'But

I think you will do better with the countess in town. I have no wish to be racketing around.'

'I dare say we shall not be out so very much,' Lottie said innocently. 'I may be gone only a short time—it depends on what I find…'

Lottie was thoughtful as she went to bed that evening. Perhaps she was a fool but there was no point in staying here pining for something that might never happen. Nicolas was obviously not going to return of his own accord. He might be furious with her, but that would be better than this silent indifference. If they were to part it would be better done now—though in her heart Lottie knew that she would never love anyone else.

She could not stand by and see Nicolas go to the devil without at least trying to discover the cause.

Nicolas stared at himself in his shaving mirror and cursed what he saw. He looked as if he had been dragged through the gutters the previous night; for all he knew, he might have been. He had visited various clubs, discovered that endless gambling bored him and returned home to lose himself in a brandy bottle.

The trouble was, he suspected, that he was missing Lottie. Her perfume seemed to haunt him and he was conscious of a hollow place inside that had been filled for a little time by her presence. He could not get her out of his mind. The drinking and gambling had done nothing to ease the ache inside him or the sense of shame he felt for having abused his wife.

She would hate him now, of course. From the very beginning he had done nothing but insult her—and that last quarrel was unforgivable. How could he go home, which was increasingly where he wished to be? Lottie's clear eyes would show her disgust too plainly and it would kill him to know he deserved her hatred.

Of course he was not in love with her. Romantic love was a myth, but he had enjoyed her company and he wanted her affection—her respect. And though he felt sure that he could never return it, he'd selfishly wanted her love.

Well, he had forfeited it and there was no going back to before that night, but it was time to bring an end to the mad behaviour of the past weeks. He would ruin himself or end up dead in the gutter.

Perhaps he would write an apology to his wife. If she accepted it, he could at least visit her sometimes.

Feeling better, he decided to visit the fencing master he sometimes patronised. It would sharpen his wits and get rid of the sluggish feeling, which was the result of too much wine of late.

'His lordship said nothing of your coming, my lady,' the startled housekeeper said when Lottie and the Countess of Selby arrived on the doorstep of the London house that morning. 'It won't take above half an hour to prepare your rooms—if you would step into the parlour and partake of some refreshments?'

'I dare say my husband did not get my letter,' Lottie said blithely, though she had sent none. Had she informed him, she was certain that Nicolas would have told her not to come. 'We shall be quite content to sit and drink a dish of tea while our rooms are prepared, Mrs Barret.'

Lottie glanced around her as they were taken into a

very elegant salon. It was furnished with delicate satin-wood furniture inlaid with porcelain plaques and looked as if it might be French in style. Perfect for entertaining one's friends, but not as comfortable as her parlour at home.

Lottie frowned, because she had been used to thinking of Rothsay as her home and that might change quite soon. She lifted her chin, putting on a brave face. Henrietta had spoken of Nicolas as being in a parlous state, but she would judge for herself when he came in later. It seemed that he was expected for dinner that evening.

What would he say when he discovered his wife had come to stay? Would he be furious and ask her to leave first thing in the morning?

Why should she leave until she was ready? Nicolas had bullied her into marrying him when she would have released him from the contract. Now he must just put up with the inconvenience until she was ready to leave.

'So what do you think of the house?' Henrietta asked. 'Nicolas had it refurbished when he was first on the town. Personally, I feel it is stylish, but not truly a home.'

'I think it is perfect for entertaining, though if I were often here I should like something more comfortable for the afternoons when I was alone.'

Henrietta laughed. 'Lottie, my dear, I can see this is your first visit to town. The whole point of being in town is that one is never alone—one is always coming or going or entertaining. I dare say your boudoir may be more comfortable.'

'My boudoir? Do you imagine I have one here?'

'Yes, certainly. Nicolas must have prepared the master suite for the comfort of the lady he intended to be his wife. You may care to sit there sometimes—if you are at home—but I am sure that once I tell my friends you are here you will not have time.'

Lottie looked at her uncertainly. The countess seemed very certain that she would be welcomed into society by everyone. As yet, Lottie was not quite so sure.

'Lottie…' The door that divided her suite of very attractive rooms from those that Nicolas used when in town was suddenly flung open and her husband strode in. Her heart caught as she saw him, because she had temporarily forgotten how very handsome he was. 'I could hardly believe it when Barret told me you were here.'

'Nicolas.' Lottie's pulses raced as she looked at him. 'I am sorry you did not get my letter. I hope you will not mind my coming up to town, but I find I cannot manage with the clothes I have. Though you were undoubtedly generous with the gowns you organised for me before the wedding, I have been entertained by most of our neighbours and if I am to take Aunt Beth to Bath, I need some town bronze. Henrietta was kind enough to say she would help me choose the right seamstresses.'

For a moment Nicolas was silent, his manner uncertain, as if waiting for something, then, 'Of course I do not mind, Lottie. I told you that you would need more clothes, did I not?'

'Certainly you did, Nicolas.' Lottie kept her expression bland, wanting to give nothing away as she searched his face for signs of the depravity the countess had spoken of. He looked tired and there were shadows beneath his eyes, but at the moment he was sober and she could see no sign of desperation. 'I dare say it will only take me a few days to be suited and then you may be peaceful again.'

'Please stay as long as you wish, Lottie.' She noticed a little pulse flicking at his temple. 'Are you quite well? I think you have lost some weight? You look thinner than I remember.'

'Perfectly well, thank you,' she replied and allowed a cool smile. 'You will not pull caps with me, Nicolas. Mr Masters said that you had given me a free hand—and I fear I have taken advantage. We have started work on the Hollow, using mostly local labour. I must tell you that one of the new houses is almost built and that terrible ditch has been covered in and drained into a cesspool.'

'Masters wrote and informed me,' Nicolas said, his eyes narrowed and intent. 'I should, of course, have seen to it years ago—but for reasons I prefer to remain private, I favoured pulling the whole place down.'

'It would be a pity to drive people from their homes when a few repairs and some rebuilding will make it a perfectly decent place to live. Now that the open ditch is gone I am sure everyone will be healthier.'

'Yes, I am certain you are right.' He hesitated, then, 'Dare I hope—have you forgiven me, Lottie?'

Lottie wrinkled her smooth brow. 'I am sorry that Sam Blake was killed, but you were not present and the law was on your keeper's side. I have offered to set Lily Blake up in her own establishment in Northampton. There is no way I can make up for what she has lost, but I hope that in time she will be able to move on and begin a new life.'

'I did not mean…' Nicolas shook his head. 'Then you

do not hate me?' he asked, an odd expression in his eyes. 'You said it the last time we spoke.'

'I must apologise for the things I said to you, Nicolas. I was angry but—I could never truly hate you,' Lottie said. 'I know that I have broken the terms of our agreement by coming here—but perhaps you will not mind too much just for a little while?'

'I find that I do not mind at all,' Nicolas said. 'Do you have enough money? If not, you must send the bills to me. I would wish my wife to appear in society in a manner befitting the Countess Rothsay.'

'Thank you, I shall try not to let you down, Nicolas.'

'How could you do that?' he said. 'I have an appointment to play cards with a party of friends this evening and ought not to cancel it—perhaps tomorrow evening we could go somewhere together?'

'Henrietta says we are invited to a soirée tomorrow evening, Nicolas. If you care to accompany us that will be perfectly acceptable—if not, then perhaps another time. You must not think that you are obliged to dance attendance on me. I am perfectly able to entertain myself—at least with Henrietta's help I shall be.'

'Very well, I shall not interfere with your plans.'

'Or I with yours,' Lottie said. 'It is not unknown for a husband and wife to attend separate affairs, I believe.'

There, she was being the perfect convenient wife.

'It is often the case. We should hold a dinner ourselves—if that is agreeable to you?'

'Perfectly. We may attend some of the same affairs, of course,' Lottie said. 'It must be just as you wish, Nicolas.'

'So we are back to that…' Nicolas nodded thoughtfully. 'Very well, my love. I see we shall go on just as before.'

'I hope that we may be friends again,' Lottie said. 'Have you forgiven me, Nicolas?'

'There was nothing to forgive,' he replied smoothly. 'I thought—but perhaps I was mistaken… I find I cannot read you as well as I imagined, Lottie.'

'Perhaps as time goes on you will know me better,' she said. 'Pray do not let me keep you from your appointment, Nicolas.'

He stared at her uncertainly, inclined his head and went back through to his own room, shutting the door with a little snap.

Lottie stared at the door and wondered. Had she noticed signs of frustration in Nicolas? Could it be that he had missed her just a little?

Nicolas's thoughts were in turmoil as he left Lottie to change for a quiet evening at home. He found himself wishing that he might stay with her and talk about the future for them—but his pride refused to let him speak too openly of his feelings. She seemed to have forgiven him for that night or at least to have put their quarrel to one side. In Lottie's estimation, it seemed, the only thing needful of forgiveness was what had happened to Sam Blake—and it appeared that she had accepted he could not have prevented it.

Nicolas was still having Larkin watched. As yet nothing out of the ordinary seemed to be happening. The man went about his work in an exemplary way—but did he know he was being watched?

Damn it! He could not worry about such things when Lottie was suddenly here and in the next room. Her manner was no different than it had ever been—it was almost as if they had never quarrelled. He could not be certain whether she was indifferent or merely making things easy for him.

Now all he had to deal with was his hunger for the woman who would be sleeping in the room next to him for the next week or two.

Would Lottie be prepared to go back to the way it had been on their honeymoon?

Nicolas's pulses raced at the thought. He badly wanted to go back now and kiss her senseless, to take her to bed and make love to her until they fell asleep in each other's arms.

Now he was being a damned fool! Lottie might permit his lovemaking, but she did not love him. She had told him she would never love him, even if he obliged her to do her duty. Why did that matter so much? Nicolas dismissed the notion that he might be in love with her. He wanted her, liked her, and appreciated her good qualities—but love? If he felt the kind of love for her that his father had felt for Nicolas's mother, it would lead to nothing but heartbreak.

He remembered the golden days when his mother had been the heart of their home and it had seemed that his father was always there, always good mannered, smiling and loving towards his son. How suddenly those days had vanished!

His mother's death and the sudden withdrawal of his father's affection had devastated Nicolas. He had not understood as a child that the silent stern man who went away for long periods and hardly noticed his son when he returned was sunk in a terrible grief that had hastened his death. Only later, after an unhappy love affair with a woman who had thought him an object of amusement, had Nicolas begun to understand his father's loss. He thought that he had not truly understood it until recently.

Surely he was not caught in the trap he had meant to avoid by arranging a marriage of convenience? Love was too painful when it ended. He had not wanted to feel that pain again. Yet he could not regret that Lottie had come into his life.

She was beautiful, but there was so much more to her—so much more to discover.

He would be a fool to allow himself to care, Nicolas reflected as he changed for the evening. If there were a chance that Lottie cared, perhaps—but her manner was so unemotional. He could not think that she cared for him in any meaningful way. She was prepared to be the mother of his children, because she had given her promise—and he knew now that she would keep it.

Why could he not just accept that and be content to live his own life, as he had intended?

Nicolas groaned as he suspected that he was caught in a trap of his own making. Yet he would not admit to it, because if he did…

Shaking his head, he took the evening cloak his valet offered and went out of his room and down the stairs. This evening he would take care not to drink more than a single glass of wine. Otherwise, he might find it too tempting to go through that connecting door.

* * *

Lottie heard Nicolas come in. She was surprised he was so early. It was scarcely much past eleven, which for a man who had reportedly been burning the candles at both ends was unprecedented.

She lay for a while, wondering if he might come to her, but the door between their rooms remained firmly closed. She wished she had the courage to open that door and go through to him, but was afraid of his rejection. If he wanted to lie with her he would surely come to her?

Nicolas had accepted her, even telling her to stay as long as she wished, and to send her bills to him if she had not enough money. Why was he so generous and yet so removed from her in every other way?

The frustration grew as she thought of him lying so close. A little moan of need issued from her. She wanted so much to lie in his arms and feel his lips on her—but she must hide her need and wait until Nicolas came to her. He would surely do so in time, because he needed an heir.

Lottie faced the fact that she was in love with her husband. She had sworn she would not love him, but she did. He was indifferent to her, though at times he had a need for marital relations. Was he still seeing his mistress? She supposed he must be—might even have visited her that evening.

The thought was so painful that she dismissed it instantly—yet it would not go away completely.

What did this woman have that Lottie did not? How could she make him want her rather than this unknown woman who haunted his dreams?

If only there was a way to make him jealous! Lottie

could not think of one, however hard she tried. She knew she was not unattractive, but it needed more than that to arouse a man's passions. Perhaps if he thought that other men were interested… Lottie's thoughts went round and round in her head. How could she convince her husband that other men thought her interesting or desirable?

She sighed as sleep claimed her at the last. It just was not going to happen…

Chapter Twelve

'Countess Rothsay.' The young buck smiled at Lottie winningly. 'I know I am late—but dare I hope there is one dance left on your card?'

'I think…' Lottie consulted and then inclined her head. 'Just the dance before supper—if you would care to write your name?'

'May I also take you into supper?' Mr Bellingham asked hopefully.

'I have already been asked several times,' Lottie replied. 'If you would care to join us all, I should be happy to see you, sir.'

'Then I shall certainly do so, Countess. May I say that we all perfectly understand why Rothsay tried to keep you hidden in the country. Were you my wife, I should not wish to share you either.'

'Oh, it was nothing of the kind,' Lottie said with a laugh. 'My aunt was unwell and I stayed until she felt much recovered. I assure you there was no such intention on Rothsay's part.'

'Then he is a fool,' Mr Bellingham replied. 'I shall return for my dance later.'

Lottie nodded and turned to her next partner. This was her first dance since coming to town, for she had needed several gowns made before she could think of attending a society ball of this size. The large rooms were overflowing and very warm, but as yet Lottie had not been tempted outside, though more than one gentleman had asked if she would like to take the air.

She had been hoping that Nicolas would approach and ask her for at least one dance, but thus far he had kept his distance. It was for his sake that she had kept the supper dance until the last, but since he was clearly not interested, she had given it away to Mr Bellingham.

Her popularity at every event she attended had made no impression on Nicolas. He had escorted her and Henrietta to a couple of card evenings and spent most of them in the room set up for cards, leaving Lottie alone to make her own friends and enjoy herself as she would.

So much for her hopes that he would be just a little jealous. He seemed not to have noticed that she was being lionised by most and that the gentlemen flocked to her side every time she stood and watched the dancing for a moment.

She smiled as her next partner presented himself, bowing to her reverently. 'My dance, I think, Countess?'

'Yes, sir.' Lottie's heart thudded. Mr Gerard Hunter was Lady Fisher's nephew. Sir Bertie had introduced them and therefore Lottie had felt obliged to accept his name on her card, but she was a little nervous of him. Of all the gentlemen she had so far met in London, Mr

Hunter was the most particular. His eyes seemed to convey a message and when he held her, there was a certain possessiveness about him—as though he was trying to draw her into a more intimate relationship. Lottie was not sure whether or not she trusted this particular gentleman. 'I believe it is...'

The dance was a waltz. As the young man put his hand at her waist, she realised that she had been unwise to allow him a waltz. His manner was altogether too intimate, his eyes seeming to burn into her as he looked down at her.

She was relieved when the dance came to an end and she could thank him and move away.

Running upstairs to the chamber set aside for the ladies to refresh themselves, she bathed her face in cool water and tucked a stray lock of hair into place behind her ear, before leaving to go downstairs. At the head of the stairs she saw Nicolas and realised that he must have been waiting for her.

'Was Hunter annoying you, Lottie?'

'Just a little,' she said. 'He seems almost too attentive at times—but he is not the only gentleman to pay me foolish compliments.'

Nicolas's gaze went over her slowly, his eyes dark and thoughtful. 'You certainly look very beautiful this evening, Lottie. That gown becomes you, though perhaps the neckline is a little revealing.' His eyes dwelled on her birthmark. 'It is unlike you to let that show?'

'I asked *madame* to make certain the neckline would cover it, but she assured me it was attractive and said the fashion was lower this year. Henrietta said I should be guided by *madame*—but perhaps a little lace at the neck would make it more modest?'

'Why should you hide your charms when every other lady in the room is revealing theirs? A gentleman must learn when his attentions are not wanted. Shall I have a word with Mr Hunter, Lottie?'

'I think it would make a statement if you were to dance with me,' she replied. 'Perhaps your indifference gives other men the wrong impression?'

'Yes, perhaps it does. Do you have a free dance on your card?'

'No. I gave the last to Mr Bellingham.'

'Harry will not mind if I cut in,' Nicolas said. 'I shall have to make it plain that you are my property.'

'Shall you, Nicolas?' Lottie replied and hid her smile. 'How very boring for you.'

'I do not think I shall find it boring to dance with you,' he replied, but his eyes were stormy and she sensed his anger.

Something told her that Nicolas did not care to see other men flirting with his wife too openly.

Nicolas cut in after Lottie had taken half-a-dozen turns around the room with Mr Bellingham, who held her in a perfectly polite manner and did not give her smouldering glances.

'Damn you, Rothsay,' the young man said, but gave way with good grace. 'You should have reserved your own dance—but I suppose I must allow you to claim her. You are a damned lucky devil and always have been.'

Lottie went into her husband's arms. Immediately, she was aware of a feeling of pleasure as Nicolas swept her about the room. How wonderful it felt to waltz with Nicolas. She wished that their dance would go on and on for ever, but all too soon it came to an end.

'Now I shall take you into supper and that should be enough,' Nicolas said. 'Forgive me for neglecting my duties, Lottie. It never occurred to me that Hunter would decide that you were available.'

'No, I am sure it did not,' Lottie replied. 'He was mistaken. I am not available, Nicolas. I am your wife and even though you may not particularly want me—I shall not conduct a clandestine affair behind your back.'

'Shall you not? I am relieved to hear that, my dear.' He offered her his arm, but frowned as if deep in thought. 'What may I fetch you for supper?'

'Oh, just a syllabub, I think, Nicolas. I am not very hungry.'

'You must not neglect yourself, Lottie. I do not wish you to become too thin—you were perfect as you were when I married you.'

'Indeed?' Her eyes sparkled. 'Now that is a compliment, sir. I have received several this evening—but what can top perfection?'

'Nothing.' His brow furrowed. 'You must know that you are one of—if not the—most beautiful women in this room?'

'How kind of you to say so, Nicolas, but you really have no need to flatter me.'

'I was not aware that I was flattering you. I imagined you knew me well enough to know that I speak as I find.'

'The shame is, Nicolas, that I hardly know you at all.'

Lottie went to sit down at an empty table while Nicolas departed to fetch some champagne and a syllabub. When he returned, he discovered that at least four young gentlemen were vying with each other to fetch Lottie some supper. She seemed to have recovered her appetite, because she was nibbling delicately at a tiny almond pastry someone had brought for her.

Nicolas joined the group about her, noticing the way her eyes lit when she responded to their teasing, and the softness of her lips as she licked a crumb from them. He was conscious of a strong desire to lean forwards and lick the crumb from her lips himself, but would not do something so revealing in company.

It was hardly surprising that half the men in the supper room were observing Lottie with barely disguised lust. Even those who were not dancing attendance on her were staring at her with admiration and at him with envy. He was torn between irritation and pleasure that his wife should arouse so much attention.

Yet the frustration he had felt the first night she came up to town was building. He hardly knew how to control himself, because if he simply walked through that adjoining door he could have what every other man in the room wanted.

He wondered when Lottie had become so very desirable—or had she always been and he just had not seen it? Was he a fool to hold back when he might have spent several nights in her arms?

Just what did he want from her?

'Nicolas, how lovely to see you.'

Nicolas turned his head as he felt the touch on his

shoulder. He saw Elizabeth's beautiful face and bowed over her hand, lifting it to his lips.

'Lady Madison, how are you?'

'Oh, well enough, I suppose,' Elizabeth said and sighed. 'My marriage is not all I imagined it would be, Nicolas. I think I made a mistake when I refused you. The years have given you a presence you did not have when we were younger.'

'It is merely age. The years have been kind to you, Elizabeth. I think you are more beautiful than ever.'

'I have been invited to visit Lord Hartwell's country house next month. My husband does not accompany me. It would be pleasant if you were there.'

Nicolas hesitated. Her meaning was clear enough. She was not the first lady bored with her marriage to hint that she would be happy to indulge in an affair.

'Forgive me, Lady Madison,' Nicolas said. 'I believe I shall be in the country with my wife.'

Glancing across the room, Lottie saw Nicolas kiss a lady's hand. She was an exceptionally lovely woman with hair the colour of jet. Turning to Mr Bellingham, she smiled and enquired the name of the beauty.

'Oh…you mean Lady Elizabeth Madison,' Bellingham said and looked slightly uncomfortable. 'She is beautiful, though before her marriage she was an Incomparable. We all wanted her, though she seemed to prefer—' He broke off, embarrassed. 'All in the past and long forgotten.'

Lottie knew at once that she must be *the* Elizabeth— the woman Nicolas cried for in his sleep.

'She is very beautiful,' she said. 'I find I am a little

warm, sir. I should like to take the air on the veranda—if you would oblige me?'

'Of course,' he said and offered his arm. 'Rothsay is a fool if he neglects you for her—she has the tongue of a fishwife.'

'Oh, no.' Lottie trilled with laughter and tapped him with her fan. 'How wicked you are, sir.'

Her laughter had made Nicolas glance her way, but she was genuinely amused and did not see his frown.

Lottie was tired when they returned home that evening. The countess had gone earlier, complaining of a headache, but insisting that Lottie remain and ask for Nicolas's escort to see her home.

'It is time he did his duty by you, Lottie. Nicolas was always a provoking man—but this time he has gone too far. He is your husband. He should act in the proper manner towards you. I wash my hands of the foolish man.'

Lottie smiled and shook her head. Henrietta did not understand the bargain she had made. No matter how much it irked Lottie that her husband remained indifferent, she would not make demands on him. She was perfectly well able to enjoy herself in town without Nicolas running after her.

However, she had been glad of his interference that evening. Mr Hunter was too insistent and it would not do for Lottie to be thought to be fast. She was Nicolas's wife and as such must remain above criticism—at least until his son was born. Yet how was she to give him a son if he did not come to her bed?

It was a problem; the longer things remained the

way they were, the more difficult it would be to resolve them.

How could she break down her husband's reserve? What must she do to bring him back to her bed? She was not as beautiful as Lady Elizabeth Madison—but she was his wife. Surely he had cared for her a little when they spent such happy times together on their honeymoon. Could she make him forget his first love?

She hesitated when she said goodnight, hoping that he might speak, but he merely inclined his head. Lottie turned away and went up to her room, feeling the frustration mount. She undressed and sent her maid away, sitting to brush her long hair in front of the mirror. It was as she was about to go to bed that she noticed she was still wearing her pearls. She reached to unfasten them at the back and discovered that they had snagged on the lace of her night chemise and would not come free. She was reluctant to send for her maid and instead went to the adjoining door. She knocked and Nicolas's voice invited her to enter. He had removed his breeches and long boots and was standing in just his shirt, which came down to his thighs. His face registered surprise as he saw her.

'Yes, Lottie—what may I do for you? You are not unwell, I trust?'

'Oh, no, I am quite well,' she replied and suddenly her earlier tiredness had fled. 'It is these bothersome pearls, Nicolas. The clasp has caught in the lace and I did not want to send for my maid at this hour.'

'Let me see what I can do,' he offered.

Lottie swept her hair up with one hand, turning so that her back was towards him and he could see the clasp.

'I did not realise they were caught until I tried…' She caught her breath as she felt his hand at her nape. The touch of his fingers sent delicious shivers down her spine and she could not speak. He had freed the lace and his hand caressed her throat as he removed the pearls. She turned slowly and looked at him, her lips parting as she saw something in his eyes. 'Nicolas…' she breathed and instinctively swayed towards him.

'Lottie—damn it…' he muttered hoarsely and caught her to him, his mouth seeking hers. She melted into his body; her lips parted to invite his seeking tongue, feeling the heat of desire begin to build low in her abdomen. 'Will you…do you want me to continue? I have not dared to ask after that night…you said you hated me.'

'Oh, Nicolas,' she murmured against his mouth. 'I told you I did not mean it, my dearest. It was a foolish quarrel that I have regretted.'

'Was that all? I thought…I might have given you a dislike of my character.'

'No, nothing like that. I was angry, but I—admire you and like you, truly.' She reached up to stroke his cheek with her fingertips, suddenly daring. 'I have missed you, Nicolas. Would you sleep in my bed tonight?'

'Yes, Lottie, I shall,' he said and grinned. Bending down, he caught her behind the knees and swept her up in his arms, striding back into her room. Placing her carefully on the sheets, he stripped off his shirt and she saw that he was naked and fully aroused. 'I have been wanting to do this for a while now. I think we will have this pretty thing off, don't you?'

He pulled her nightgown up over her head and let it

fall to join his shirt on the floor. His gaze feasted on her naked flesh and then he bent his head to kiss her lips. In another moment he was beside her on the bed, lying with his heated skin touching hers, his hand stroking the satiny arch of her back as he pulled her closer still.

Lottie sighed with content, allowing him to stroke and touch her for a few minutes, then, because she could no longer hold back, she began to stroke his shoulders and to kiss his neck. Her nails lightly raked his flesh as she arched and moaned, not trying to hold in the feelings he was arousing in her. Nicolas did not want a clinging wife and she had done her best to keep something back, but her need was too great. She had lain alone too many nights, knowing that he was close and that she loved him, wanted him. Even if he guessed that she loved him, she could not hide her pleasure in his loving. Her screams and the desperate need she felt to have him inside her again and again had driven all else from her mind. He was her husband and she wanted his loving. She wanted him to possess her, to own her, to be a part of his flesh.

She wanted to make him forget the beautiful Elizabeth if she could.

Nicolas seemed to respond to her wanton need, driving into her again and again relentlessly, their cries mingling until at last she shuddered, gripped in a climax that was almost like dying, and he suddenly collapsed against her, his seed deep inside her.

For quite a long time they lay still, silent, holding each other, the desperate need satiated.

'Nicolas,' she whispered at last. 'You won't leave me again, will you?'

'Go to sleep, Lottie,' he said and kissed her brow. 'I have to think. Tomorrow we shall have time enough to talk.'

Lottie woke and stretched. At first she could not remember why she felt so good, then she ran her tongue over lips that still tasted of Nicolas and everything came back. They had made love in such a tumultuous fashion, and then they slept. In the night she had woken once to find Nicolas still at her side. He had wanted her again, making love this time with a slow, sensual tenderness that left her weeping. He had hushed her, stroking her hair as her tears wetted his shoulder, and she mumbled something about love and then hoped he had not heard.

Nicolas would hate it if she tried to put chains on him. She had begged him not to leave her again and then told him she loved him. She would have only herself to blame if he asked her to go home or ran away himself.

Getting up, she wrapped a lace peignoir about her and went to his room. There was no sign of him and she guessed that he had gone out to ride, as he often did early in the morning. He had told her he needed time to think. Was he trying to find a way to tell her that he did not love her?

He had wanted her. Lottie was in no doubt of his need the previous night—but perhaps seeing that other men were attracted to her had aroused his interest. Or perhaps there was some other reason. He had been speaking with Elizabeth and been desperate because he could not have her. Lottie had gone to him, offered herself to him and he had taken advantage. That did not mean he loved her.

She must not expect it…even though he had said things as they lay together.

Lottie used the water her maid had brought her and dressed in a pretty yellow silk gown. She would go down to nuncheon in a moment, for she had slept late. A jewel case was lying on the dressing table, but it was not one Lottie recognised. She opened it and discovered a beautiful diamond necklace. The stones were so large and so white that she gasped with amazement. Then she saw the little square of paper.

Family heirlooms. I had them reset for you, Lottie. You deserve the best. Nicolas.

Lottie stared at the note. She held the necklace to her throat. The diamonds were certainly fabulous, far more valuable than anything else Nicolas had given her. Why had he left them here? She felt a little nervous for they should certainly be locked away in Nicolas's strong room except for special occasions.

She closed the box and stood up, remembering that she had left her pearls in Nicolas's room. She went through and saw them on the dressing table. Picking them up, she returned to her own room and then halted as she saw the woman standing there. She had her back to Lottie but she knew her at once.

'Clarice—what are you doing here?'

Her sister turned. She was wearing a racy hat with heavy veiling. As she lifted it, she revealed an oddly guilty look on her face. 'I wondered where you were. Is that Rothsay's room through there?'

'Yes. I was retrieving something I left there last night,'

Lottie said and felt defensive as her sister's eyes went over her with a flash of jealousy. She was aware that Clarice's gown looked a little outdated, as if she had not had a new one for a while. 'Why have you come, Clarice?'

'Do I have to have a reason?' Clarice asked. 'That isn't very nice, Lottie—considering you have me to thank for all this...' Her eyes travelled round the room and there was jealousy in them.

'Yes, I know. I am grateful that you pushed me into it, Clarice. I did not expect to be happy, but I am.'

'Aunt Beth told me he spoils you.' Clarice fingered the pearls Lottie had placed on the dressing table. 'These are nice. I suppose you have plenty of pin money—you couldn't lend me a couple of thousand, could you?'

'I don't have anywhere near that much, and, as I told you at Rothsay, even if I did I couldn't give it to you.' Lottie said. 'Are you in trouble, Clarice?'

'Philippe is—he owes thousands. If he doesn't pay some of it, he will be arrested and imprisoned. What shall I do then, Lottie? You have all this and I have nothing.'

'This...' Lottie indicated the room about her. 'This belongs to Nicolas. He shares it with me but I do not own it. I cannot give you a thousand pounds, Clarice—at the moment I have no more than two hundred pounds.'

'Give me that, it will help for now.' Clarice said. 'Don't be mean, Lottie. You would have none of this if it were not for me.'

Lottie felt guilty. In much the same way that she always forgave her father his faults, she loved her twin just as dearly. To see her suffer broke her heart. After all, she was so lucky to be Nicolas's wife and she owed her happiness to Clarice. If she had not spent so much on clothes she could have given her sister more. She opened the top drawer of her dressing chest and took out a wooden casket, opening it to remove the small bag of gold coins.

'There you are, Clarice. I am sorry it isn't more, but I have spent my allowance for this quarter.'

'I'll come back for the rest another time,' Clarice said, flew at her and kissed her cheek. 'Goodbye, Lottie. Remember that you owe me.'

She pulled the veiling over her face again and turned to the door. She opened it, looked out and then disappeared through the aperture, leaving Lottie staring after her. She felt slightly sick. How on earth had Clarice managed to reach her room without being seen or announced? Her reminder that she could have been Lady Rothsay had she chosen had left Lottie feeling uneasy. She wished her sister had not come.

Something made her look at the jewellery case that Nicolas had left lying on the dressing table that morning. Her stomach clenched and she reached for it somehow knowing what she would find. She opened it and saw that the necklace was missing. Clarice had taken it. Her own sister was a jewel thief. She had taken a priceless heirloom and then had the effrontery to ask for money.

Rising to her feet, Lottie went out and ran along the landing to the top of the stairs to look down at the hall. Clarice had gone. She must have fled the instant she left the room, knowing that Lottie would look for the necklace sooner or later.

How had she managed to get into the room while

Lottie's back was turned? She had been wearing veiling over her face. They were identical in build and height. If the servants had seen her walk up the stairs they would have assumed she was Lottie; Clarice had probably even been admitted to the house and mistaken for her. It was likely that no one would know she had been to the house.

What was she to do? Lottie sat staring at the empty jewel box, then opened a drawer and slid it inside. Could she contact her sister and demand that she return the necklace? Clarice would simply deny having taken it and Lottie could prove nothing. If no one had seen her, there was no proof that she had ever been in the house. Besides, how could Lottie admit to Nicolas that her sister was a thief?

She remembered that he had accused Clarice of stealing some guineas from his friend's pocket in that gaming house in Paris. He had been disgusted by her behaviour then—what would he think if he knew that Clarice had come here on purpose to rob them? Lottie wondered uneasily if her sister had taken anything else. She glanced around the bedchamber, but everything else seemed to be in place.

'Oh, Clarice,' she whispered. 'Why did it have to be the diamonds?' If it had been her pearls or something less important, it wouldn't have mattered so much—but Nicolas was bound to ask about the necklace.

Nicolas would expect her to thank him. He would naturally expect to see her wearing them—and what could she say?

Lottie was close to tears. She had hoped that they would be closer after last night—but if she told Nicolas that Clarice had stolen the diamonds he would be so angry. He might accuse her of having given them to her sister—or of being the thief herself.

She did not know what to do for the best. Feeling restless, Lottie decided that she would go out for a walk. She could not go shopping because she had no money left, but she was too upset to sit in the house and wait for Nicolas to return.

When she met Mr Hunter as she was entering the park, Lottie was glad that she had brought her maid with her. It had been tempting to go alone, but it would not be thought proper for the Marchioness of Rothsay to walk alone.

'Lady Rothsay,' he said, sweeping his hat off and making her an elegant bow.

'Mr Hunter.' Lottie inclined her head coolly, hoping to be allowed to walk on, but it was not to be. He stood deliberately in her path, making it clear he meant to make the most of this chance meeting.

'I shall join you on your walk. It is a pleasant day, is it not—though I believe a mite cooler than of late?'

'The summer has deserted us,' Lottie replied. Since he would not take a hint and leave her to walk in peace, the weather was a safe topic. 'I dare say you will soon leave for the country, sir?'

'Oh, no, I have every intention of staying in town for a while.'

'I plan to return to the country quite soon. Excuse me, I see Lady March and I must speak with her. Good morning, Mr Hunter.'

She beckoned to her maid, who had dropped behind,

and headed for a young woman she had met recently whom she rather liked. Mr Hunter had accepted his dismissal this time, but she was conscious that his eyes still watched her as she walked away.

What she did not know was that the brief interlude had been seen by a man on horseback.

Nicolas was frowning as he left his horse in the mews and walked back to his house. Why had Lottie been walking in the park with Mr Hunter at this hour of the day? He had left her sleeping and had imagined she would not go out before the afternoon, when he had intended to take her shopping.

The diamond necklace he had left on her dressing table was only the first of several gifts he intended to give his lovely wife. He was thinking that they might take a short trip to Paris, which was where he should really have taken her after their wedding. There were so many plans in his head concerning the future that he had gone out for an early ride to blow the cobwebs away.

Why had she slipped out in the early morning to meet Hunter in the park? He had only caught a brief glance of them, talking earnestly, it seemed to him, and had no idea of how long they might have been together.

He fought his unworthy suspicions, forcing them to a small corner of his mind. Lottie might have met with Hunter by chance. He must not jump to conclusions, but it had made him realise that he did not care for other men paying his wife too much attention. Yet there was surely no harm in what he had witnessed. Just because Elizabeth had led him on, allowing him to believe that she loved him, only to laugh in his face when he proposed to her, it did not mean that other women were the same. Lottie was warm and loving and the previous night he had believed that she truly cared for him.

He still hesitated to use the word *love*. Lottie had enjoyed their lovemaking and clearly felt something for him. Since Nicholas did not believe in love he would name it affection and admit that he felt the same for her.

Yes, he was fond of Lottie. She had somehow managed to get beneath his skin and he would hate to lose her now.

Chapter Thirteen

Nicolas returned in time for nuncheon. He smiled as he joined Lottie at the table in the smaller of the two dining parlours. Since there was just the three of them the formal dining room would seem awkward and too large. He took his place at table and smiled on the two ladies already seated.

'Forgive me if I have kept you, ladies,' he said. 'Tell me, what are your plans this afternoon?'

'We must call on some of my friends,' Henrietta told him and nodded to the footman serving soup. 'Thank you, Henderson, just a little.' Her gaze transferred to Nicolas. 'Had you a particular reason for asking?'

'I thought Lottie might like to go shopping with me?'

'Thank you,' Lottie said, her cheeks a little pink. 'I should like to go another day, Nicolas, but Henrietta thinks I should meet some ladies who do not often go into society. Also I must thank you for the beautiful gift you gave me, Nicolas.'

'I am glad you liked the necklace, Lottie. You should wear the diamonds tomorrow evening when we attend the Duchess of Argyle's annual ball. It is one of the largest of the summer and generally means that she will be leaving town. After next week only the hostesses who seldom leave London will be entertaining. Their dinners are usually for politicians and academics and rather dull affairs—unless you have an interest in such things?'

'I must say that I do prefer a gathering of artistes and musical evenings, but I dare say some such company may still be found?'

'Then you do not intend to return to Rothsay just yet?'

'Perhaps I may stay another week or two,' Lottie said and helped herself to a dish of turbot. 'If that does not inconvenience you, Nicolas?'

'Why should it? I was thinking of inviting a shooting party to Rothsay for the autumn, but that is a few weeks away yet.'

'In that case I shall return a week ahead to make sure everything is in order.' Lottie glanced at Henrietta. 'Will you remain in London, dearest?'

'Not after you have gone,' Henrietta said and smiled at her. 'I visit occasionally, but stayed longer this time for the pleasure of introducing you to society, dearest Lottie. I think we may say that your début has been successful—would you not agree, Nicolas?'

'Yes, Lottie has caused a stir, especially amongst some of the gentlemen.' Nicolas looked at his wife. 'Did you enjoy your walk this morning, Lottie?'

'Yes, I walked in the park for a while, Nicolas. Did you happen to see me?'

'Just for a moment or two, Lottie. I like a ride first thing, you know—but I was surprised to see you. I thought you might have wanted to sleep in a little?'

'Oh, well, when I woke I felt the need of some exercise.'

'I see…' Nicolas inclined his head. 'I shall not see you this evening. I have a card party and may be late. Do not wait up for me, Lottie.'

'We have a soirée,' Lottie said. 'If you are late, I shall see you in the morning, Nicolas.'

Lottie glanced down at her plate. The succulent turbot tasted like dust in her mouth. It seemed that nothing had changed. She had imagined that after last night Nicolas would suddenly become the charming lover of her dreams, but he seemed to have withdrawn once more and she had no idea why.

If she had not been feeling so guilty over the loss of the diamonds, Lottie thought she would have excused herself to Henrietta and spent the afternoon with her husband. It was becoming increasingly obvious to her that they must talk seriously. Nicolas could not blow hot and cold for ever and expect her to accept his moods. They must come to a proper arrangement so that she understood what he expected of her—did he want a wife who was always willing to welcome him to her bed or not? Last night he had taken her with such passion she could swear he cared for her, but this morning the mask was in place once more.

She saw him looking at her, his eyes dark and

brooding, and she sensed that he was angry, but fighting his anger. What on earth could she have done to make him angry? Surely he couldn't know about the diamonds already?

What on earth was she to do about them? If Nicolas had not suddenly gone cold on her again she might have told him the truth, but she was afraid that he would not believe her. Something was definitely troubling him.

True to his word, Nicolas was out late that evening. Lottie heard him come in well into the early hours of the morning. She lay listening for a few moments, hoping that he might change his mind and come to her, but he did not.

She could not bear this a moment longer! Getting out of bed, Lottie went through into her husband's room and saw him lying fully clothed on the bed. He had not even bothered to take his boots off. Had he been drinking again?

Lottie frowned as she bent over him, but could not smell excessive wine on his breath. She pulled off his long boots and peeled back his hose. His feet looked white and soft; tempted beyond bearing, she bent her head and kissed one. Then she pulled a cover over him and sat on the edge of the bed, gazing down at him. Her hand reached out to brush hair that was a little too long back from his forehead.

'My dearest love,' she whispered, then bent and kissed his forehead. 'Please try to love me, Nicolas. I do love you so.'

She got up and walked to the door between them,

shutting it softly. Behind her Nicolas stirred, but did not wake from his pleasant dream.

Lottie had spent the day visiting and taking tea with ladies she had met and liked. They were, like her, interested in improving the lot of the poor and under-privileged and she had been asked if she would join a debating society. She had explained that she would be leaving for the country soon, but would be pleased to join them in Bath later in the year.

Returning home with Henrietta, she went upstairs to change for the ball that evening. She was standing in her petticoat when the door to Nicolas's room was flung open and he came striding in.

'You may attend your mistress when she sends for you,' he flung at the maid, who shot a terrified glance at Lottie and scurried off. 'Well, Lottie,' Nicolas fixed his angry gaze on her. 'I see you are not yet wearing your diamonds. May I fasten them for you?'

Lottie swallowed hard, hesitating. 'I...the clasp was not quite right for me, Nicolas. I have sent them to the jeweller's to be mended.'

'Indeed?' His mouth thinned to a hard line. 'Then it is as well that he sent for me and I was able to collect them for you, was it not?' He took something from his pocket and she saw the glitter of diamonds hanging from his fingers.

'Oh...' Lottie gasped, her heart sinking. She had been hoping she might somehow recover them—that Clarice might repent and return them to her. 'Where—I mean, how did you find them?'

'The jeweller recognised them. It was not clever of

you to take them to a prestigious London dealer, Lottie. Unfortunately for you, his was the firm I used to have them cleaned and reset. He knew them instantly and you, my dear. I suppose you have run through your allowance. You should have asked me for more money if you needed it—they are worth far more than he paid you, perhaps because he knew he would need to return them to me—for a small consideration, naturally.'

'He couldn't have...' Lottie said but knew that her sister was enough like her for a stranger to be certain he was dealing with the Marchioness of Rothsay. 'Nicolas... it wasn't the way it seems...'

'Was it not, my dear?' His voice cut her like broken glass. 'In my opinion, theft is always as it seems, a most sordid business. I told you the necklace was an heirloom. You must have known that meant you had no right to sell the diamonds.'

Lottie turned away from the accusation in his eyes. 'You should not have left them where you did, Nicolas. I did not ask you for such a valuable gift—they were a temptation for anyone.'

'Are you saying you did not sell them? The man told me he served you himself.'

'Well, I am sure he was right,' Lottie said. 'You called me a thief when we first met, Rothsay. It is your own fault for marrying me. You knew that I was as bad as the rest of my family, did you not? I am sorry it has cost you money to get the diamonds back. Perhaps in future you will not leave them lying around. I certainly have no wish to wear them.'

'Lottie?' Nicolas looked at her uncertainly. She turned on him then, her eyes blazing. 'What? You are angry—but if you did not…your sister? Did she ask you for money?' Lottie was silent. 'No…has she been here? Did she take them? Or did you give them to her? Has that been the plan all the time—to get what you could from me for your wretched family?'

She recoiled as if he had slapped her. How could he think that of her—how could he?

Lottie refused to answer him. 'Please leave me now, Nicolas—and take your diamonds with you. I have a headache and shall not be attending the Duchess's ball this evening. If you intend to go, please make my excuses if you will.'

'Not go?' Nicolas glared at her. 'Why will you not answer me? If I have accused you falsely, tell me.'

'I feel most unwell. Please allow me to rest.'

'Very well.' He inclined his head stiffly. 'If I was misinformed, I apologise.'

'You are forgiven. Goodnight, Rothsay.'

Nicolas stared at her in silence for a moment, then turned and walked from the room. Lottie stood where she was for a moment, staring at the door. She was hurting too much to weep. There was no relief for her in tears after what Nicolas had said to her. She had thought that he had begun to care a little, but even after she had given him all the love inside her he could still believe that she was a thief. Yes, she ought to have told him the truth at once. Lottie acknowledged her fault, but he ought to have known that she would never steal from him. Why should she when he had been so generous? It was obvious that she had still to gain the trust of her husband.

She looked about her, wondering what to do. She could not stay here a moment longer. Nor could she return to

Rothsay Manor. Her pride had been hurt as well as her heart. She wanted to be alone for a while. The only place open to her was her father's house—she wanted nothing that Nicolas had given her. At this moment she did not know what she would do in the future, but for now she wanted to be as far away from Nicolas and those cold, cold eyes as possible.

She would send for her maid, pack a small trunk with the most inexpensive clothes she could find and leave tonight while Nicolas was out. She would take none of the jewels he had given her, but she must borrow a horse and carriage, for she had given all her money to Clarice. The future looked bleak, but at this moment she could only feel; her mind was too numb to imagine what she would do with the rest of her life.

Much later that night Nicolas knocked at the door of his wife's room. There was no answer. Frowning, he opened the door and walked into her bedchamber. It was empty, as was her boudoir, as he discovered a moment or two later. A cold shiver went down his spine. Lottie had claimed to have a headache, so where had she gone?

He rang the bell and a few moments later a maid appeared. He did not think she was the one who usually waited on Lottie.

'Where is my wife?'

'She left earlier this evening, my lord. She sent for the carriage and went out with Rose, her ladyship's maid. They took a small trunk and a portmanteau with them, sir.'

'Did my wife receive bad news? Did she say where she was going?'

'I do not think so, my lord. I do not know if she received a letter, but I think she did not leave word of where she would be.'

Nicolas swore beneath his breath, then, 'Thank you, girl—do you happen to know if my wife had any visitors yesterday?'

'I'm not sure, sir. Shall I ask Mrs Barret?'

'No, I will do that myself, thank you. You may go.'

Nicolas waited until she had gone, then went to the closet and opened it. Most of Lottie's things were still there. Her jewel case was lying on the bed. He picked it up, opened it and saw that everything he or his relatives had given her was still there. The only things she had taken were her aunt's pearls, the diamond star her father had given her and various trinkets she had owned before she married him.

'No!' he cried in anguish. 'Lottie, damn it. Why didn't you tell me the truth?'

Nicolas felt the cold seep through him. He should have known Lottie would not sell those wretched diamonds. Why on earth had he lost his temper and accused her of being a thief? His anger had been a mixture of annoyance at the jeweller's manner in confiding in him that the marchioness had pawned her jewels and the meeting he had seen between Lottie and Hunter in the park.

What had he done? Nicolas was certain that she had left him—but where would she go?

Surely she would be at Rothsay? She was angry with him, but she wouldn't just leave him without saying goodbye—would she?

He had left her without a word. Why should she imagine he would care two pence where she was when he had accused her of a crime she had not committed?

She had lied to him, pretending that the necklace was having the clasp repaired. No doubt he had taken her by surprise. She must have been protecting her sister.

The jeweller did not know Lottie. If he saw Clarice he would assume that she was the marchioness. They were enough alike to be mistaken for one another if you did not know them. Nicolas would not be fooled for a moment, but he imagined that many people might.

The servants were not sure there had been a visitor on the morning he left the diamonds lying on the dressing table, but seen from a distance they also would take Clarice for her sister.

What a fool he was not to have known that at the start. It was the fault of his damnable temper—and the suspicious nature that had not quite believed in Lottie's goodness despite all his senses telling him that she was as sweet and good as she was beautiful—and he loved her.

He had been hiding from the truth for months now. Lottie was the woman he loved and he prayed that she loved him in return—a real, true abiding love that should have lasted for a lifetime.

Had he destroyed it by his careless words? Would Lottie forgive him once more? He knew he had hurt her too many times. Why should she care for him? He knew that he did not deserve she should—and yet he could not give her up.

Striding into his own bedchamber, he summoned his valet. He would go down to Rothsay. If she was not there, he would search for her until he found her.

* * *

'No, Lottie has not come here,' Aunt Beth said and frowned when Nicolas asked if his wife was upstairs. 'I thought she was enjoying herself in London with you?'

'She was—we quarrelled and she left without a word.'

'Whatever did you say to her, Rothsay? That is not like my Lottie. You must know that she is the most loving, caring of women and a true lady.'

'Yes, she is,' Nicolas admitted. 'It is all my fault. I said things—things that I had no right to say. It is hardly to be wondered at that she grew tired of me and left me.'

'Are you sure she has left you?'

'She took only a few clothes and jewels that came from you or her father. Everything I had given her was left behind. I have had it all sent down here, but if she is not here...'

Aunt Beth looked at him accusingly. 'You must have hurt her badly, sir. Lottie could not have done anything to deserve it. I know her. She is honest and loving, as different from—' Aunt Beth broke off and shook her head. 'Where can she be?'

'Would she have gone to her father's house?'

'If she has, it will avail her nothing, sir. Her father has closed the house and put it and the land up for sale. He says that he sees no point in trying to keep up appearances now and will manage better without the estate somewhere abroad.'

'What of Lottie's sister?'

'Clarice visited the house just before I returned here. She said she needed money, but I had only a few pounds

to give her. I had given her money before and so had
Lottie. She did say that she was going to ask Lottie
for money—apparently, she believed it was owed her,
because Lottie had everything and she had nothing.'

'Indeed?' Nicolas's mouth thinned. 'I suppose that
means she intended to blackmail Lottie?'

'Lottie is fond of her sister, despite all, and would give
her any money she had to spare, sir—but she would not
give her anything that belonged to you.'

'I all but accused her of doing that very thing! What
am I to do, Aunt Beth? Will she forgive me?'

'Most women would not, but Lottie has a tender heart
and she may—but first you must find her.'

'Yes, I must,' he said. 'I shall go to her father's house
immediately. If it has not yet been sold, she may have
let herself in. After all, where else could she go?'

Where could she go now? Lottie looked at the
boarded-up windows of the house where she had spent
her childhood. The notices proclaimed that it had
been sold, which meant it was no longer her father's
property.

She could perhaps manage to get in and spend the
night, but she would be alone without a fire or food.
There was nothing for it but to find an inn and take a
room for the night.

'I am sorry, Rose,' she told her maid. 'I had no
idea that my father had sold the house. I am not sure
where we can stay tonight. I do not have much money,
only a few shillings. Perhaps we can find lodgings for
that—or maybe the landlord would accept a piece of
jewellery?'

'You will never sell your jewellery, my lady,' Rose said. 'There's no need, for I have three guineas in my reticule. I was paid before we left London and I can pay for our lodgings for one night.'

'In the morning…we shall go to Rothsay,' Lottie said and sighed. 'I have some things of my own there that I can sell. I shall repay you, Rose. Rothsay is your home and you must stay there, for I shall not be able to pay you a wage. It is very good of you to share with me like this.'

'You would do as much for me,' Rose said and smiled at her. 'We'd best tell coachman to take us to the nearest inn, mistress. It is getting late and we could all do with something to eat.'

'Yes. How sensible you are,' Lottie said and sighed. 'I should never have given my sister Clarice all the money I had—but I felt so guilty, because I had so much.'

And now, because of what Clarice had done, she had nothing. Without Nicolas the world was an empty place. The money and jewels had never meant that much to her, but they were a part of his world—and she had wanted to belong to him.

Rose nodded. 'Sisters are always trouble, miss. Mine used to get into scrapes all the time when we were little and because I was the eldest I got the blame.'

'Poor Rose. Clarice and I are twins. When we were small no one could tell us apart.'

'She would be the lady I saw coming from your room then, my lady. She was wearing a hat with veiling, but from a distance I thought it was you—but she didn't answer when I spoke to her, just ran down the stairs, as if she were in a hurry.'

'Yes, I dare say she was.'

Lottie's heart ached. Why had she not put those wretched diamonds away when she went into Nicolas's room that morning? It had not occurred to her that anyone would steal them—and only her sister would have dreamed of it. Rothsay's servants were all too honest.

She climbed back into the coach and gave the driver the order to find the nearest inn. She had been in acute distress when she left London, but now despite the pain in her heart, she could think more clearly.

What was she to do with her life? As Rothsay's wife she had had a purpose: the clearance of the Hollow and the setting up of a school for the tenants' children were just two of the plans she had made. Even had Nicolas visited only a few times a year, it would have been enough—or would it?

If Lottie were honest with herself, she knew that she wanted much more. She wanted Nicolas to love her as much as she loved him. He wanted her. His lovemaking had been passionate, even desperate at times, but he did not love her.

There was also Aunt Beth to consider. She knew her aunt could not live on her small income. Lottie would have to find work and support them both. Her pride had prevented her taking anything that Nicolas had given her, but perhaps she might accept a small part of the allowance he had made her for her aunt's sake.

No! She wanted nothing from him. He thought her a thief and a cheat. Somehow she would manage alone—but she must return to Rothsay and collect her things. Perhaps Aunt Beth could remain at the estate until Lottie had had time to find a small cottage for them and a position of some kind, though she hardly knew what she was fitted for. Unless she could be a teacher in a charity school? The wage would be very small, but there might be some accommodation with the job.

The worrying thoughts went round and round in her head. She must find a way of making her living somehow.

Nicolas stared at the empty house. The sold notice meant it was too late. If Lottie came here, she would know she could not stay. Where would she go then?

He wondered how much money she had left from her quarterly allowance. He doubted it could be much after her visit to the fashionable seamstresses in London. Besides, her aunt said she would have given what she had left to Clarice.

How had her sister managed to steal those wretched diamonds from under Lottie's nose? She must have turned her back or left the room for a moment, of course. It was his fault for leaving the necklace on the dressing chest instead of giving it to Lottie when he saw her. He wished that he could go back to that day—he would do anything if he could only unsay those awful words.

Lottie might go to Bath—but she had never visited her house there and could not know exactly where it was situated. Besides, if she had not taken her clothes and jewels, she would not think of living in the house he had given her.

Would she try to find work? Had she stayed at an inn? Or would she go to Rothsay? Many of her things were stored there. She would need them if she intended to live independently.

How foolish of her! She could not hope to survive on the wage that she would earn as…a teacher. Yes, he imagined she would try for something of the sort. However he had assuaged some of his guilt over his wife's hasty departure—he had told Aunt Beth that she was on no account to think of leaving his house.

'You will oblige me by living here, ma'am, and I shall make certain that you have an allowance—unless you are too proud or angry with me to accept it?'

'I have no intention of cutting off my nose to spite my face, Rothsay,' Aunt Beth told him. 'At my age I cannot afford to be too proud. Besides, I shall pray that Lottie will come to her senses. I feel that she really loves you and would be miserable apart from you. She would be greatly missed here, you know. Everyone loves her.'

'Yes, I am certain she was meant to be mistress of a house like this and why should she not continue as before? If she cannot forgive me, I will promise to keep my distance—but she is my wife and I shall not divorce her or permit her to divorce me.'

'That is foolish talk, sir.' Aunt Beth sighed. 'Have you learned nothing? Lottie may be coaxed, my lord, but she will not be bullied.'

'I did not mean…' Nicolas looked rueful. 'It is my damnable temper again.'

'You must learn to curb it, sir.'

'You are very right, ma'am. I must.'

Should he return to Rothsay and wait for Lottie—or should he make a tour of the district and discover if she had stayed at a local inn?

If she returned to Rothsay, Aunt Beth would do her

best to keep her there until he returned. She would be safe and comfortable, but if she were staying at an inn without much money she might be in trouble.

Chapter Fourteen

'Lottie, you foolish girl!' Aunt Beth rose from her chair and went forwards to embrace her. 'I have been worried out of my mind. Rothsay was here. He was convinced that you had left him.'

'Well, I have—or that was my intention,' Lottie said. 'Father has sold the house, but I suppose you knew that?'

'Yes. He gave me twenty-four hours to leave so I came here.' Aunt Beth looked at her anxiously. 'What else could I do, Lottie?'

'You did exactly right,' Lottie told her. 'I want you to stay here, dearest, just until I can find somewhere for us to live.'

'Could we not live at your house in Bath, if you will not stay here?'

'The house belongs to Rothsay. I want nothing of his, Aunt. He accused me of stealing his diamonds.'

'I don't know exactly what went on between you, my

dear, but I do know that he is sincerely sorry for what he said to you, Lottie. Do you not think you could forgive him?'

'You do not understand, dearest,' Lottie said and held back a sob. 'It is not just because of the diamonds. Oh, Aunt Beth, I love him so much. I thought I could accept this marriage of convenience, but it hurts too much.'

'Of course it does,' her aunt said. 'You have been in love with him almost from the start, I think?'

'Yes. I thought I could pretend to be the kind of wife he wants and needs. Rothsay does not want love from me. He merely desires a complaisant wife and an heir. I do not think I can be what he needs, Aunt.'

'Are you certain that he wants only that, Lottie?'

'What do you mean?'

'He has gone to your father's house to look for you. He seems genuinely distressed, my love. Could you not allow him to apologise to you? He has been good to us—to me. He has given me an allowance and told me this is my home. Even if we went elsewhere I should have a decent living. There are not so many men who would be as generous in the circumstances, Lottie.'

'No, Nicolas is the most generous of men—that is why it hurts all the more. How could he imagine that I would want to steal from him?'

'I dare say he is very sorry for having thought it, Lottie.' Her aunt gave her a shrewd look. 'Have you thought what will happen to the people here if you leave just like that? There may be no more improvements to the Hollow and certainly no school for the children.'

'Oh, do not remind me,' Lottie said. 'I feel so guilty. If I stayed for a few days just to make sure everything is in order… Perhaps it would be best to discuss the future with Rothsay. He may wish to divorce me. He must have an heir and he will need a wife.'

'Just so,' her aunt said and smiled. 'Besides, you must think carefully where you wish to go and what you will do. If you have a situation when you leave here, it will be more comfortable for you—and of course you will have to revert to your own name, Lottie.'

'Yes, I suppose I shall.' Lottie looked at her left hand. She would hate to take off her wedding ring, but it would probably be for the best. 'I shall wait for a few days at least. In the meantime I must find a way to sell a few of my possessions. I have some silver items that were my share of Mama's things…'

'You would never sell those, Lottie?' Her aunt looked shocked.

'I may have to. It is either that or the brooch Papa gave me for my wedding.'

'Better that than your mother's things. Besides, I have a little money left. What do you need?'

'I owe Rose three guineas. She paid for our lodgings—and I should like to give her a little more.'

'I will give you five guineas for her, Lottie. You can always repay me when you have money again.'

'Yes…' Lottie frowned. 'I had promised Lily Blake money for her dressmaking establishment. Perhaps I could ask Rothsay if he would consider giving her the money himself.'

'Did you not know?' Aunt Beth looked surprised. 'Lily came here while you were away. She wanted to tell you that she had the money and had decided to go to

Northampton and set up in business for herself. I thought you must have sent it to her?'

Lottie shook her head. 'No, I meant to do it when I returned. I wonder…do you think Nicolas could have sent her something?'

'I imagine he thought recompense was needed after what happened, though it was scarcely his fault, Lottie. Sam Blake was a fugitive from the law and any of the landowners around here would have told their keepers to shoot on sight. Rothsay did not instruct Larkin to do that, but the man acted within the law.'

'It is a bad law and should be changed. If I were a man, I should do something about it.'

'Well, perhaps your husband will one day, Lottie. If you guided his thoughts, he might do a great deal of good—as you could yourself if you stay here.'

'What are you up to, Aunt?'

'I am only asking you to reconsider,' her aunt said. 'I understand why you ran away—but men are sometimes wrong-headed, Lottie. They make mistakes. My husband was often misguided and even careless, but I forgave him—and I loved him. Your mother loved your father until the day she died, and she forgave him far worse.'

'Yes…' Lottie's throat caught with emotion. 'I know. Mama said we must always give others the benefit of the doubt—but Nicolas thinks *I* am a thief. How can I stay with a man who has such a low opinion of me? Papa always knew Mama was good, even though he let her down so many times.'

'Well, you must decide,' her aunt said. 'But at least let him have the chance to apologise.'

'I suppose I ought to speak to him. We must try to be civilised and make certain that the scandal is kept to a minimum.'

Lottie decided to walk to the lake. She had been back for three days now and Nicolas had not come home. Perhaps he had gone back to London. She was not certain what she ought to do for the best. Aunt Beth insisted she should wait for a while and speak to Nicolas and the servants were all so pleased to see her back home.

It was her home. She felt relaxed and comfortable here even though her heart ached. Having visited the Hollow and seen how much improvement had been made in the past weeks, she knew that it would be a crime if the work did not continue. The vicar had called on her, asking if she meant to set up her school and begging her to consider his curate for the post of teacher.

'Bernard is a good man and would do well in a local school, my lady. His stipend is very little and the poor lad cares for his sick mother. He cannot hope for preferment for some years, because he has no influential family to help him. If you could see your way to giving him a chance, he would repay you.'

'Well, I shall certainly interview Mr Bernard,' she said.

The young man did indeed sound exactly what she had hoped to find. His duties would be light and would not prevent him carrying out his work at the church, for the hours were compatible.

If only she could continue as she had been until the disastrous visit to London. Lottie wished that she had not taken it into her head to try to make Nicolas jealous.

The last night she had spent with him had shown her how very much she loved him, and left a constant ache about her heart. She was no longer satisfied to be a complaisant wife. She wanted to be loved and needed. Nothing less would do for her now. It would probably be better if she left before Nicolas returned. Aunt Beth was settled here and she need not worry about her. Lottie could establish herself somewhere and then her aunt…

Her thoughts were suspended as she saw a man walking towards her. For a moment she thought it was Nicolas and her heart raced. Then, as he came nearer, she saw that it was Bertie Fisher.

Lottie liked her friendly neighbour, but at the moment she would have preferred to be alone.

'Lady Rothsay,' he said and swept off his hat. 'I thought I might find you here. There was a great deal of talk when you did not attend the duchess's ball. People were speculating that you had left Rothsay. I decided to come down and investigate.'

'I am grateful for your concern, sir. It was just a little headache that kept me from that engagement. I am much better now.'

'You must know that I am your good friend, Lottie. If you are in some trouble, it would be my pleasure to help you.'

'You are very kind, sir.' Lottie smiled as she saw his earnest expression. 'I think I have been a little foolish, but there is nothing you can do to help.'

'Is Rothsay treating you properly? When he first announced the marriage, I thought it was merely because the family needed an heir, but I've changed my mind.'

'Have you—why?'

Lottie took the arm he offered and they turned back towards the house. She smiled up at him, because he was a good friend.

'Oh, because of the way he looks at you, and the way he acted on the night of the duchess's ball. He seemed like a man in torment.'

'Perhaps he was thinking of his lost love?'

'Lady Elizabeth Madison?' Bertie shook his head. 'I happen to know for a fact that she received a rebuff from him quite recently. I have it on the best authority—her own—that he turned down the offer of an affair. She was most put out and told me in a fit of temper. I do not think you need concern yourself about that lady. Any man who preferred that scold would have to be mad.'

'Oh, Bertie, you are a darling.' Lottie reached up to kiss his cheek. He grinned and kissed her back. It was not until they resumed walking that she realised Nicolas was coming towards them and had seen their embrace.

'Lottie—' Nicolas's expression was cold and angry '—I have been looking everywhere for you. What am I to infer from this—are you leaving me for Fisher?'

'Come off it, old chap,' Bertie said. 'No need to jump to conclusions. I'm a great admirer of your wife, but wouldn't dream of coming between you. What you saw—well, it wasn't what you think.'

'I was speaking to my wife.' Nicolas glared at her. 'If you will grant me a few minutes alone with Lottie, sir. I need to clear the air.'

'Not if you're going to bite her head off again.' Bertie squared his shoulders. 'I ain't one for quarrelling, but I ain't prepared to stand by and see you make Lady Rothsay's life a misery.'

'Going to challenge me to a duel? You can't be serious, Bertie. You know you don't stand a chance against me.'

'Have a damned good try.' Bertie looked stubborn. 'Lady's honour and all that…'

'Please do not be stupid, either of you!' Lottie lost her temper. 'You are both being ridiculous. I refuse to be a bone of contention between friends. It was a friendly kiss because I was miserable, Rothsay—and if you can't believe that, it is best I leave at the first opportunity.'

Lottie ran past them and into the house.

How dared they fight over her? Lottie was furious as she went up to her room. Why was Nicolas always so swift to think the worst of her? First he accused her of selling the diamonds, now he imagined she was conducting a clandestine affair with Bertie Fisher, of all people! He must still believe she was truly like Clarice.

She felt so ashamed. Aunt Beth thought she should continue to live under Nicolas's roof, but how could she? If Clarice was back in England for good it would only be a short time before people discovered that Lady Rothsay had a sister—and Clarice's reputation could ruin her. Between them, they would bring shame on Nicolas's proud name and his family.

She must leave as soon as she had spoken to Nicolas. It might be better if she went abroad. Nicolas must be regretting the day he offered marriage to Clarice and then ended up with her sister.

Sitting on the edge of the bed, she bent her head, covering her face with her hands. She could no longer hold back the tears. It had been foolish to come back here.

She should have found somewhere to live and sent for her personal things. When the door opened, she refused to look up.

'I am sorry, Lottie. Bertie is a good friend to us both and I am a fool for being jealous of any man who looks at you.'

'No, please, Nicolas,' Lottie said and looked at him. She wiped the back of her hand across her eyes. 'It is mere foolishness. I understand why you despise me—my sister is a thief. Her morals are not those of a decent young woman and you think me her equal. I am sorry. I should never have agreed to take her place.'

'Do you regret it for your sake or mine?'

Lottie's eyes closed for a moment, then she looked at him. 'For both our sakes, Nicolas. I find it does not please me to be the kind of wife you require—and I am certain you must wish you had never seen either Clarice or me.'

'Your sister is certainly a problem,' Nicolas admitted. 'I had hoped she might stay in France and not trouble us, but I dare say a way to control her excesses may be found.'

'What do you mean?' Lottie wiped her cheeks with a lace kerchief. Her eyes widened as he sat on the edge of the bed beside her. 'Clarice cares for no one. She must have known I would guess she had taken the diamonds.'

'She thought you would not give her up to the authorities. Do not fear, my love. I have no intention of handing your sister over to a magistrate. For one thing it would cause a scandal for us, and another—I owe her something for tearing up the contract, as I did. Though she herself did not sign it, she could have found a way to sue me for breach of contract had she chosen.'

'If she guessed that, I dare say she might,' Lottie said and gave him a watery smile. 'You were right, she is a thief. I am sorry you were forced to buy back the diamonds, Nicolas.'

'Be damned to the wretched things. They mean nothing to me. I would have left them in the bank, but I thought you might like to wear them.'

'I should have done if Clarice had not stolen them.'

'Why did you not tell me at once, as soon as you discovered the theft?'

'I knew only Clarice could have taken them. I went into your room to recover my pearls, which I left the previous evening—and when I returned she was there. She asked for money. I gave her what I had—and then after she had gone I discovered the necklace was missing. I wanted to tell you but I was ashamed of what she had done—and even if she is a thief she is my sister...'

'You thought I might have her arrested for theft?' Nicolas nodded. 'I had Blake arrested, didn't I? You could not know that I would have given him a lenient sentence and had him released early on promise of good behaviour. Believe me, Lottie. I had no wish to see the man hang or be given a long prison sentence.'

'I should have known—but you were so angry...'

'I have a wicked temper, my love. At first I resented being preached to by a woman—and then I began to know that woman and I understood that she spoke from the heart. I am very sorry Sam Blake was killed. If I could have prevented it, I would.'

Lottie nodded, looking up into his face. 'Did you send Lily Blake some money?'

'The twenty guineas you gave her and another hundred. I told her that she might apply to us for custom for her business when she was ready and we should recommend her. Was it enough for her to start up do you think?'

'A hundred and twenty guineas is a fortune to someone like Lily, Nicolas. She will have a fine establishment and should soon be famous and wealthy.'

'Will it make up for what she has lost?'

'I cannot speak for Lily—but if I lost a husband I loved and my children lost their father no money would be enough.'

'No, I feared not.' He sighed and looked regretful. 'What more can I do, Lottie?'

'Nothing,' Lottie smiled. 'You have done all that could be expected of you, Nicolas. However, you can continue the work at the Hollow and set up a school for the children.'

'Will you not stay and do those things? You are so much better at seeing what people need than I am, Lottie.'

'Do you mean that we should continue as we planned at the start?' Lottie could not look at him. Her heart was racing and she felt that she could hardly breathe.

'No, not as it was at the start, but as it could be between us now—if you can forgive me?' His hand reached out to lift her chin so that she looked at him. 'I care for you, Lottie, much more than I expected I should. I want you to be my wife, not because I need an heir but because I want to be with you. I want children with you, but I want so much more.'

'Are you sure, Nicolas? I do not think that I could bear it if you made love me to me and then rode off to London to the bed of your mistress the next night.'

'I have no mistress, Lottie. I gave her up once I'd agreed to your father's marriage deal and there has been no one else since, I promise you. Once I had tasted your sweetness I knew that no other woman would ever content me. You are the woman I need in my life—can you bear to give me another chance?'

He still had not said that he loved her, but Lottie knew that perhaps this was the closest Nicolas could come to telling her he cared. Elizabeth had hurt him so badly that there was a barrier inside him that would not let love in. He had lowered it partially, but it was still there.

'If you truly want me, I shall stay,' Lottie said after a moment. 'I must tell you now that I love you, Nicolas. I have loved you almost from the start. If you do not want my love, it would be fair to tell me now.'

'I thought I had forfeited all right to your love,' Nicolas said. He leaned forwards to kiss her on the lips. It was a long, lingering kiss, sweet and tender. 'You are my wife and I care for you as much as I am able to care for anyone, Lottie. I am not sure it is love as you know it, but I will not lie to you. There is something locked inside me that just will not come free, much as I might wish it. I want you, need you, care for you—is that enough?'

'Yes, I think so,' she said and touched his cheek. 'Perhaps in time you will feel able to love with all your heart, Nicolas.'

'Perhaps I love, but cannot express it.'

Lottie gazed into his eyes. 'Yes, perhaps that is so,' she said softly. 'Come to me tonight, Nicolas. For the moment I think we should go down—Aunt Beth will be worrying.'

Nicolas smiled. 'Wash your face, my love. You have a dirty mark just there.' He kissed the spot. 'I shall go down and tell her the good news.'

Lottie decided to change her gown before going to tea with her husband and her aunt. She went behind the screen and took it off, pulling on a fresh yellow silk gown. Hearing someone enter, she thought it was Rose and called out to her.

'Rose, will you brush my hair for me, please…?' She stopped and stared as she came out from behind the screen and saw the woman standing by her dressing table. 'Clarice! What are you doing here?'

'I came to see you, of course,' Clarice said. 'Are you not pleased to see me, Lottie?'

'Should I be—after what happened last time?' Lottie opened her jewel case, which was lying on the table, then held out her hand. 'Aunt Beth's pearls, if you please. I know you have them, Clarice. If you do not return them, I shall have you arrested. Aunt Beth would hate it if they were sold. Her husband gave them to her when she was married.'

Clarice reluctantly took the pearls from inside her glove. 'Give me some money, then. I don't mean two hundred pounds. I told you last time that I need at least ten thousand. Philippe is in such trouble. If he doesn't pay up they may kill him.'

'Has your lover been gambling again? He should learn

to play within his means, Clarice. I cannot give you such a sum, for I do not have it—and even if I had I should not give you Rothsay's money for a gambling debt.'

'You may be sorry if you don't. I need that money, Lottie, and I do not mind what I do to get it. Your precious Rothsay would not be happy if the truth came out, I think.'

'What are you talking about?'

'Why, I will tell all the world about the little deal that Father made with Rothsay. That the marquis bartered for a bride, and to make matters worse for both of you he was duped into marrying the woman he hadn't even bargained for. Imagine what everyone will think of you both then? Rothsay would not care for that to come out, I imagine.'

'You wouldn't, Clarice.' Lottie felt sick. She had just made things up with Nicolas and now Clarice was back making trouble. 'Rothsay will respond for sure. He could have you arrested for the sale of that necklace.'

'Really? I doubt it. I told the jeweller I was you. He believed me—and after all it is true, is it not?'

'No, actually it is not,' a voice said from the doorway. Both sisters turned to look and saw Nicolas standing there. He looked furious as he came into the room, and Lottie's heart sank. 'The original deal I made with your father was off before the wedding even took place. I married Charlotte Stanton, not Clarice—and I thank God for it every day of my life.'

Clarice scowled, her lovely face ugly with rage and bitterness. 'You think yourself so clever, Rothsay—but I have proof of the deal in the original contract and that is sufficient to cause a scandal. Do you want everyone to laugh behind their fans and say that Lottie was second choice?'

'They would not say that if they knew you, Miss Stanton.' Nicolas glared at her. 'However, you are correct in thinking I owe you something. Had Lottie not come in your place, it was my intention to offer you compensation for your loss.'

Clarice's eyes gleamed with avarice. 'I want twenty thousand pounds or my contract goes to *The Times* along with a lot of interesting gossip that would blacken your name, sir.'

'You may publish and go to the devil as far as I am concerned, but I shall not have Lottie harmed.' Nicolas was silent for a moment. 'I shall give you ten thousand— and I'll want the contract and a signed document that says this business is at an end.'

'If I gave you that, I could go to prison for blackmail.'

'How would that serve to protect Lottie and her good name? You, Miss Stanton, will go to Paris with ten thousand pounds in your pocket—and the promise of two thousand a year as long as you stay there. I shall offer this once only. Give me your word now or do your worst.'

'Damn you,' Clarice muttered. 'I need that money. I'll sign and I'll stay out of your way—for as long as I receive the two thousand a year.'

'It will be money well spent,' Nicolas said, his expression harsh. 'Go down to the parlour, Lottie. You aunt is waiting for you. I shall deal with this lady and then I shall join you.'

'Yes, Nicolas.' Lottie glanced at her sister. She felt

numb with shock. Surely Nicolas would never forgive this? 'Goodbye, Clarice. I hope we shall not meet again—until you have learned to respect others, at least.'

Chapter Fifteen

Lottie took tea with her aunt. She was apprehensive as she waited for Nicolas to join them, but he was a long time coming and when she asked the housekeeper where his lordship was, she was told he had an urgent message and had gone out. Too restless to stay in the house, she pulled on a warm pelisse and went out into the gardens.

It was chilly and she was about to return to the house when she heard the sound of gunfire quite close and then a man came charging at her. She hardly had time to see that it was the keeper Larkin when he pointed a shotgun at her, gesturing wildly in the direction of the park.

'It's your fault with your high morals, poking your nose in where it is not wanted and causing trouble from the moment you got 'ere,' he muttered. 'Well, he'll be sorry for what he's done—if I go down, I'll take you with me.'

Lottie shivered, a chill creeping down her spine as

she looked into the man's crazed eyes. She was alone and Larkin was clearly desperate.

'I have no idea what you mean, sir.'

'Don't you pretend with me, woman. I had a nice little thing going on until you turned up, laying down the law and getting folk on your side. Well, you'll pay for it and Dickon Blake will too, fer it's 'im wot told on me.'

'If you have been breaking the law, then you deserve to be punished,' Lottie said, standing her ground. If she turned and ran he would no doubt shoot her. 'You were swift enough to kill Sam Blake, and that, sir, was no accident. I would swear you might have shot him in the leg had you not wished to kill him.'

'Blake were in with us from the start, but he wanted out on account of his missus telling him she would leave 'im if he didn't give it up. Dickon and me both warned 'im, but he wouldn't listen so he had to be shut up—the way I'm going to shut you up now.'

'If you shoot me, you will certainly hang.' Lottie told him. 'My husband might be lenient with you if you come to your senses.'

'And very likely he won't fer it's 'im wot 'as 'ad me watched, spied on—and that rogue Blake 'as gone over to 'is side an' all…'

Lottie heard a rustling sound in the shrubbery. She did not dare to turn her head to look, but knew that someone was behind them. Larkin had become aware of it, too. In the moment that he turned his head, she rushed away to the right, fleeing deeper into the shrubbery. She heard Larkin shout, then another man's voice, and then the sounds of a struggle and finally a shot, followed swiftly

by a second. Lottie gave a little cry of fear. Who had
been shot—and would Larkin give chase?

'My lady,' a man's voice called as she hesitated, hardly
knowing which way to go for the best. 'Larkin cannot
hurt you. You are safe now.'

'Dickon—Dickon Blake, is that you?'

Lottie moved towards the spot where the sounds had
come from and saw that Larkin was lying on the ground,
bleeding profusely from a wound to his leg but still alive.
He glared up at the man who stood over him, holding a
shotgun at his head. Lottie saw that it was indeed Dickon
Blake and that he also had a superficial wound to his
arm.

'You are hurt, Mr Blake. What happened here?'

'He shot at me, but his gun misfired and I took him
down,' Dickon replied. 'I'll not lie to you, Lady Rothsay.
I've been a poacher and proud of it. In my opinion the
woods should be open for a man to take a rabbit for his
family—but I am not a murderer and I could not stand
by and see him murder you the way he murdered my
cousin.'

'I owe you my life, sir,' Lottie said. 'I think we should
go back to the house and—' She was about to say that
she would bind his wound and send someone to fetch
the more seriously injured Larkin, who appeared to have
passed out, but, before she could say more, several men
came crashing through the shrubbery.

'Lottie!' Nicolas cried as he saw her. 'My God! I
thought he might have killed you.' He glanced from her
to the man on the ground, then at Dickon Blake. 'What
happened here?'

'Larkin intended to murder me the way he murdered

Sam Blake. Sam wanted to make an end to the poaching. He was going to try to find work and look after his family, but Larkin couldn't allow that because he was the one masterminding the serious poaching in these parts—is that not so, Dickon?'

'Yes, my lady…' Dickon hesitated as if he would have said more, but Lottie frowned and he was silent.

'Mr Blake happened to be nearby and he heard what Larkin intended—and he shot him in the leg after he was shot at. Is that not how it was, Dickon?'

'I couldn't let him hurt you after what you've done for us at the Hollow, my lady. I thought you were like all the others at the start, but you ain't—and I couldn't let him do it, even if does mean I spend the rest of my days in prison.'

'I doubt you need worry about that,' Nicolas said. 'My agent told me you had been most helpful over the investigation into the poaching. I know you have had difficulty in finding work—perhaps you would care to take on Larkin's work? I shall expect you to deal honestly with me—and a man in need may be warned twice. After that he must be brought to me and I will see if he is a thief or just desperate.'

'Your gamekeeper?' Dickon stared as if he did not believe his ears. 'I've been one of them what stole from you, my lord—but if I take your money I'll serve you well. I never thought you would give me half a chance…'

'No doubt I should not have done so once,' Nicolas said and put his arm about Lottie's shoulders. 'My wife has taught me better manners, Mr Blake. You deserve no less than respect after what you just did, sir.' He beckoned to the keepers who were staring in astonishment. 'Take Larkin back to the kitchens and have him patched up. He will be arrested and tried for murder—and in his case I shall not be lenient. He will hang for the murder of Sam Blake and the attempted murder of my wife. You, Mr Blake, must also be attended. We shall talk later, for I am sure that a man like you will know what injustices have taken place in the past and should be righted—and I shall consult you concerning the affairs of the people at the Hollow. My wife has begun the task but it will be for me to make certain that things do not come to such a pass again.'

'Thank you, my lord.' Dickon bent to gather up Larkin's fallen weapon. 'I reckon it was a lucky day for us when you married her ladyship.'

Nicolas turned to gaze down at Lottie. There was an odd expression in his eyes as he replied, 'Yes, it was the luckiest day of my life—even though I did not know it then.'

'I think I should go back to the house,' Lottie said. 'It is most strange, but I feel a little…' She moaned and started to crumple at the knees.

Nicolas caught her in his arms. He turned and walked towards the house, carrying his precious burden and followed by his men and Dickon.

Aunt Beth had seen them from the window and came fluttering into the hall, her expression anxious. 'What has happened to her? We heard shooting—is she hurt?'

'No, it was a keeper who was shot—but she might have been had Dickon Blake not been there to help her. I have had an agent watching over things while I was away, but this afternoon everything came to a head.'

Lottie's eyelids moved. She opened her eyes and looked up at him. 'How foolish? Did I faint?'

'Bring her into the parlour,' Aunt Beth said. 'I dare say she will be better in a moment. These faints do not as a rule last long.'

'What are you talking about?' Nicolas asked, puzzled. 'I dare say it was the shock of being attacked by Larkin and then seeing two men wounded.'

'I very much doubt it,' Aunt Beth said as he set Lottie gently down on a daybed in the parlour. 'I do not know if Lottie is aware of it herself, but all the signs are there—though perhaps I should not say.'

'Now you have completely lost me.' Nicolas was exasperated. 'Is Lottie ill? Please have the goodness to tell me, for I have no idea what you mean.'

Lottie caught Nicolas's arm, as he would have moved away. 'I think what my aunt is hinting at is that she thinks I am with child, Nicolas. I have not mentioned anything, because I was not perfectly certain—though I have not seen my courses since…I left London.'

'You are with child?' Nicolas stared at her, then a smile showed in his eyes and his mouth curved into a huge grin. 'That is wonderful, Lottie. Do you suppose the night before you left…?'

'Yes, I would think so, though it is too soon to be sure, Nicolas. I could begin my courses tomorrow, though I am late and I think…I truly feel that I may be with child.'

'Here, Lottie dearest. Hold this to your nose,' Aunt Beth said and gave her a kerchief heavily soaked in lavender water. 'It may help you with the headache you may have after a nasty faint like that, my love.'

Lottie took the kerchief and inhaled the perfume

gratefully. She had been feeling a little queasy, but the strong lavender helped and she breathed more deeply.

'Should you not see what is happening elsewhere, Nicolas? You will need to send for the constable and have Larkin attended by a doctor. Even a man as despicable as he should be properly cared for, do you not think so?'

'Had I fired the gun he would probably be dead,' Nicolas admitted grimly. 'He is lucky that Blake got to him first. My keepers and agent will do all that is necessary, Lottie. I have no intention of leaving your side until I am assured that no other villains lie in wait for you. Forgive me for not protecting you properly.'

'It could not be expected that Larkin would try to kill me or that he would be in the rose gardens.' Lottie was sitting up now. She smiled and took his hand. 'Sit here beside me, Nicolas. Tell me just what has been going on here, please.'

'You were so certain that Sam Blake was innocent of any crime other than taking a rabbit or two. Therefore I had to wonder if Larkin was a dishonest servant as you'd suggested. When I went off to London I engaged agents to come down to Rothsay and discover what they could—and also to make sure that nothing happened to you. After what you'd said, I thought that it might possibly have been Larkin who took a pot shot at us that day. He probably wanted to give you a fright, but when you became involved with Lily Blake and took too much interest in things that could be dangerous for him, he decided to kill Sam.'

'Dickon told me that Sam wanted out of the large-scale poaching. Larkin would not let him give it up, because he thought he might betray the rest of them. I do not know who else was involved, but I think he was the ringleader.'

'He will be punished for the crime of murder. I shall give the others a warning—but I believe Dickon Blake will sort things out. A reformed poacher makes the best gamekeeper of all. My father once said that, but I fear I had forgotten much of what he told me. He went away from me when I was very young, you see.'

Lottie saw that Aunt Beth had left them alone. She patted the seat beside her and Nicolas sat down, reaching for her outstretched hand. 'Were you lonely as a child, Nicolas? Someone told me your mother died when you were very young?'

'She was very like you in some ways, Lottie, always wanting to help others. She had been nursing one of the young mothers at the Hollow and caught a fever. The doctor could do nothing and she died swiftly. Both my father and I were devastated. I think he could hardly bear to be here afterwards; he spent long periods away, and he scarcely seemed to know he had a son until just before he died. He apologised to me then, but it was too late. I had grown a protective barrier inside.'

'That isn't all of it, though, Nicolas?' Lottie's eyes were on his face. 'I know something of your affair with Elizabeth.'

'I did love Elizabeth in my way, but it was not enough for her. She once told me that the only time I came alive was when I played the pianoforte.'

'You do lose yourself in the music, which is why you play so well—but if she had loved you, she might have found a way to tear down the barriers you had built around your heart.'

'The way you have, Lottie?'

'Have I—truly?'

'Yes. I thought some of the hurt might still remain. I wasn't sure if I wanted to love completely, because it hurts to lose those you love—but I could have lost you today, Lottie.' He took her hand, lifting it to his lips to kiss the palm. 'I know that my life would be empty without you. You have made my heart your home, Lottie— and you rule both in my heart and my home. Without you I think I should be like my father and simply fade away.'

'What nonsense,' Lottie said and leaned forwards to kiss him lightly on the lips. 'For one thing I have no intention of going anywhere without you again, and for another—I want your promise that if in the future I should die and leave a child or children, you will love them and give them all the affection they deserve. Only a weak man gives up when he loses something, Nicolas, and I know you are not that. If my children live, then I shall live on in them—but it is most unlikely to happen. I dare say that you will be stuck with me for many years, perhaps the whole of your life.'

Her eyes twinkled with mischief and Nicolas laughed. 'You have my word, Lottie. You are right. I am not my father. I have my mother's spirit and she was brave like you. I promise that I shall always love our children—and now, my dearest, should you go up and rest?'

'Not yet, Nicolas. I shall change my gown for the evening, but it will be months before I shall need a nap in the afternoons. First thing in the morning, I intend to inspect the village hall and make sure that a part of it will do for my school.'

'And if it will not?'

'Then I shall expect you to build me a little school of my own, Nicolas,' she replied. 'I already have a very good master in mind and the sooner it is ready for the children the better…'

Lottie was brushing her hair before the mirror when the connecting door opened and her husband entered. She smiled and laid down her brush, standing up to receive him.

'Are you too tired, my love?'

'No, indeed I am not, Nicolas. Please do not imagine that I shall break if you touch me. I may be in a certain condition, but I am not delicate, and I do not think that making love will harm our child at this early stage. Perhaps later we may need to be more careful, but for the moment I am perfectly well and not in the least tired.'

He came to put his arms about her, gazing down at her face for several moments, before bending his head to kiss her. His lips were soft, tender, yet with an underlying passion that spoke of his hunger.

'How did I become so very fortunate?' he asked huskily. 'I was so careless in the way I chose my bride—and I found myself untold treasure in you.'

'Had you chosen more carefully I think we should never have met.' Lottie frowned. 'I am sorry about the things Clarice said and did. I hope she will stay in France and not trouble us again, Nicolas.'

'I have her receipt, and she knows that if she breaks the terms of our agreement she could find herself in prison. I believe she will stay away, but if she comes again, just tell me, Lottie. You must not feel sorry and give her money. Let me deal with her. Your sister is an adventuress. I regret to say it, for it must pain you, but you should face the truth.'

'I have,' Lottie said and sighed. 'I did not wish to believe you when you told me what she did in Paris, but I should have known. I shall not be foolish enough to give her money again. She must manage with her allowance or fend for herself.'

'We do not need to talk about her, my love.' Nicolas's hand stroked her hair, then her cheek. 'Come to bed, my darling. I want to show you how very much I love and worship you.'

Lottie gave him her hand, letting him lead her to the bed. Her heart was beating wildly as she lay down and drew him to her. Their kisses were sweeter than ever before, because for the first time both gave everything. All the barriers had been swept away, and Nicolas's eyes were free of shadows.

As Lottie surrendered to the tumultuous feeling of desire that overwhelmed her, she loved and knew that she was loved. Her nails raked his shoulders, her mewing cries of pleasure mixing with the rasp of his breath as he cried out and shuddered at the end. They lay together, flesh to flesh, lost in the wonder of the new happiness they had found, and then they slept.

* * * * *

Harlequin® A *Romance* FOR EVERY MOOD™

Harlequin®
American ★ Romance®
LOVE, HOME & HAPPINESS

Harlequin® *Blaze*™
red-hot reads!

Harlequin® *Desire*
ALWAYS POWERFUL, PASSIONATE AND PROVOCATIVE

HARLEQUIN® HISTORICAL:
Where love is timeless

Harlequin®
INTRIGUE®
BREATHTAKING ROMANTIC SUSPENSE

Harlequin®
MEDICAL™
Pulse-racing romance, heart-racing medical drama

Harlequin®
n♥cturne™
Dramatic and sensual tales of paranormal romance.

Harlequin® *Presents*®
Seduction and Passion Guaranteed!

Harlequin®
Romance
From the Heart, For the Heart

Harlequin®
ROMANTIC
SUSPENSE
Sparked by danger, fueled by passion

Harlequin®
SPECIAL EDITION
Life, Love & Family

Harlequin®
Super Romance®
Exciting, emotional, unexpected!

Want to try **2 FREE** books? Visit: www.ReaderService.com